ON A CLEAR DAY, YOU CAN SEE BLOCK ISLAND

GAGE GREENWOOD

THE SUPERSTARS OF PATREON

The following people make this writing career of mine possible. If you enjoyed this book, thank them. Without their support, it wouldn't be possible. They truly are my heroes.

WHITE WOLVES: Mandee, Jamie McFarland, Carli Love, Molly Mix, Kirsty Williams , Michael Casey, Emily Morash

WINTER'S LEGENDS: Savannah Fischer, Mary Trujillo, Trudy Meiser, Jennifer Sweet, Teresa, Damaris Quinones, Carrie, Chaz Williams, Amy Porter, Meghan Burns, , Kelly Jobes, Erica Kennedy, Tracy Allen, Engilbert Egill Steffonsson, Deven VanKirk, Kylee Jones, Lisa Vasquez, Chris Knickerbocker, Angie Valentine, Kristina Lee, Rhonda Bobbitt, Ali Sweet, Kendall OConnor, sarajaye, Hope Haugstad, Megan Stockton

DEMIGODS: Trina, Charlotte Stevenson, Javaneh Jones, Jason Artz, Matt StPier, Ashley Harvey, Janalyn prude, Crystal Cook, Chandra Greco

LAMPPOSTS: Shannon Ettaro, John Lynch, Lindalaine, NRD, Kate Stevenson, Aaron, Jennifer Bonges, Alexandria Bracanovich, Elyn Noble, MacKenzie Meade, Stephanie Huddle, Nicole Laudij, Roth Schilling, Kate Forsman, Kelli Hahn, Sally Feliz, Tina Coley, Bryan

Walsh, Justine Manzano, Kelly Kujawski, Adrian Mathis, jl courtney, Sarah D'Ambro

HUSKS: Stacie Denise, Kristina Lebedeva, Dagan Boyd, Tiffany Riggs, Kelsey stokes, Chiara, Summer Smith, Brooke Conley, Jaxon Lee Rose, S.P. Somtow (Somtow Sucharitkul)

For Kristina Lee,
A reader who became a friend who became a best friend.

I
WELCOME HOME, YOU PAINS IN THE ASS

A new house meant new fun, and Jackson had high hopes for the game Brian invented. It wasn't very original, basically just a more complex version of Telephone. However, instead of children whispering to one another, this version took advantage of their new space and the massive number of rooms spread out along the upstairs hall.

One person, called "The Wordsmith," came up with a sentence. Jackson took that role, figuring the kids should get first shot at the actual game. He wrote his sentence down on a slip of paper and handed it to player one.

Charlie begged for that position. As the middle child, he'd grown comfortable staying away from the spotlight, fitting squarely between other shadows. The first player simply had to read the sentence out loud—in song form—to the next player. The catch? Each child stood in a different room. Thick walls separated the players, and those walls muffled the hell out of the song. A person could decipher the words if the speaker sang clearly, slowly, and distinctly. All hard things to accomplish for children between the ages of eight and seventeen.

Charlie slipped into the room farthest left. The bathroom. Once inside, the rest of the kids ran to their designated rooms for the game. Jackson sat on a ridiculously old chair, a gift that came with their new home, and a reminder of how out of his element he felt in his new standing. The chair's splat gave a slight creak as he leaned into it. He found the thing uncomfortable, a relic from a time when people enjoyed suffering for aesthetics.

He both loved and hated the house. Loved it because he could afford it. No more bunk beds for the kids, jockeying for the single bathroom, fighting over remote controls, punching elbows at the kitchen table. Finally, they could move about freely, go to their own worlds, and all it took was corporate negligence to the tune of ten million dollars. Sorry we killed your wife, bub, but hey, have some cash. He hated it for the gaudy style and cold openness. The creaky wooden floorboards and dank, dusty corners. And that it came at the price of his wife.

Status was ugly. Freedom had mold.

He sighed, leaned back, and crossed his legs. The fun part about the hallway gig was he could hear his children clearly. Somehow, the narrow corridor stole the sounds from all the rooms and carried them out like a loudspeaker. A trait he found convenient for a parent whose oldest children were bringing home dates and slinking them into their bedrooms under promises they were "just watching movies." Well, the kids now knew how much the sound carried, so they would probably keep themselves from any activities that might cause embarrassing noisemaking.

Charlie sang the sentence with the expected level of timidness, "Welcome home, you pains in the ass." Jackson chuckled to himself. He knew the kids would get a kick out of it, him not only allowing them a cuss word, but encouraging it.

Chrissy, nine years old and by far his most bizarre child, giggled as she listened to the sentence on her side of the wall. Her laugh made Jackson smile, so out of place for the quiet girl always face down in an Anne Rice book. Yes, she read Anne Rice books at nine years old. Lately, she'd taken to wearing puffy shirts, which to her meant vampire royalty, but to Jackson meant *Seinfeld* pirates.

Chrissy shuffled from one side of the room to the other and sang her song through the opposite wall. To Jackson's surprise, she nailed it. "Welcome home, you pains in the ass," she sang like a bard entertaining a royal court.

Next up was Brian, the inventor of the game. He turned fifteen two weeks ago, and his face showed the war signs of teen growth, riddled with acne scars and greasy mustache bristles. At school, he'd quieted, growing more aware of his looks and feeling embarrassed by them. Jackson knew this by the way his son sank within himself the second he exited their Prius and slowly walked to the building every morning. Here, at home, Brian played the opposite, speaking loudly and proudly, pushing himself into a leadership role only he took seriously.

His footsteps marched from one side of the room to the other, and he boomed his voice through the wall into the most contentious bedroom, "Welcome home, you pains in the ass."

Impressive, Jackson thought.

The fourth room down the line had caused quite the stir upon moving into the house. It lay directly in the middle of the hallway, which might have made the room the weakest if not for how large it was. Wreath claimed it first—and being the oldest, Jackson figured she deserved it—but Brian and Angela fought tooth and nail for it. Brian insisted he deserved it more because Wreath would move out too soon to take over any room. "She can handle a second-rate room for a year," he said. And he, being the next oldest, would still have a good three years to enjoy the comforts of the large room. Jackson considered it a fair argument. Wreath didn't. Instead, she stomped and screamed like one of the younger children.

Angela had no real argument, but at eight years old, thought saying, "I want it" repeatedly was a worthwhile counterpoint. Eventually, Jackson solved the fight by giving it to Wreath, promising

Brian he could move in the day Wreath left for college, and giving Angela a couple of peanut butter cups.

A part of Jackson appreciated the kids bickering over a room. It was a normal thing for kids to do, and since their mother died, normality wasn't part of their routine. Children react to grief differently than adults, ranging in a variety of emotions with no rhyme or reason. At Elaina's calling hours, the kids cried in the receiving line as a series of people hugged them and gave their condolences, but after the service, the kids ran around the funeral home playing tag. One minute, they were fine, thinking about school, toys, television shows, whatever, and the next, a switch would flip, and they'd explode with anger or sadness. Grief was a viral infection. It was as if someone injected them with extreme emotions by the syringe full, and it swam in their blood, pumped through their heart and brain, and coated their stomachs until they'd vomit it out, confused and scared by the sickness. They didn't know what was happening inside of them; they only knew it didn't feel good.

Since moving into the new house, Jackson had tried hard to make it their place, more than just a space he had moved them to. And that's why Brian's game excited him so much. It gave the kids an opportunity to forget everything else and enjoy each other, while also adapting to their new surroundings. Their siblings and the house layout all played together, working as a unified force to get the message sent.

Wreath didn't giggle at the sentence the way the other kids did. *Too cool*, Jackson thought. He listened as her gentle footsteps tapped from one side of the room toward the other, but they surprised him by stopping at the midway point. Silence. Jackson furrowed his brow.

Was Wreath ruining the game?

A sound, low and weak, came through the door. A soft croak, followed by a gurgling.

Jackson's heart lunged into his throat. He shot out of his seat and ran to the door, knocking and pushing to open it. "Wreath, are you okay?"

As a child, Wreath had suffered from epileptic seizures, but as she grew up, they became less and less frequent until they had all but disappeared. Jackson remembered the sounds, the horrifying groan and gurgle that Wreath would release.

"Wreath?" He slammed his shoulder into the hard wood, but unlike the splat of the chair, it gave nothing in return. "Wreath, honey, open the door."

The other children shuffled out of their rooms. Angela first, followed by Charlie and Chrissy.

"What's happening, Dad?" Charlie asked.

Fear took over the hallway. Brian finally joined them.

"Wreath, what's going on?" Jackson shouted.

The children talked over one another, trying to figure out the problem. Jackson hushed them. He leaned into the door, pressing his ear to the wood. Nothing. The gurgling had stopped. For a brief second, a wave of relief washed over Jackson, until he realized the silence was more disquieting than the noise.

"Wreath, open the door now."

"Dad?" Angela shook his pants leg.

"*Shhh*," he said, trying to pick up any sound from the room, waiting for some sign it was all a false alarm. Footsteps approached the door, coming closer to him. He moved his ear around, trying to get the best spot for hearing into the room over the loud cacophony of children's breathing.

Closer. Closer.

"Wreath, what are you doing? I can hear you walking." His pulse settled. If she walked, she was fine.

She breathed against the door, loud and harsh, as if she stuck her mouth against it flush and exhaled deep into the wood.

"This isn't funny. Open the door. You messed up the game."

The rest of the children froze outside of the occasional itch or twitch. The inability of a kid to stay in place.

"Open the fucking door, Wreath." He knocked hard once with his fist.

And then the blood rushed to his head in a crash, so rapid and unexpected, he nearly collapsed to the floor.

Not one voice, but two, one gruff and harsh like a tree branch cracking, and the other soft and feminine, but wholly unlike Wreath, said, "Welcome home."

The children screamed, and their high-pitched wailing made the horrific nature of what unfolded even more unnerving.

"What was that?" Charlie screeched.

"Dad!" Angela said.

Chrissy's eyes grew wide, and she backed up until her head hit the wall on the opposite side of the hall.

"Charlie, take your sisters downstairs. Brian, help me get this door open."

He slammed his shoulder into the door again, and Brian lifted his foot and kicked.

Charlie grabbed his sisters, but as he took Chrissy's hand, she yanked him closer to her instead of following him away.

"Chrissy, come on."

But she didn't move.

Jackson and Brian kicked and slammed. The door didn't budge, proving as stubborn as Chrissy.

The voices came again, saying, "Welcome home." No, not saying it. Singing it. Taunting the words in a sing-songy "nana nana poo-poo" way.

Then, an awful crunching. The horrid sound sent shivers down Jackson's spine.

"Welcome home." *Crunch.*

"Welcome home." *Crunch.*

"Welcome home." *Crunch.*

Brian kicked in rapid fire, and the wood cracked slightly. Jackson joined in with his foot until finally the wood around the doorknob splintered and gave way. It slid open with a whiny creak.

Jackson knew horror, had lived through plenty of it. He knew the feeling of leaving your body, seeing a tragedy unfold from way up high. When his mother shot herself in the head, he found her, not by entering the room as a small child, but overseeing from the ceiling with God's omniscient view. Of course, that wasn't right, but that's how it felt after the fact, how it played out in his memories.

When the children lost their mother, Jackson took the call and transferred the message to each of them. The factory burned down, midday. An accident. Jackson lost his wife, and five children lost their mother, simply because she worked at the wrong place at the wrong time.

When Jackson had taken the call from some middle manager of the company, he listened to the man's words as he floated through the future, an empty white space, futile to understand without Elaina in it. He saw nothing but emptiness.

Whenever tragedy struck, he floated. That's how a person survived real-life horror. They floated, feet peeling off the hardwood.

None of those horrors took him down, though, because they were real, and genuine horror happens every day. You can float away from it by moving forward.

What he saw when Wreath's door opened was different. It wasn't a real horror. It was fiction, and he wondered if something had broken so deeply inside him that his brain conjured it into existence.

How else could one explain a creature inhumanly tall, gaunt to the point of skeletal, with gray, leathery skin wrapped around its bones? What else but insanity could make sense of such a creature eating a teenage girl, crunching on bone, smiling as it sucked on sinew and meat?

Thin strips of mist spindled off the rug surrounding the creature like weeds.

Around Jackson, lost to the thrumming of his heart, his children screamed and panicked, grabbed him, pulled on him, begged him to explain what they were seeing. Some scattered down the stairs and out of the house.

But Jackson, he stayed perfectly still, hearing louder than the surrounding chaos, the blood coursing through his heart and head. Jackson froze. He didn't rush to save his daughter, didn't shuffle his family to safety. He stared, feet planted on the floor. No floating.

Because nothing made sense anymore. The most frightening thing to know. Nothing made sense anymore.

2
AN ATLANTIC FOG

FOUR YEARS LATER

Charlie took his shoes and socks off and kicked them behind a large donation box. He stepped onto the sand, searching for a place to sit farthest from other people. The night had cleared out most beachgoers, leaving just a few couples and some obnoxious teenagers. An older couple walked holding hands on the shoreline, close enough for the surf to slip under their feet. Another couple sat on a beach blanket with two unleashed golden retrievers scuffling beside them. The teens sat around a small fire dug into the sand in a far corner of the beach, just before the private property line. They'd tucked their circle behind some dunes, hoping to avoid visibility, but they were impossible not to see. They were probably drinking and too stupid to know no one gave a shit.

Charlie found a place near the private property line on the opposite side from the teens, but the beach was so small he could nearly make out their conversations, anyway. He sat on his butt, knees up, and dug his heels into the gravelly sand, paying attention to the way the sand filtered between his toes, picturing the spaces between as little sandglasses.

The moon hovered over the silhouette of a water tower on his left, and the water lapped against the breachway on his right. Somewhere in between those two objects, shrouded by night and a low fog, was the island he lived on for two whopping months. Block Island. From the Charlestown beach, on a clear day, a person could make out the outlines of the island. It had two lighthouses on each side, two little thumbtacks. Charlie imagined plucking them and watching the island curl up into a scroll.

"Whatcha staring at?"

Charlie shot up straight. He turned his head slowly, trying to recover from the embarrassing jolt he had just made. Behind him, a girl his age stood with her arms crossed. Trouble, Charlie knew. She had short brown hair flowing just below her ears. Her lipstick was blue, and her eye shadow black. She wore a Gorilla Biscuits tee shirt, and her shorts were just a few threads more than a pair of underwear. He assessed her before responding, debating whether it was best to ignore her or to offer a short answer—whatever it took to avoid her calling her friends over for a round of humiliation.

"Well?" She put her hands out as if offering him help.

"Nothing," he unintentionally whispered, which he tried to correct by clearing his throat and trying again. "Nothing."

She tilted her head, stared for a beat, then sat down next to him. She wrapped her hands around her knees and gazed deeply into the ocean.

"What are you doing?" Charlie asked, still trying to figure her out. Obscure punk tee, sorority girl shorts, cutesy haircut, goth makeup.

"You seemed unwilling to give me answers, and I'm a curious type who can't accept not knowing. It's like a neurosis. I need to know what you were staring at."

"No, I mean, I'm really not staring at anything."

She shook her head but kept her eyes focused on the water.

"Unacceptable. Even if that was your goal. Your eyes focused on something, a wave, a rock jutting out, something. For the record, I understand why you didn't answer. Guy sitting alone sees a bunch of douches around a fire, and one of them comes over. Smells like the start of trouble. Totally get it."

The surf lapped. Every five seconds, another slurp hit the shore, and it dug into Charlie's skull as it disrupted this bizarre interaction he both hated and loved.

The rhythm of his heart lost its beat and doubled in speed, reminding him how much he disliked conversations, even good ones. He enjoyed people, their company, and hearing their thoughts, but the art of speaking, of knowing what to say and how to say it, what sounded sincere and what came across as sarcastic, all the navigational tools for speaking sent waves of anxiety deep within the pit of his belly.

"I was staring at Block Island."

She scrunched her forehead. "I can't see it."

"Me neither. I was trying to. There's too much fog."

"So, you came here at night to see Block Island? They have ferries that run like, all the time. You can just take one for a day trip."

"I've been there. But I wanted to see it tonight. It's hard to explain."

She brought her chin to her ribs and with a low growl, said, "Oh, come on, dude. Did you not listen to a thing I said? I need to know now. Tell me. I can't handle not knowing."

He wiped his hands down his face, pressing his palms deep against his skin. "I may not be someone you'll enjoy knowing, then. I'm not very expressive."

She frowned and stared at him. "Fair enough. Then let's be more superficial. You live in Charlestown or just visiting?"

He sighed. "I live about half an hour from here in Tanner's Switch."

She laughed. "No shit? Me too." She pointed to the kids at the fire. "We all do. You go to Tanner's Switch High School?"

He wiggled his toes under the sand, finding comfort in the sensory overload. "I will. First year. Can't wait to be the new kid. Wonder what I'll get mocked for. I'm weird, shy, mediocre at sports, oh, and I'm dirt poor."

A smile crept up one side of her face. "You're new to the area, huh? We're all weird, mediocre at sports, and oh, dirt fucking poor. It's Tanner's Switch. Not Newport. It's a shit town. We're like, last in every sport, so even the athletes suck at playing, and there's gotta be some shit in our drinking water because it's like the island of misfit toys in school. A bunch of fucking weirdos."

"I'll probably be the king weirdo."

She pointed both hands at her face. "Hello. Have you been listening to me? Is this conversation normal to you? Do I come across as the picture of normality?"

A tall dude, who Charlie noted looked very athletic, stood up by the fire and shouted, "Yo, Tiffany, are you gonna leave that dude alone or what?"

She waved him off and turned back to Charlie. "Don't worry, that's just my brother, so if you were interested in me, he's not my boyfriend. Your bigger problem if you're interested in me, will be that I'm a lesbian. Sorry to disappoint you."

Charlie broke the wall he had tried to build and let out a laugh.

"What's so funny? I wasn't kidding. I *am* a lesbian."

He couldn't hide the panic in his face. "No. No, not that. Your sexuality isn't a joke. That is not who I am. It's just, you talk in a funny way. I don't know how to do that."

"I knew you weren't mocking my sexuality, but I already enjoy making you uncomfortable, even though I hardly know you. What do you mean you 'don't know how to do that'? Do what?"

"Just say whatever you want. I can't do that. My brain needs to think things through, over and over, until the conversation has moved past whatever it was I was thinking about. Then, I just say nothing."

She tilted her head, and he had to admit to himself that he would have been interested. Very much so. "You seem to be talking just fine right now."

He put his head down. He couldn't explain himself, and he wanted to cry. "It's really hard."

She smiled and put her hand out. "I'm Tiffany."

Charlie shook her hand. "Charlie."

She stood up and dusted sand off her butt. "I hope it gets easier, Charlie, because I want to keep talking to you." She stepped back. "Until next time." She turned to walk away.

The farther she walked, the more his muscles loosened, and his fingers unclenched from his palms. *No*, he thought. *No. Don't take the easy way out.*

"Hey, Tiffany," he shouted.

She turned back to him.

"When I lived on Block Island, my sister died. Today's her birthday. That's why I wanted to see it tonight."

She bit her lip. "I hope you see what you need to bring you peace. I'm sorry for your loss."

As she walked back to the fire and her friends, Charlie considered what she had said. Of course, his decision to tell her the truth was far from it. She could never know why he was here, the ritual he had on Wreath's birthday.

First, the couples left. Then Tiffany waved goodbye to Charlie, and the teens were gone too. Once he was certain he had the beach to himself, he stood up, inhaled, and walked to the shoreline. The surf spewed past his feet, and Charlie stared down into the water. His fractured reflection stared back at him.

"I can't see Block Island tonight, but it's there. I don't need to see it to know it's real because I've seen it before. So, you can keep hiding, but it changes nothing. I know you're there. I know you're real. One day I'll find you. One day I'll fucking kill you for what you did to my family."

The water shrunk back into the ocean. Nothing happened. Nothing changed. Charlie walked back to his car alone, questioning his own words. Four years, and he'd never seen the monster again. He didn't even know if he believed his own memory. Detectives. The media. They all spent months drilling into the children, trying to dig up the truth, and maybe they were right not to believe the story. Maybe the entire family convinced themselves they saw something they couldn't explain because they didn't want to know the truth. Maybe Block Island itself was nothing more than a myth he'd created in his mind, and the fog protected him from the real memories.

3
A TORN PAGE

Chrissy's back dug into the wrinkled, hard bark of the large oak in front of Tanner's Switch Middle and High School. Hastings kissed her, pressing her harder into the tree. His groin pushed forward, bumping into her stomach, and she fought back the desire to laugh because she wanted him to keep kissing.

The first day of school went well and making out with a dude in front of just about everyone, including some faculty members, would improve her stature even further. Of course she wasn't using Hastings. She was into him and enjoyed the fooling around. But what really turned her on was knowing everyone else saw it and either revered her or reviled her for it.

A car horn honked, and Chrissy opened her eyes. Behind Hastings' stupidly perfect brown hair idled Charlie's beat-up Volvo 240, now more beige than white after years of neglect.

She pushed into Hastings' chest, and he slowly pulled away. "Gotta go. Brother's here."

"Okay, I'll text you later." He smiled at her, the geeky smile of a horny boy in love.

She nodded, picked up her book bag, and walked to the car. When she got in, Charlie was staring at her with a fatherly anxiety in his eyes.

"What?" she asked.

"What happened to you? You used to be a nerd, and now you're making out with dudes in front of the school."

She checked her hair in the passenger side mirror. "Still a nerd. Just a sexy one."

He stuck his tongue out and made a gagging noise. "Never use that word again. You're my sister, and you're fucking thirteen."

"Wah, wah." She dug into her bag and pulled out her book, now finely bent at the spine. As she peeled it open to its latest dog's ear, she put her feet on the dash.

Charlie sighed and set the car in motion. "So, how was your first day?"

"Good," she said, not looking up from the page.

"Don't get used to it."

Chrissy's eyelids drooped. "Yeah, Auntie will lose her job in six months, and we'll be off again."

"Hopefully not back to fucking Cranston."

Chrissy laughed. "Oh jeez. Yeah. Never again, please."

"And me?" Charlie said. "How was my first day? Well, thanks for asking. I skipped."

She dropped the book on her lap. "You skipped on the first day of a new year at a new school?"

He snapped his fingers and pointed at her. She rolled her eyes. "You're an idiot. Why?"

"I woke up. Ate breakfast. Took a shower. Ready to go. Then . . ." He made an explosion sound. "Panic attack. Big time."

She frowned. "I'm sorry. That sucks. You know, of all the places we've lived, this is my favorite so far."

He stopped at a red light. "You're making out with dudes on your first day. Not surprised you like it."

Chrissy laughed. She found a sick joy in being more successful with people than her brother. "Not because of that. And I didn't just meet him today, you know. We met like a month ago. We've been dating for two weeks. But I just like it in Tanner's Switch. The people are nicer here. More chill. And the history is all sorts of fucked-up."

Charlie nodded. "It is cool. Everything is old. Plus, even I made a friend."

Chrissy pointed in the opposite direction from where the car's blinker flashed. "Let's go that way. I hear they have a cool library. We should check it out."

"We've lived here for two months, and you haven't been to the library yet? That new boyfriend is destroying you." He switched the blinker in the opposite direction and turned the car.

They drove in silence for a few minutes after she dropped her head back into her book. She knew her brother relied on her for conversation, that she was the only person he could open up to. She was an outlet for him to vent to about his anxieties and thus eased his stress. But she also knew when to back off and let him slouch back into himself. This was one of those times.

He was taking them to a new place, and that meant a fresh level of fear boiling inside him, and any wrong move could topple him, forcing him to change course and take the safe route back home.

She flipped a page.

"What are you reading?" Charlie asked softly.

She eyed his hands on the wheel, the way he gripped it and shifted his fists as if he were revving a motorcycle. "It's called *Winterset Hollow*, and it's amazing. You can borrow it when I'm done."

"Is it horror? You know I can't read that. I don't know how you can."

She shrugged. "Some people lean into their trauma."

He grabbed an old napkin from the center console and threw it at her. "What thirteen-year-old talks like that? You're so fucking weird."

They pulled into the library parking lot and both Charlie and

Chrissy slowly tilted their heads upward, gawking at the towering gothic display.

"Jesus, this place is enormous," Charlie said.

Chrissy bit her bottom lip and released a giddy giggle. She gripped Charlie by the shoulders. "It's fucking heaven."

She jumped out of the car and skipped through the lot. Before she opened the front door, she turned back to her brother, who walked slowly, still staring at the large front façade. "I'll meet you by the front when I'm done."

He waved for her to go. "Just don't take forever."

She flew past the oval-shaped librarian's desk and searched the end caps for the horror aisles. She found a sign listing the genres by floor and realized she needed to take an elevator to get to her favorite section. While she wished horror was popular enough to demand a first-floor spot, the glee of knowing she stood in a library so massive it required elevators took over any disgruntled feeling toward a society that preferred romance to horror.

When she arrived on the third floor, she found the size of the horror section underwhelming, just one aisle long. Fantasy, which nestled in the aisles next to horror, had three long walkways all to itself. But what horror lacked in size, it made up for in substance, and Chrissy came to understand that someone who loved horror worked there. Had to. No library would order fantastic books like *BETA* by Sammy Scott, *Anathema* by Nick Roberts, and *Experimental Film* by Gemma Files without having an employee who knew, understood, and loved the genre. These weren't books that the mass public fed on, but the types that nurture a genuine sense of horror, feeding the diehards of literary trauma.

She flipped through a Bachman book and to her surprise, discovered the old, tattered thing had *Rage* in it. The book could score her about a hundred bucks or so on eBay if Chrissy had the desire to steal a library book. Luckily for Tanner's Switch Public Library, Chrissy had no interest in doing any such thing. She did, however, want to read it, so she curled the book into her arms and went thirsting for more. She found four books by Ketchum, which she thought impressive for a library, but she'd read all of them. Still, it made her happy to know they sat there waiting to be devoured by someone like her, someone who would find peace in violent words.

Horror wasn't a spotlight on evil, it was control. If a person could create beautiful sentences from horrific events, then any person could weave their way through life's trauma. You just had to make the grime shine.

And as if a spirit wanted to remind her that not all people handled the grime in the same way, she heard a gentle whimper in the aisle next to her. She didn't need to look, knew exactly who it was. Her brother found the horror section, knowing she'd be there, but didn't want to disturb or rush her. The building, being as large and cold as it was, had probably brought him a bout of anxiety and he wanted to be near her. It was sweet, she thought, and it filled her with pride that she could be her older brother's rock.

She noticed a book out of place and grabbed it on her way to her brother, feeling a compulsive need to fix the error. She crept around the corner and peeked at Charlie, who pretended to read a fresh copy of *The Color of Magic*.

"Never took you for a fantasy reader."

Charlie looked up, surprised, and tossed the book back on the shelf. "I'm not. You checking up on me?"

She shrugged.

"Thanks."

Chrissy grabbed the book she'd found in the wrong place and shoved it onto the shelf where it belonged. "I had to come over here anyway. Someone had put *Winter's Myths* in the horror section when it clearly belongs over here in fantasy."

Dissatisfied with collecting only one book, she debated asking for more time but saw the weary bags under her brother's eyes and wanted to bring him peace in the way he needed, which was to get him home where he could lock himself into syndicated sitcoms.

She gave him a nod and locked her arm around his. "You okay?"

He peered around, as if staring at looming ghosts only he could see. "I'll be fine. It just feels like a lot."

They took the elevator down to the front desk. Even the enclosed space smelled like old paper and dust, and Chrissy sniffed it in, soaking in the joy of it.

At the front desk, the librarians were chatting up a couple of elderly women about Broadway musicals, so Chrissy perused the new release stacks. A small section in front of it showcased books by local authors. She scanned past the Christa Carmen books, which she'd already read, and a book on the Richmond boat train accident. On the bottom shelf, she spied a book called *Langblasses and Other Block Island Lore* with a picture of a shadowy creature coming through a wooded area. The creature might have been her monster, but the artwork only gave outlines and shadows. With more detail, maybe the demon could have crawled off the cover and eaten her up. She itched to snatch the book but knew her brother would see it, and it would upset him.

She wished she could feel the same way, but she had no recollection of the monster that killed their sister. In fact, the entire night is one black stain in her memories, a torn page from her biography. She'd tried so many times to remember the events that haunted her siblings, wished she could truly feel their unrelenting fear, but all she could cling to from that night was that she had a sister named Wreath, and then she didn't.

As she and her brother made their way to the car, *The Bachman Books* in her grasp, she knew she'd have to sneak back here to get the Block Island book. If she was being honest with herself, maybe that was why she went from an Anne Rice fan to full-on horror obsessed. It wasn't a way to ease a trauma by leaning into it, but rather to jostle the trauma free, to find something so haunting in her books that it unleashed a chained-up memory of a monster, because the older she got, the more she questioned her family's collective memories.

The monster her family clung to didn't frighten her; the fact it might not be real did.

In one scenario, they had a night of insanity.

In the other, they've been insane ever since.

4

THE BREAKFAST GUEST

J ackson woke from a deep slumber that blurred the lines of reality for a few moments upon awakening. A clinking came from the kitchen, as if silverware fell to the floor. He sat up, rubbed his eyes as the sun sliced through the blinds onto his face.

The clink came again, and paranoia splashed like cold water in Jackson's face. It wasn't a dream noise invading reality. It was a real noise waking him up.

His legs came off the bed, and he stumbled to his feet. He needed a screwdriver to take away the heart palpitations and chest tightness, but first he had to figure out what the fuck was happening in his kitchen.

He wondered if he had accidentally left the door open and let a raccoon rampage his cupboards. He wasn't worried about theft. No one was going to traverse his lawn filled with collected junk just to break into his shitty manufactured home and steal, what? His fine kitchen china?

When he crossed into the living room and saw the small portion of the kitchen counter next to the sink devoid of his dinner dishes, he knew who the intruder was.

As he crossed the threshold into the kitchen, he sighed. "You have to stop coming here, Charlie."

"No, I don't," Charlie said without looking up from the sink as he dutifully scrubbed a handful of forks and knives.

Jackson opened the fridge and took out a bottle of Smirnoff. He grabbed one of the freshly cleaned glasses and poured some.

"Jesus, Dad. Can you even pretend to try?"

Jackson swirled the glass as he went back in the fridge for a carton of orange juice. "What do you think is gonna happen, bud? You think I'm going to stop drinking today and magically become a wonderful dad again?"

Charlie laughed, slammed the faucet off, and turned to him. "You're delusional if you think you were ever a wonderful dad."

Jackson finished making his screwdriver and took a sip. The instant it hit his lips, his chest untightened. "Is that why you came here? Wanted to dig the knife in?"

Charlie sat down at the table and slid a plate of eggs over to his dad. "No, I came here to avoid going to school for the second day in a row. But are you really going to host a pity party here? You were a shitty dad, you're still a shitty dad, and you're probably going to be a shitty dad for a long time. Boo hoo. Cry about it, or ya know, just stop being a shitty dad."

Jackson took another swig and exhaled the detox away. "Chrissy told me you're quiet and get anxiety when you talk to people. Why can't you be like that when you're here? And by the way, go to fucking school. I'm still your dad."

Charlie forked some eggs onto his own plate. "I'm trying to work on my shyness. Congrats on being my test audience."

Jackson crossed his arms. He wished he had done better by them. He knew Charlie told the truth; Jackson had always sucked as a parent, but at least the kids used to know he cared about them.

"Why are you avoiding school, then? Do you need a lecture on avoidance from the alcoholic?"

Charlie smiled. "I'm gonna go. I just need to calm my nerves. I'll be a little late."

Jackson nodded, not wanting to press him anymore, allowing himself to be the cool person in Charlie's life who didn't make him feel guilty for being flawed. They sat in silence for a few minutes, both wolfing down the eggs.

"How's everyone doing?"

"The same as last time. Chrissy's good but getting a little promiscuous. Angela is still a little brat. No one talks to Brian anymore, but when we do, he's still the same asshole."

Jackson nodded. "I know they all think . . ." he trailed off, unwilling to finish the thought.

"No, they don't."

Jackson swallowed the rest of his drink. "You said it yourself months ago. Everyone doubts what happened."

Charlie stood up and tossed his backpack around his shoulders. "Yes, they do. We all doubt it, but no one thinks you did anything. No one. Not even Brian, and he fucking hates you more than he hates combing his stupid hair."

A wave of nausea crept up Jackson's belly. He rushed to the bathroom, clicked the light on, and tossed up his breakfast. Charlie walked in, opened the bathroom closet, and tossed his dad a hand towel.

"Don't you ever want better than this?"

Jackson took the towel and wiped his mouth. A rage soared through him, and he debated grabbing his son by the shoulders and throwing him out the window.

"Shut the fuck up, Charlie."

Charlie scoffed. "You're such a coward."

"Says the kid hiding in my house so he doesn't have to go to school."

"Well, it's been a pleasure, as always. I'll see you in a few days." Charlie walked out.

Jackson wished he had the courage to stop his son, to draw him in for a hug and tell him everything would be all right. But he knew he would keep drinking and nothing would ever change. He'd gone to therapy, taken medications at night to help him sleep, and different pills during the day to quell his anxiety, but nothing worked to dull his constant fear quite like alcohol.

It all seemed so impossible, and the anger increased at the unfairness of his situation. He charged to the door, and as Charlie walked head down to his car, Jackson yelled, "I don't care if you all doubt it. It happened. You can pretend it didn't, so you sleep better at night. But it happened."

Charlie lifted his head, turned around and walked back to the side steps where Jackson leaned out from the kitchen door. "It doesn't matter if it happened or not, Dad. We're all still alive, and the rest of us don't have the luxury of pretending that's not true."

"What do you want me to say? That you're all better than me?"

Charlie craned his neck to the sky, as if searching the clouds for answers. "I just want you to say you'll be better than *you*. Try, Dad. Just quit for a week. Clean your house. Have us over for dinner or games or something."

For a moment, he considered saying yes. The way Charlie laid it out, it sounded feasible, until Jackson remembered the nighttime, how every creak kept Jackson alert, how every kiss from the wind against the window slapped him from sleep. He remembered the countless nights tucked in a ball on his couch with the television playing reruns of *The Office*, and how his eyes fought against him, his body pleading for rest, but his brain saying, "Stay awake or it will kill you."

When Charlie was five, Jackson took the boys on a hike in the woods. Jackson led the trek while Brian and Charlie trailed behind. At one point, Jackson heard Brian yell, "Whoa," and by the time Jackson had turned around, Brian held Charlie and ran with him, a plume of bees surrounding them. Brian ran away from the danger with his little brother in his arms, and when they reached Jackson, he handed Charlie off. Jackson darted away with his son for about a half mile, with Brian keeping in step.

Charlie cried his eyes out, screaming that he didn't mean to do it. Jackson ripped Charlie's clothes off, searching for bees. A few flew out and went on their way.

Charlie screamed, "I can't let go! I can't let go."

Jackson noticed Charlie had a fist gripped around something. He gently pried his son's fingers open to find an acorn clutched so tightly it had broken the skin on Charlie's palm. The poor kid thought he held another bee.

When it ended, Jackson counted eleven stings, and Charlie cried for another hour, overwhelmed and scared to death of any further apocalyptic bug attacks. Brian avoided a single sting, and so did Jackson. Apparently, Charlie had stepped on a nest, and Brian ran *into* the bees to get his younger brother.

Jackson always assumed if he had noticed the situation when it happened, he would have run into a swarm of bees to save his son. Of course he would have, right? What father wouldn't?

But here he was with four children covered in bees, and he just wanted to close the door. A fucking coward through and through.

"I think it would be better if you just moved on, Charlie. Forget your dad and find happiness elsewhere. It won't happen here. I'm unchangeable."

Charlie stared for a moment, turned, and walked off. Jackson closed the door and locked it, went to the couch, and opened the shade. A blizzard of dust motes danced around his face as he watched Charlie drive off.

After his son drove out of view, Jackson walked to the fridge for another drink.

5
CREEPING IN THE CORNERS

Angela sat at her desk with her legs folded, holding in her pee. It pressed on her stomach, and every movement threatened to open the floodgates. It made her sweat.

Why had this happened? As always, she'd avoided drinking anything before and during school, and she emptied her bladder before leaving the house. She hated school, and she especially hated this school, where the teachers talked super slow and placated even the most bizarre of disruptions with an even voice and a creepy smile.

They'd forced her to go to this shithole because the public schools said they didn't have the resources to care for her the way she needed. What they meant was, they didn't want their teachers getting punched and bit anymore.

Her leg shook, which increased her need to pee, but she couldn't stop it. It begged her to stand up and go go go.

But she couldn't. No friggin' way. If she went into the bathroom —those weird-ass school bathrooms with little to no light—she'd see *the thing*. It'd creep out from the corner and come at her, singing its stupid song, "Welcome home."

Fuck that. School wouldn't be over for another couple of hours, but the lunch bell would ring in twenty minutes, and the bathrooms would fill up with kids. She'd be good if other kids were in the room.

Twenty minutes.

Her hands trembled. It took a lot of work to hold in pee, and it didn't thrill her muscles. She brought her attention to the teacher. What subject were they discussing? Oh yeah, life as a colonist. Most of the other kids weren't listening either. They doodled in their notebooks or played with rubber bands or fiddled, fidgeted, stared blankly at the ceiling.

Nineteen minutes.

Why did she have to live this way? Tears formed in her eyes. Her life was a prison of her own design. Pee schedules, showering with the bathroom door open, sleeping in the living room with the television on, and the ceiling light. Her whole fucking day planned around not being alone in the dark.

And did anyone give a shit?

Nope. No one cared.

She wasn't even afraid of the monster. If she saw it in real life and not just some conjured projection in her head, she would stab the fucking thing in the eyeball. Unlike her father and Chrissy, who both just froze up and did absolutely nothing. And her dad continued to do nothing, stopped caring about how maybe that shit traumatized his children. Nope, all he cared about was himself. He gave away all their goddamned money to feel better or something, not thinking how it would affect his kids' lives and how they'd all be shoved into their aunt's apartment, moving every time the woman lost her job, and having to make peace with whatever new dive she moved them into. No matter where they moved, they were living off tuna sandwiches and peanut butter and fluff. Then, they all sat around talking in circles about how maybe the creature was a fever dream, a group projection to make sense of something they couldn't comprehend. Yeah, it was something they couldn't comprehend. A fucking monster. But Angela could comprehend it; because unlike those other morons who barely remembered what the thing looked like or blocked it out entirely like Chrissy, Angela still saw it all the fucking time, everywhere she looked. Even now, it hovered in the classroom corner staring at her with a grotesque grin. And did anyone try to find out how Angela was feeling and dealing with all of this? Nope. Brian was too busy moping in a mound of pills, Charlie sulking to himself about his lack of personality, Chrissy reading a stupid amount of books, and her dad drinking himself to hell. Where was Angela in all this? No one cared. All they cared about was how disruptive she was, and how she always whined and complained. Well, you fucking try living when every time the lights went out, a monster jumped in your fucking face, singing the same horrible song he sang when he chewed on your sister. You see if you turn out normal.

Fuck.

Fifteen minutes.

Fuck.

She openly cried now, cold tears rolling down her cheeks, but just like always, no one noticed.

The teacher, Mrs. Marcotte, a pleasant woman in her forties, droned on about fishing in Rhode Island during the colonial days. Jesus. Who cared? Cod. Mackerel. Herring. Angela hoped it was worth it, stupid colonists, because half the state lived off canned tuna sandwiches now. Economic growth. Everyone just drowned in work and died with no healthcare. Who gave a shit? Mackerel. What the fuck was mackerel, anyway? Did people eat that? Did McDonald's have a McMackerel?

Twelve minutes.

The monster hung in the corner, clung to the ceiling by its claws, hanging down, staring at her with an upside-down face and a crooked smile made of jagged teeth. With a class full of people, it'd stay there, wouldn't sing its stupid song, or crawl toward her. Just taunt her by existing, mocking her with its smiling face, the face of someone who always won, who owned her.

Eleven minutes.

She whimpered, just a small one, not enough to attract attention. But the pee that splashed down her leg and dripped against the linoleum floor attracted all the attention. Kids laughed. One girl screamed. How fucking dramatic. Like, did she really need to scream? The teacher ran over. The pee didn't stop. It wasn't a little making its way out, but the full bladder pouring down her leg, the seat, onto the floor.

Angela kept her head forward, refused to see the looks on the kids' faces. She bawled, embarrassed, angry—no furious, sad.

"What happened, Angela?" the teacher asked.

Angela stayed the course, not moving her head, keeping her eyes directly on the chalkboard. "I'm fine. Just keep teaching."

"I can't do that. We have to clean this up. We'll send you to the office so you can call home."

The teacher stood up and yelled, "Enough" to the laughing chorus.

"Mrs. Marcotte, seriously, I'm fine. Can you just keep teaching? I'll clean it up after." She sniffled and wiped the wet streaks on her cheeks.

"No, Angela. You need to go home. You can't wear those clothes all day. Okay, honey? You're not in trouble. We just gotta get you home and cleaned up. We can figure this out tomorrow."

Angela placed her hands over her face, as if she could disappear into the shadows of her palms. "Please, just keep teaching." The force of her hands muffled her words.

The teacher bent down. "Angela, honey. It's okay. Go to the office, tell them what happened, and just relax. Enjoy an early release."

Angela slapped her hands on the desk. "Please, just keep fucking teaching." The words left her throat like a bomb, and the explosion caused a thick quiet in the room.

For the first time at her special school, she made a teacher raise her voice, "Angela, go to the office now."

Angela slid her chair back, her sneaker sloshing in the puddle of piss. Her feet squeaked with each step as they left wet footprints on the linoleum. She slammed the door on her way out and ran down the dim hall. The monster darted right beside her. "Welcome home," it sang as her feet pitter-pattered down the empty corridor.

6

CHRISSY, THE REBEL

Chrissy read some of the Bachman book on her lunch break. Hastings huffed while she read. It wasn't a possessive need for attention but an inability to enjoy silence and a good book. He needed to talk and to have others talk to him.

He tapped on the front of her book, bouncing it enough to make her eyes slip from their momentum. She slapped the pages shut. "You need to get a hobby so you can stop disrupting mine."

He tilted his head, trying to play cute. "I have a hobby, but they don't let me play baseball in the cafeteria."

She made a fart noise with her tongue.

"You told me you were reading adult books about vampires in like, fourth grade, right?"

"Yes, Anne Rice. I still read Anne Rice. You should too. But I do more than read books, you know? I watch a lot of YouTube! I'll sit there for hours watching Cahlaflour play horror games. She's probably the coolest person ever. And Katieplaysstuff is awesome too! But yes, I also love reading. You should give it a whirl."

He made a pouty face. "You know, I tried once. For you. Not

Anne Rice, but some other horror writer, and I just don't have the attention span. I end up reading the same line over and over because I get distracted, and my brain goes away to somewhere else."

"Porn?"

He laughed. "Probably. But seriously, how do you do it? Like, why did you even get into those books when you were a kid?"

"Long story."

He slid her book closer to him. "I want to know everything about you."

She sighed, reached over the table, and took her book back. "You'd have to understand my family. My mom was this super cool ex-cheerleader. Everyone loved her. Like, even years after high school. She had so many friends, and everyone loved her."

Hastings lifted his hands like he was an evenly balanced Lady Justice. "Okay?"

"My dad was always trying to get in on the fresh new thing. He couldn't hold down a job, so he went after every get-rich-quick scheme he could find. He'd get us kids excited when he ran in all, 'We are going to be millionaires!' But he just kept finding himself at the bottom of a new scam."

Hastings tapped the table. "I love you, but what's this got to do with reading?"

"My brothers and sisters were all the same way, always trying to be cool and in on the next big thing. Fighting for new video game systems we couldn't afford. Spending hours in the bathroom prettying themselves up, always trying to be cool. And it got them nowhere. My dad never found a steady, decent-paying job but lost us tons in shitty investments. My brothers were never cool, no matter how many brand-new video game systems they got. Wreath, well, she was beautiful and smart, but all she ever found were douchey dudes who used her. And my mom worked for almost no money, never happy, always broke and stressed, and she did that until it killed her."

Hastings leaned back in his chair as if those last words physically nailed him in the face. "Wow. I'm sorry."

"I saw all this as a kid. I knew when I was super young that the way they all lived wasn't worth it. One day my dad takes me to the library so he can check some shit out on the computer. I don't remember what, but probably some new MLM scam. So I'm walking through the aisles when I see this teenage girl sitting at a table reading an Anne Rice book. She was kind of ugly. Large, pimply-faced, hair all tangled. And these two bitches, clearly some girls she knew from school, they were just relentlessly mocking her."

She paused for a second, and Hastings lifted his eyebrows, very interested in the rest of the story.

"She didn't give a fuck. Didn't look up from her book. Didn't even show a change in her eyes or smile. You know how people do that when they're uncomfortable? They make weird-ass pretend smiles. She did nothing. She just licked her finger and flipped the page. That was the first time I'd ever seen someone not give a fuck about what other people thought. I decided I wanted to be that girl. I didn't want to give a fuck. When the two girls left, I went up to her and asked what she was reading and if she could tell me about it. She smiled and talked to me like I was smart enough to understand her. Which, like, nobody did back then. When you're a kid, it's like they just want to talk down to you."

Hastings smiled. "That's such a cool story. So this girl, she was a nerd, but she was also really cool?"

"That's how I saw it. I checked out my first Anne Rice book that night, and I didn't know how to read it or understand it. But when I got home, all my siblings busted my balls about it and talked shit, and that made me need to read it even more. The more people talked shit or mocked me, the more I leaned into it. I even bought shirts like Tom Cruise wore in *Interview with the Vampire*. Those stupid poofy shirts. I hated them, and everyone laughed at me when I wore them, so I kept wearing them. It was like I needed to prove to myself that I would do everything in my power to not care what people thought."

"That's so awesome."

She rolled her eyes and put her hands on top of his. "No. It wasn't. By actively trying to get people's attention, to make them not like me, it was the same as everyone in my family trying to get people to like them. We were all putting in the same effort toward something that didn't matter. If I really didn't give a shit what people thought about me, I wouldn't think about other people enough to try."

"Oh."

"But I read a lot of books and I learned a lot. Which led me to be introspective. So, at least I know that I have a weird, stupid desire to get people's attention by annoying them or pissing them off or grossing them out. Unlike the rest of my family, who refuse to change or even see the need for it, I can work on myself and be a better person."

Hastings gave up responding and reverted to head nodding instead.

"Anyway, I have to go." She stood up and yanked her book from Hastings' grasp.

"Where? We still have ten minutes of lunch before social studies."

"No, you do. I'm leaving for the day. I have something to do."

"What?"

"I need to get a book from the library."

He laughed, catching the attention of some girls sitting nearby. "You're cutting school to get a book? Only you. All right, let's do this." He stood up and crumbled his paper bag filled with an empty Hi-C container and a sandwich wrapper, then tossed it into a nearby container.

She opened her mouth to argue but decided she enjoyed having a boyfriend willing to face detention or suspension to cut school with her. Especially one who would do so just to hit up a library.

Leaving school turned out to be rather simple. They walked out the front door and hopped on the town bus. No sneaking necessary. It turned out people didn't give a shit if kids went to school in Tanner's Switch, apparently.

At the library, Chrissy went right to the front shelf where she'd seen the Block Island book, and luckily, there it stayed. No surprise. It's not like it was an Oprah's Book Club pick.

She dragged Hastings into the elevator, and he moved in for a make-out session, but while elevator kissing might be a kink for some, she preferred a crowd. She pushed him off her and giggled. He put his hands up, relenting. She liked that he never pressed, stopped the second she said to, and kept a smile on his face. No whining, no begging.

They rode to the fifth floor, all the way to the tippity top. The fifth floor housed a special selections room, an art room, and an auditorium. Why did they need an auditorium in Tanner's Switch? What big-named speaker would fill that room? Wouldn't someone noteworthy go to Providence or Boston? She shrugged. No matter.

Hastings gave her a kiss and promised to see her soon. He wanted to explore the other floors and leave her to her reading uninterrupted.

She peeled open the book and read the first chapter. She wanted to flip through, see if any of the stories had parallels to her own, but thought it best to respect the author enough to read a little of what he wrote. The first yarn talked about a fiery ghost ship phenomenon called the *Palatine* Light. Apparently, the residents of Block Island had a pirate streak in the 1700s and they lured the *Princess Augusta* to its demise before robbing the German immigrants aboard of their worldly possessions. The passengers bound for Philadelphia were killed, and according to the book, their spirits haunted the island. Many townspeople reportedly saw an apparition of the boat on fire during dark nights. Since the immigrants were Palatine Germans—natives of the Palatinate region—the *Princess Augusta* was described in documents of the time as the *"Palatine Ship,"* which caused confusion over its name and why the phenomenon was dubbed the *Palatine* Light.

She rolled her eyes. No one had ever mentioned any of that to her before, and she doubted many people who lived on the island even knew about it. This story mattered little to her and upended her search for answers to her own life, but something about the tale felt all wrong, and she wanted to know more.

She went to her favorite place for answers: Wikipedia. There she found a very different tale, stating that Block Islanders helped the *Princess Augusta,* and a few of the ship's passengers even ended up living there. Many of the immigrants aboard died on the ship from foul water.

The Wikipedia article also told a much more frightful tale about a woman named Mary Van Der Line who refused to deboard and went down with the ship. Those who claim to see the ghost ship also say they can hear her screams.

That sent a shiver down Chrissy's spine. After further reading, she discovered the boat never caught fire and most likely went through repairs before heading off to Philadelphia. So much for fiery ghost stories.

She slid the book away and dug deeper on the internet, searching for Mary Van Der Line. Unfortunately for her desire to find answers to her own life, she also loved a good rabbit hole.

Mary Van Der Line had limited hits on the good ole interweb, as Chrissy's dad called it, but she found a weird case study about someone with almost the same name. It didn't take long into reading it before Chrissy's heart thumped with a little more ferocity.

Mary Vanderline, a twenty-one-year-old woman on Block Island, suffered from seizures, but unlike normal seizures, these lasted for up to two hours. Somehow, her brain and, well, life remained unmarred. Hence, the medical miracle worthy of a case study.

This Mary Vanderline came from the 1970s, so not the same as the boat lady, but here's where it really sent Chrissy's adrenaline rushing. Mary Vanderline, while not suffering from massive brain damage from the seizures, hallucinated, claiming every time she had one of her episodes, a monster crawled closer to her, and eventually, she knew it would reach her.

Chrissy did a dance in her seat, unbalanced by the creeps worming up her back, the feeling that the monster was closing in on her as well. She looked behind her, giggling at herself for being such a geek. Two librarians chatted and rolled a cart filled with returns. No monsters, although one lady looked like the type who enjoyed yelling at children.

She took a breath and read more, hardly able to hold her composure as she reached the sentence about Mary's uncle claiming she had a seizure in the locked bathroom, then screamed about a monster. When her uncle crashed through the door, his niece was nowhere to be found.

Chrissy cried and shut the phone down. None of this jarred the images of the monster loose in her head, but the parallels were insane, and she couldn't wait to tell Charlie about it. Still, parallels did nothing to bring her clarity.

She sighed and headed for the elevator, carrying her Block Island book with her. The elevator dinged after the doors closed, and with a small bounce, she descended to the bottom floor.

The lights flickered and fizzled out.

"Welcome home." The echoes of memory played in her mind like an old cassette tape.

She startled and dropped her book. As she pressed her back against the wall and slid downward onto her butt, the sounds freshly excavated from her mind dug up more memories. The visuals stayed blurred outside of her mind's capabilities, but that voice—the choral quality of its speaking—it flooded in like a tsunami. A single voice split in two, one masculine and gruff, the other feminine and sing-songy, yet somehow, they were entwined, coming from the same cavernous throat.

The lights clicked back on, and Chrissy reached for her book, which lay splayed in the center of the floor. She gripped its center and turned it over, only to scream anew. A black-and-white picture looked back at her from the pages of her cheesy book of hauntings. A slender, gray face, as if it were smoke-worn wallpaper. Its eyes, swirling black pools. Its mouth, a swath of bladed teeth.

The monster.

Wreath's monster.

She remembered it now. Holy fuck, she remembered it now, and wished to the gods she'd never tried to unearth it. She stared at it, frozen just as she had been as a child. Her fingernails dug into her palm, her throat closed, and her muscles ached from temporary tetanus throughout her body.

Ding.

She jolted as the doors split apart. Hastings stood at the threshold, staring in shock at the sight of his girlfriend curled in the fetal position in the elevator's corner.

"What happened?" He ran to her, bent down, and rubbed her back.

She brushed his arm off her and stood, grabbing her book. "I need to check out this book and get the fuck out of here."

"Were you screaming?" He followed her to the front desk, where a few librarians stared with wide eyes and nervous grins.

Chrissy wiped the water from her eyes. "Nope. I'm fine. Just need to get home."

With trembling hands, she gave the book to the red-haired librarian.

Hastings rubbed her back again. "Are you sure you're okay?"

She pushed his hand off again. "I'd be fucking fine if you stopped touching me."

She regretted taking out her anxiety on him, and especially the way she yelled, causing all eyes to turn toward him. She'd villainized him to the crowd, and an embarrassed shade of red swam across his cheeks.

"Okay. I'll just head back to school." He walked out, head down, a defeated puppy.

"Do you need us to call someone?" the librarian asked, staring at Hastings as he walked out the door.

7

PAREIDOLIA

Tiffany had told Charlie that Tanner's Switch was all misfits. At the time, it provided him zero relief, but as the bell rang, ending *his* first day at school, she may have been right. No one mocked him, no crazed bullies stood out as future threats. All in all, it was a perfectly fine day. Sure, he ate alone at lunch, no one really spoke to him all day, and he never ran into Tiffany—his only chance at a friend—but he also avoided punches, or even verbal assaults. A win's a win.

He hated conversation, anyway, so not making friends was A-OK by him.

As he stepped through the double doors, and the sunlight dropped on his face like a hammer, his day of no talking ended abruptly. A muscular hand slapped his back and gripped his shoulder.

"What's up, buddy?"

He turned to find Tiffany's older brother smiling at him.

"You're the kid from the beach, right?" the guy asked.

Charlie nodded his head. "Yeah, you're Tiffany's brother?"

He held out his beefy paw. "Yup. Doug. What's your name?"

"Hey, Doug. I'm ah, Charlie."

They shook hands.

"You're new to Tanner's Switch, right?"

Charlie nodded. "Yeah. Tiffany is the first person I've ever talked to here. I was hoping to see her today, but I guess she's not in any of my classes."

Doug shot him a stern eye. "Why, you don't like her, do you?"

"Oh, no. I just, ah—" He shrugged, hoping that would settle it. But when Doug kept staring, waiting for his reply, he sighed and continued, "I just don't have any friends. Ya know?"

Doug clapped. "Well, it's good you don't like her. She's a lesbian. Not interested in you, okay, pal? So don't try anything."

Charlie put his hands up. "I promise."

"Anyway, me and some friends are about to head to the management area for some beers. You want to join us? Tiff is gonna be there."

Charlie shook his head. "No. I would, but I gotta get home. I have some stuff to do."

Doug frowned. "Okay, well, if you change your mind, that's where we'll be until it gets dark." He walked away and high-fived some other massive human male.

Charlie's eyes watered. The strain of keeping up a conversation with someone so vastly different from him flooded him in anxiety. His heart raced, and he worried at the straps on his book bag.

Part of him wanted to go. So rarely did he make friends, and Doug's offer seemed genuine enough. In the back of Charlie's mind, he wondered if it was a prank. Drag the new kid into the woods and beat him up a little, let him know not to fuck with Doug's sister. Or maybe something less sinister but equally awful, like a hazing ritual. Welcome to the club. You just have to down ten beers and swim across the bay.

He opened his phone and headed toward his car. Twelve text messages. All but two texts were from his aunt, ranting about Angela getting into trouble at school and needing Charlie to pick her up. The last two were from Chrissy rambling about how she needed to speak to him immediately and wanting to know if he could give her a ride home, but she wasn't at school, she was at the fucking library.

He put the phone back in his pocket and rubbed his eyes. Why did everything fall into his lap? Why did people assume Charlie would be the one to fix everything? He couldn't even take care of himself, yet he was supposed to pick everyone else up when they dropped the ball.

He typed a few replies but deleted what he wrote, never quite landing on what he should say. Finally, he responded to his aunt and to Chrissy: *No.*

He put the phone away and chased after Doug. "Hey, hold on. I want to come with you."

THE HANGOUT SESSION in the woods wasn't a prank or a hazing ritual. It was, in fact, just a few dudes hanging out along a cut path while drinking beers and telling raunchy jokes. It was so mundane, Charlie almost wished he had just picked up his sisters.

Charlie had drunk beer before when he visited Brian at college, which was probably a dumb decision, knowing how his father turned out, but he'd only ever sipped on it. He started that way with Doug and his friends, too, but after a little while, he matched the sip frequency of the other guys as if they were practicing for a synchronized drinking tournament.

Two or three beers in, his head swam, and his voice slurred, something he recognized because the other symptom the beer provided was a new ability to speak freely, his nerves destroyed by tinny tasting cheap-ass medicine.

Tiffany showed up around half an hour after the boys started drinking. She had a friend with her, or maybe a girlfriend. They weren't holding hands or acting cuddly, but the closeness between them was apparent in the way they giggled with one another. The special bond between two people who knew each other so well, they could laugh at nothing and know the shared punchline.

"Charlie?" she asked at the sight of him.

He crossed his legs and bowed with his arm across his chest. "The one and only."

Had he truly just done that? Jesus. Yeah, the beer opened him up, but it also turned him into a king idiot. No one laughed at him, though. Not even Doug and his Neanderthal friends. In fact, the guys had shown nothing but kindness the entire time, laughing at Charlie's jokes and making him feel like one of the gang. Of course, he didn't tell the kind of jokes he normally enjoyed, shooting more for Brian's crasser humor, but whatever. He told them well enough to get big guffaws from a group he never suspected would enjoy his company.

Tiffany hugged him. "How did you get here?"

He took a swig. "Doug invited me."

Doug smiled. "Sorry, Tiff. I stole your friend. He's my friend now."

Tiffany tilted her head and gave him a wide-eyed stare. "You can only be friends with one of us. Choose wisely."

Charlie stumbled back, exaggerating his surprise. He pointed to Doug's friend, Corey. "I choose Corey. He brought the beer."

Corey ran up to him and slapped him on the shoulder. "Good choice!"

Tiffany sighed. "Boys. So easy to please. He didn't even bring good beer. If you're going to pimp yourself out for alcohol, at least choose someone who brings something stronger than water."

Corey whispered to Charlie, but loud enough for everyone to hear, "Tiff's just jealous because my girlfriend is hotter than hers."

The new girl slapped him. "Hey!"

So, yeah, the new girl was Tiffany's girlfriend.

Charlie put his hand out awkwardly. "I'm Charlie."

She shook it. "Beth. And I am way hotter than Corey's girlfriend, who, by the way, is a literal golden retriever."

Everyone laughed, and while Charlie didn't get the joke, he joined in and found it genuine.

Tiffany turned to Doug. "Are we going to the boats?"

Doug shrugged. "Sure. Let's go."

"Where?" Charlie asked.

Doug picked up the last case of beer with full cans in it. "*We* are going to the boats, but you and Corey can go somewhere else, you goddamn traitor."

They marched on an offshoot path, cut and worn from use, but thin and unmarked. Branches and vines stretched over the route, slapping against Charlie's legs and chest as the group trudged through.

At the end of the trail, an enormous stone the size of a truck jutted off the land and hovered over the edges of a lake. The sun shined on the water, and a fractured line of light stretched from one side of the lake to the rock.

Tiffany kicked off her sneakers and rolled up her pants before sitting on the ledge, letting her feet dip into the water.

Charlie cracked another beer and took a long pull. His brain turned from swimming to drowning in seconds, an analogy he didn't enjoy making so close to the water. Maybe this was where his new friends would turn on him. If he proved himself a lightweight, the new fish showing blood to a pool of sharks, he could lose them quickly.

He tried not to speak, containing the deepening slur in his speech to the depths of his throat. As the group goofed off on the rock, drinking, laughing, shoving each other, Charlie sat on the edge, staring into the water. Every few minutes, he'd catch himself swaying left and right in rhythm with the gentle sloshing of water against the stone.

While the rest of the group focused on a thumb wrestling match between Corey and Beth, Tiffany stayed on the edge of the rock next to Charlie, splashing water with her feet.

He pulled his hands away from his cheeks and asked, "Swearza boats?"

"Huh?" She giggled.

"The boats. You said boats." He put his head back down.

"The rocks. There's a few more around the lake. We call them our boats. We aren't stupid enough to go in the water when we drink. It's just our dumb name for them out here."

His brain didn't comprehend what she meant. He stared into the lapping green water, too sludgy to see more than some floating particles. He blurred his eyes as he focused on his reflection, waiting for the corrupted image to grow a smile too large for his cheeks, a shadow of the monster, the broken bits of its structure releasing from Charlie's memory into a crude pareidolia from hell.

It never came, though. In fact, he couldn't pull even a distorted version of the monster into his mind, let alone into a visual projection.

Not only had the alcohol loosened his tongue, but it had freed him of the creature. His pulse didn't drumroll, his palms didn't sweat, and his heart kept a steady thrum.

Maybe he understood his father after all. No. The difference between Jackson and Charlie was the responsibility. Jackson had children who needed him, who had been through the same horrific event and needed an adult hand to guide them through it. He failed them. Charlie had no responsibilities. He could get drunk and forget the monster, and it changed nothing. No one looked up to him. No one cared about Charlie.

He remembered his phone, which sat in the pocket of his backpack, which sat in the back seat of Doug's Camry. Angela, ignored, left to handle her own trauma with no one protecting her. Chrissy, who texted and asked for his help. Maybe he had responsibilities and people who needed him after all.

But for right now, Charlie couldn't stand, and for once, he enjoyed only caring about himself.

"Let's go," Doug said.

Charlie leaned back until his head rested on the stone. "You shouldn't drive drunk."

Doug laughed. "Beth's driving us all home. She didn't drink."

Charlie squinted his eyes toward the sky. "I think I'm just going to rest here for the night."

Doug scooped Charlie up like a baby and placed him on his feet. When Charlie leaned, Doug caught him and put his arm around Charlie's back. "Come on, kid. You can do it."

Why weren't they laughing at him?

"Why are you guys so nice to me?"

That made them laugh. He picked up Tiffany's chuckle above all else.

Doug slapped his shoulder. "Welcome to Tanner's Switch. We take care of each other. It's fucking weird here."

"It's very bizarre," Charlie said, although he knew the words came out jumbled.

"Well, I also slipped a bunch of drugs into your beer, so we can take you to the hotel and steal your organs."

The group laughed again.

"You're joking with me. I think."

"You'll see."

THE TRIP back felt quicker than the trek into the woods. They were at the car in no time. Doug grabbed Charlie's backpack and tossed it to him. As promised, Beth drove everyone home, and Charlie wondered how Doug would get his Camry back, but he was too tired to ask. Instead, he leaned his head against the back seat window and fell asleep.

He woke up with the car parked in front of his house and Tiffany shaking his knee from the front seat. His eyelids pulled apart, and he took a deep breath.

"Go eat some food to soak up the alcohol." She smiled at him.

He nodded and opened the car door. The first step was shaky, but after he took a few more, he regained his walking skills.

Before he opened the front door of his aunt's house, he turned back to the car. "How'd you know where I lived?"

Tiffany leaned over Beth and yelled, "We used your face to unlock your phone and checked your PayPal account for a mailing address. Also, I bought some new shoes."

Charlie smiled. "At least you didn't take my organs."

"Lift your shirt," she said as she flopped back into her seat.

He peeled his tee shirt up to reveal a series of crudely drawn stitches made with black marker. He laughed.

"See ya," Tiffany said and waved goodbye as they drove off.

He waved to nothing. "See ya."

He turned and opened the door as everyone inside welcomed him with a chorus of yelling.

8

MOVING ON

Angela sat at the kitchen table with her arms crossed. In the reflection on the fridge, she saw her distorted face, red and streaked with tears. Auntie Clara yelled at Charlie for not picking Chrissy or Angela up from school, but she more yelled *at* Charlie *for* Angela. Auntie *C* had worn herself out hollering at Angela, frustrated at how skilled Angela was at turning into a hollow void when someone screamed at her.

Of course, like always, no one gave Angela the chance to speak her truth. No one cared what it felt like to pee yourself in front of your class, only to spend the rest of the day in the nurse's office with wet pants because not a single person in your family wanted to pick you up. Angela wasn't a human in the family. She was a chore.

Chrissy, too, yelled at Charlie for not picking her up, but unlike with Angela, Auntie Clara gave her space to speak.

Charlie smiled a little. It looked insulting, but Angela knew him enough to understand it was just a nervous thing. His eyes were bloodshot, and he kept leaning into the door frame. Maybe Auntie Clara didn't want to come to terms with it because she didn't bring up the obvious fact that Charlie was drunk or stoned. Even Angela could see that.

Charlie just stood and took it. He didn't argue, just kept repeating his life's mantra, "I'm sorry. I'm sorry."

When the whole thing blew over, everyone stormed to their rooms, leaving Angela alone in the kitchen. The lights were on, at least.

Auntie watched something in her room. Angela could tell by the annoying laugh track echoing through the hall. Chrissy probably read a book because her room went quiet. Charlie played music in his room. Trampled by Turtles, Angela thought. She picked all this up from the kitchen table by staring down the slender hallway, bedrooms flanking each side. At the very end of the hall, staring at her with its half-opened maw, stood the dark bathroom.

The noise coming from the other rooms helped ease her anxiety a little, making her feel less alone, more protected, as if noise created a natural barrier from the bizarre and ethereal.

She ate alone. A packet of ramen noodles and a cut-up hot dog. She wondered if Charlie had dinner, or Chrissy for that matter. Auntie C probably ate something at work. She usually did or ate fast food in the parking lot of the Mickey D's, unwilling to bring it home out of shame. A two-dollar cheeseburger, too much of a luxury to flaunt in front of children.

Angela gulped her meal down, eyeing the bathroom the whole time. When she finished, she planned to hit the couch in the living room to watch something but caught Chrissy sneaking from her room to Charlie's. Assuming a fight lingered on the horizon, Angela slunk down the hall for a little snooping. Her Auntie had fallen asleep with the television on, which relieved Angela. One less person to catch her spying.

She crept to the threshold of Charlie's room and leaned against the wood-paneled wall. It bowed from her weight.

"I'm sorry I didn't pick you up. I just . . ." He said something else, but Angela lost it while focusing on leaning in enough to see them without them seeing her.

Charlie sat on his bed, head resting on the wall facing away from his door. Chrissy sat on the edge of the bed, facing Charlie, but with a slight shift of her eyes, she could probably catch Angela in the act.

"It's fine. I was annoyed, but I'm over it. I'm too fucked up about my day to stress about it. I just need to talk to you."

"Okay."

"Are you drunk?"

"Is that what you want to talk about? I won't become Dad. I promise."

Chrissy waved her hands. "No. No. I know you won't. That's not it. I just have something kind of big."

Charlie sat up. "Oh, no. You're not pregnant, are you?"

"What? No. You *must* be drunk to ask that."

He laughed. "No. I drank, and it turns out I'm a huge lightweight, but I feel fine now. Funny, I figured I would have puked, but I feel good."

Angela shifted forward and gave a quick glance toward the half-open bathroom door before returning to the conversation in Charlie's room.

"I'm proud of you for having fun."

"So, what do you got?"

Chrissy lifted a book and showed him the cover. Charlie flopped back down dramatically.

"Please tell me you don't want to talk about that. You're never going to get me into horror."

"No. No. Listen. I did some research today."

Chrissy droned on about her research, boring stuff about pirates and boats burning and blah blah blah.

Angela couldn't see Charlie's eyes, but she could feel them rolling back into his brain.

When Chrissy brought up the woman with the seizures, Charlie sat up, and Angela nearly fell over. When she continued about the woman seeing a monster and disappearing in her bathroom, Angela held back tears. Charlie, however, did something unexpected.

"Okay?"

"What do you mean, 'Okay?'"

"I mean, yeah, you found an urban legend with some similarities."

Chrissy pushed her head forward, as if her neck were trying to remove it from her body. "Are you kidding me? First, it wasn't an urban legend. It came from a fucking medical report. Second, it's not similarities, it's damn near identical."

Angela's jaw dropped. Charlie had always been a steadfast believer, eager to find any proof of the monster, and now Chrissy presented him with a very similar case, and he shrugged it off. It made no sense.

"But that's not even it," Chrissy said. She slid the book to Charlie. "Flip to the page I dog-eared."

He did and within a second, he dropped the book to the floor. "Jesus fucking Christ."

"Right?"

The book landed with its cover up, and despite that, Angela leaned forward as if she could magically see through it.

Charlie's fingers trembled, and he tapped them on his knees. "I think we should just let it go."

Chrissy's jaw dropped. "You've got to be kidding me. You make friends for one day, and suddenly you're all about moving past this? This is everything we've been looking for. It's validation."

Charlie sat upright, turning his body into an *L*. "We don't need validation. Our worth isn't tied to the fucking monster. We just keep giving it power by caring. We should just move on from it."

Chrissy shook her head as if trying to rattle those words right out of her brain. "You're kidding me. Are you serious?"

A rage built inside Angela, boiling from her gut and spewing from her mouth. She charged into the room, all caution lost. "Move on? Move on?"

She came to the bed and shoved Charlie. "My whole life. It's always there. Always."

"Were you spying on us?" Charlie asked.

Chrissy still had her jaw dropped, and she glanced between Charlie and Angela.

"Fuck you. Yes. I was spying on you turning into a coward. You always talk so much shit about killing that monster if you ever saw it, and it's all bullshit. She finally found something worth looking into, and you turn into a wimp."

"Get out of my room."

Chrissy jumped in. "Hey, she's right."

"No. She isn't, and neither are you. What did we find out? That someone had a seizure on Block Island and saw a monster? Great, let's just go to Block Island and give ourselves seizures. Sound good? You found out nothing. Okay? I hope your little stories make you feel better, but they do nothing to help us. What do we do with that information?"

Chrissy stood and picked up the book. "The story with the picture talks about people on the island seeing the monster on foggy nights. They call them Langblasses. The painting of it in the book came from an artist who lives on the island. We can start by going to talk to her."

Charlie shook his head. "This isn't a movie. We aren't *The Goonies*. I'm not going on an adventure with you to lure out a monster that ate our fucking sister. What the hell are you and I going to do? Go to this lady's house and say, 'Ah, that monster you drew ate our sister. Can we ask you some questions?' Do you not remember what we went through? The police and detectives, and having to give our story over and over, and the newspapers, and the mocking. All the bullshit. Why would we ever go back to that island? Did you honestly think you would show me that book, and we'd just go back?"

"And me," Angela said. "I'm going too."

They both turned to her and in unison said, "No."

She stomped her foot. "You guys don't get to be the only people affected by this. I'm going with you."

They both yelled at her at the same time. She couldn't understand them when they spoke together. A mishmash of obnoxiousness. "You're too young. You're a pain in the ass. We don't want anything to happen to you. You shouldn't have been spying."

They wouldn't stop, and she couldn't get a word in, as always. So, she reverted to the only thing that eased her frustration when she had words to speak but no one to speak them to. She screamed. She screamed like an ignored teapot. Charlie covered his ears and yelled at her to leave the room. Chrissy frowned, and she tilted her head.

Auntie C ran in, her eyes bloodshot and drowning in black pools. She grabbed Angela by the arm and dragged her out of the room. As Auntie C pulled her down the hall to the living room, Angela turned around to see the monster peeking from the half-opened bathroom door with a smile on its face.

9
A DOZEN WASPS STINGING

Charlie sat in the back seat of Doug's Camry, his body bouncing from the pockmarked dirt road. Tiffany sat in the passenger seat, fiddling with her phone's music app, which she had synced to Doug's stereo. Her tastes were eclectic, but no matter the genre, all the songs had one thing in common: upbeat. Charlie preferred music that sent him spiraling into a moody pool of existential dread, but to each their own.

Right now, he surely wasn't in the mood for cheerful tunes. While Tiffany and Doug sang along to "Sound System" by Operation Ivy, Charlie fumed over his sisters, who had berated him all morning about the monster.

He spent years in a cycle of depression, paranoia, and desperation because of that one night. He clung to it, needing it, despite its poisonous bite. In that way, he hadn't differed from his alcoholic father. He'd refused to give up on something he knew was killing him.

He wasn't a hero for thinking about the monster all the time. It didn't bring his sister back or glue his family into one happy piece. All he'd done was sulk deeper into his shell, and in reality, that probably only hurt his family. If he'd moved on, he could have guided them to do the same.

No good could come from going to Block Island. Most likely, they'd be chasing ghosts, resulting in nothing other than more pieces that didn't fit together. Or worse, they could find their way to the monster, and then what? Get eaten too? How the fuck could they stop a monster that eats humans and then vanishes into nothing?

"Charlie?"

Tiffany's voice snapped him out of his sulk.

"Yeah."

"Were you listening? Doug wants to hit up the ice cream shop in Watch Hill, hobnob with the wealthy in their salmon-colored beach slacks."

"Sounds fancy. I'm in." Funny how it only took one day of hanging with these two for him to gain enough confidence to converse with them. He still felt awkward and anxious, but he could do it. He could do it.

They pulled into the bustling parking lot. It was filled with an eclectic mix of people. Rich older men, some indeed in salmon-colored slacks, which Tiffany, Doug, and Charlie got a good giggle out of. Some girls Charlie had to pry his eyes away from. Lots of young kids too.

A group of guys in their early twenties walked by Doug's Camry, and Charlie's heart rose in tempo, forewarning his fight-or-flight response. Trouble. The dudes wore dirty clothes. A few of them had jeans covered in paint and grime. One of them wore khakis two sizes too big without a belt, and he had to keep pulling them up as he walked. They all had beards and long hair.

Doug and Tiffany, less worried than Charlie, hopped out of the car while the guys were hanging in front of it. Charlie sighed and joined his friends.

As he moved around the car, he tucked his arms in, working to avoid any unnecessary confrontation. The guys weren't doing anything wrong, but the way they shifted their eyes and constantly wiped their noses put Charlie on high alert.

Turns out they smelled like shit too.

He let the air out of his chest as he passed them. Tiffany skipped as she walked, and Charlie turned his focus on her. What was it about her that put him at ease?

One guy said to his buddies, "We should head to Providence. I don't want to be here all day."

Charlie's legs turned to jelly. His eyes filled with water. He'd been right about that group. They were trouble. Every instinct told him to keep moving, but the stupid part of him that believed in unbreakable bonds and other fairy tales forced him to turn around.

He whispered, "Brian?"

The group of guys turned to him, and the one with the khakis too big smiled. His teeth were beady, yellowed things, half dead like the body they clung to. "Charlie?"

Brian pushed his friend out of the way and hugged his brother. Charlie hadn't expected the kindness. Brian was more of the arm punch and wisecrack kind of guy, but here he was, hugging his brother as if he just got back from a long stint in the military.

Brian, of course, wasn't in the military. He had no discipline.

Charlie hadn't thought about the embarrassment of introducing his brother to his new friends, but it hit him now. He'd eventually have to explain to two siblings who were best friends how *his* brother was a meth head piece of shit.

Brian let go. His eyes were watering too. "I miss you, brother."

Charlie stepped back, examining Brian. His skeletal frame, the gray bags under his eyes, long, yellowed fingernails, and dirty clumped hair came together as if Brian were attempting to *become* the monster.

He wanted to say he missed Brian, too, but his throat filled with chalk powder, and all he could muster was, "Hey."

"Let's go for a walk?" Brian asked.

Charlie turned to his friends, unable to hide the sadness on his face. "You guys go without me. I'll meet you back here soon."

Tiffany's smile melted away, and her eyebrows drooped with worry. "Are you okay?"

Charlie nodded. "Yeah, this is my brother, Brian. We haven't seen each other in a while."

Doug nodded. "I'll buy you a cup of banana ice cream because that's just randomly what I expect you to like."

Charlie shrugged, not in the mood for jokes. "Sounds good."

Brian guided Charlie through his group of friends, who all stayed in place chatting. Each one of them looked punch-worthy, and Charlie hated knowing his brother associated with them.

They walked to a concrete ledge overlooking the ocean. Boats lined the docks around the wall, bobbing gently with the lapping water. Charlie and Brian leaned against a metal rail, the salty air blowing against their faces with the cool ocean breeze.

"What have you been up to, Charlie boy?" Brian smiled.

This newfound kindness in his brother made the deathly pallor on his face even more horrific. If only his brother were still an asshole, maybe Charlie wouldn't have to mourn another sibling.

"I've been good. Made some friends." He pointed toward the corner of the shops where Tiffany and Doug had disappeared.

"Yeah, that's awesome. Is that chick your girl? She was hot."

"No. Just a friend."

"How's Chrissy and Angela? I miss them."

Charlie nodded. "They're great. Chrissy has a boyfriend. Still reads nonstop. Angela's having a tough time. Dad's still the same."

Brian jerked his head away, toward the ocean, as if the very mention of their father was a fist to the mouth. "Fuck Dad. I'm glad Chrissy's doing well. She was always the better one of us. No offense. She's just, you know."

Charlie nodded again. "Yeah, she has a gift. She's special. No offense taken. I agree. You should come by while you're here." Charlie regretted inviting him instantly. Brian wouldn't come, never had before. In fact, the only time Charlie had seen Brian since he moved away to college was when Charlie visited Brian's dorm, long before Brian dropped out. Whenever Brian called, Charlie vomited out an invitation, like he was begging his brother to come home. Charlie always told himself he'd stop trying, but every time, he always said the same thing.

"Yeah, that's a good idea. Maybe I'll swing by tonight. I just have some business to handle in Providence. Me and my boys are working on something. I can't say what it is, but let's just say if you think Dad was rich after Mom died, this is going to put that to shame."

There were two constants in every conversation with Brian. The first was a half-hearted acceptance of an invitation. The second was talk of a secret plan he worked on to make everyone rich. To his credit, whenever he spoke about getting rich, he always brought the siblings up, as if his fortune would be theirs as well. Chrissy assumed the get-rich-quick schemes were drug-related, but Charlie suspected not. Brian was big into art and film. At least he was before the drugs splintered his mind. Charlie thought Brian believed he could walk up to a guy who knew a guy and pitch his movie idea, and just like that, he'd have studios throwing cash at him.

"That sounds great. I hope it works out. I could use a newer car." Charlie wished he could slap his brother and say, "Snap the fuck out of it. How many times are you going to do the same thing before you realize it's never going to work out for you? Clean the fuck up." But Charlie wasn't that kind of person. He placated to avoid confrontation.

Brian scratched his ghostly white arm, and thin layers of skin flaked off like ash. "Yeah, maybe I'll stop by after my meeting. Could be good. I'd like to see everyone. You all treating Auntie well?"

"Yeah, to be honest, we all hardly see her. She's working so much, ya know? Always working. She flipped out on us last night, though."

Brian reached into his pocket and pulled out a pack of cigarettes. As he took one out, he looked at Charlie. "Want one?"

Charlie shrugged. "Sure."

Brian's eyes widened. "You smoke now?"

"No, but it's a good time to start." He took the cigarette.

Brian lit Charlie's and his own. Charlie took half-inhales, not wanting to cough like a geek. He'd been around cigarette smoke enough, with his dad and his aunt, that he thought he could manage without a hacking fit.

"So, what's going on? You look stressed. You're smoking. Auntie's yelling at you all. What's up?"

"You don't want to know."

Brian raised an eyebrow like the Rock used to do when he wrestled. "Yes, I do."

"Trust me, you don't."

Brian exhaled a stream of gray smoke from his nostrils. "Dude, I'm a shitty brother who abandoned you all like Dad did. Let me feel like I can help. Talk to me."

Charlie put his head down and inhaled a small sliver of smoke. It felt good, the way it bit at his lungs, a dozen wasps stinging. "Chrissy found a book about Block Island, and it has a picture of the monster in it. Our monster."

Brian jerked back. "You mean it looks like our monster? Our monster looks a lot like horror movie creatures, dude. It could just be a similarity."

"Yeah, no. This was our monster to a tee. Chrissy has this entire plan. She wants us to talk to the artist who drew the monster. Blah blah. I told her to stop, to just forget about it. Our lives would be easier if we just stopped."

Brian rubbed his forehead. "What the fuck is wrong with you?"

"What?"

"Our lives would be easier if we just stopped? This wasn't a bad day, Charlie. A fucking—" He paused, looking around at the faces turning toward him as his voice rose. He leaned in and went back to whispering, "A goddamn monster ate our fucking sister. We were all

ON A CLEAR DAY, YOU CAN SEE BLOCK ISLAND

kids, but Chrissy and Angela were super little. They can't just move on from that."

He leaned back and took a pull from his smoke. "Look, you're not wrong. It would be better if we all could just move on. But we can't, and they especially can't. Poor Angela probably can't close her eyes without seeing the fucking thing. Hell, I can't. Take them to Block Island. It won't result in anything. The monster won't come back because you talked to some chick who paints pictures. But it *will* make them feel better. Their father failed them. I failed them. You're their only hope."

He stood up and dropped his butt. His foot mashed it onto the pavement. "You're a good kid, Charlie. Tomorrow is the weekend. Get on the 12:30 p.m. ferry and go to Block Island. Get a ticket for me too. I'll meet you guys at the docks." He handed Charlie a wad of cash.

Charlie didn't count it in front of him, but he could see it was enough to pay for all their tickets. Brian's clothes told Charlie his brother wasn't rolling in dough, so if he handed over a stack of cash to solidify a promise, it felt like gold in Charlie's hand.

"Are you serious?"

Brian smiled and walked away.

Charlie stayed on the concrete wall for a while, holding in the scream he wanted to unleash.

10

THE EXCLUSIVE CLUB

B anks pulled in front of a large white house. Brian couldn't tell what glowed brighter, the lights coming from the windows or the unnatural green of the lawn. He never understood why anyone rich would choose to live in Providence, even in the nice Blackwood neighborhood. The dude who owned the place probably owned twelve other houses, and Brian idolized the guy for a multitude of reasons, but Brian still thought him a sucker for spending millions on what looked like nothing more than a nice suburban house with neighbors so close you could pop open the window and toss them a bag of sugar from kitchen to kitchen.

It didn't matter. Banks didn't drive him here to assess the man's real estate. Brian reached into his pocket and pulled out a bottle of pills. Prescribed. He popped one and swallowed it dry. Hopefully his nerves would temper before the meeting began.

Banks had dropped their friends off on Thayer Street so they could get a bite to eat, and he and Brian could attend the meeting alone. Technically, Banks shouldn't bring anyone along for this kind of deal, but he'd already bargained for Brian to be there.

They walked up to the door, and a large man in a Hawaiian shirt opened it before they could even knock. He tipped his head, indicating they should come in, but he stopped them at the entrance and frisked them good, with an extra special focus on Brian. The man made him strip to his underwear, patted him down, and even checked under his ball sack. When he finished, he made Brian bend over and spread his ass cheeks. Humiliating sure, but worth it if the meeting went well.

Hawaiian Shirt Guy escorted them to the living room, where a balding, middle-aged man with chubby, red cheeks sat on a leather couch, glasses scooted down his nose as he penciled in an answer on a crossword puzzle. Brian couldn't believe how close he stood to someone he worshipped.

The room was beautiful. Leather chairs to match the couch, bright paintings framed on the walls, a shiny piano in the corner.

Banks stood by the chair but didn't sit, so Brian followed his lead, standing behind his friend. Brian had never done one of these meetings before and didn't want to make some minor mistake that could blow the entire thing. Banks was a professional.

The man finally looked up from his crossword and tossed the paper down next to him. "Kevin Banks. Have a seat, old friend," he said. His voice was a tinge whiny. He looked more like a middle manager than one of the largest drug dealers in New England. Nothing like how he appeared in interviews on television.

Banks sat on a leather chair facing the couch. Another chair waited for Brian right next to Banks, but he still didn't want to sit until given permission.

The man stood up, giving Brian a full appraisal. "You must be Brian. I'm—"

"—Caleb Jones. I-I-I know, sir. I'm a big fan." Brian put his hand out.

Mr. Jones shook it and smiled. "Well then, have a seat." He waved his hand toward the empty chair.

As Brian sat, Banks said, "Brian's a genius. You know I'd never bring someone to one of our meetings if I didn't think it would bring you value."

Mr. Jones grinned and sat back down. He put his hands behind his head and crossed his legs. "Before we get into your friend's pitch, I just want to clarify our deal. Ten percent comes off and all I have to do is listen to his pitch. Just listen. I make no guarantees I'll sign off on anything. Correct?"

Banks nodded. "That's right. I know you'll sign off when you hear his plan."

Mr. Jones clicked his tongue. "We'll see about that. And as for the rest, I'm paying half in cash, half in Oxys?"

Banks nodded again. "Yup. Works for me."

Mr. Jones inhaled deep. "All right then. Why don't you go do the exchange with Walter, and I'll have a nice one-on-one with your friend."

Banks hopped up and walked over to Hawaiian Shirt Guy who waited by the door. The man grabbed Banks by the arm and led him out of the room. Now that Brian sat alone with Mr. Jones, knowing he was about to deliver his pitch, his heart slammed into his ribs. This was it. His last hope.

"Well, let's hear it." Mr. Jones sat forward, grabbed a glass of water from the coffee table, sipped it, and placed it back on the coaster.

Brian's mouth turned to cotton. "Well, sir, as I said, I'm a big fan of yours. I was watching a show one day a few weeks back, and they had on a list of the best horror movie scenes of all time. And of course, a couple of your movies were on there, like *We Are All Dead, Anyway*, and the original version of *Bunker Dogs*, before they rebooted it with Kevin Bacon as the White Wolf. But that's not what struck me. It was when they cut to the industry people talking about the scenes, and you were there, and not just to discuss your own movies, but just about every movie they listed, they always had a quote from you. More than anyone else on the show."

Mr. Jones spun his hand, telling Brian to get on with it. "I know the work I've done. I don't need a recap."

A woozy spell hit Brian, a combination of the drugs wearing off, and knowing he was rambling during a pitch that needed perfection. "I'm sorry, sir. My point is that even though you don't make movies anymore, you're a legend in the genre, and your opinion is of the highest value to the fans. I looked you up, and I saw you mention in a couple of interviews that you and your wife love escape rooms, go to them whenever you can. And as I'm sure you're probably aware, the most popular genre for escape rooms is horror."

Mr. Jones put his elbow on the couch arm and propped his head in his palm. He was getting bored, and Brian was all over the place.

"Escape rooms are cool. I like them too. But it seems to be a touch and go industry. Some companies are thriving, while new ones pop up every day and close a month later."

"Because half of them, if not more, are absolute shit," Mr. Jones chimed in.

Brian snapped his finger. "Exactly. And I've been working with the numbers. It's a hard business to profit in, unless you plan your builds really well, factor in the needed staff to run it, so many things. It's almost a consumable product. People play it once and unless they're hardcore enthusiasts, they likely won't come back. I know a few owners have combatted that with games that have different pathways based on the choices you make, so players could come back and play the same game with a different experience, but to create that, you'd need more products, more tech, more space. All of this puts the owners in a position where they feel the need to change out their games quickly, bring in a new room to lure in old business. But if they don't keep the rooms up long enough, they risk losing all the value. If the props and tech aren't worn out, how long can you keep it up before it runs dry? If you change it out, will the new theme sell as well as the last?"

Mr. Jones sat up. Interest sparked in his eyes. Brian had found something in his rant that intrigued the man. "I'm confused. When you started talking, I thought you were going to pitch an escape room idea to me, as if you wanted to see if I'd open up a business, but now it appears you're talking me out of it. To be honest, I love the conversation. Believe it or not, I've considered opening an escape room company. I could invest a lot of money into it. And I could make a good buck back. But what's the point? I'd be doing it just for the passion. I go to rooms with my wife and think up all the ways I could make it better, so I've considered doing just that. But I don't think it's a wise business decision. I don't have faith the industry isn't more than a fad. The pandemic proved how many of these companies, even some of the big-name ones, were just surviving on a wing and prayer."

Brian nodded furiously. "Yes, and I'll be honest, I *am* trying to talk you into it. Escape rooms on their own are too difficult, too much effort for a lot of risk, that even if it pans out, only leads to more effort to keep the momentum going. My idea is different. You know how Facebook started, right?"

Mr. Jones grabbed his glass of water, twirled his wrist, letting the ice spin in the glass. "Invite only. I see what you're getting at, but it's gonna need to be bigger than that."

"If there's an industry parallel to escape rooms, it's probably haunts, right? Haunted houses. I was reading a book once about extreme haunts. I stole it from my sister. She's a crazed horror fan. This book was called something like *The Death House*. Anyway, in this book, they had these traveling haunts you could only attend if you were invited to them, and they were known as the best around. Getting in was extremely difficult, which made people thirst for it even more."

Mr. Jones put his hand out like a crossing guard telling a child to stop. "You just said an escape room costs a lot to make, and has a limited window to make its money back, and now you're about to pitch the idea the window should be shorter? A pop-up, invite only escape room? Seems damn foolish."

Brian smiled. "Ah, you're on to me, but hear me out. You write the story, create the design, plan out the puzzles. You! The fucking great Caleb Jones. And that's how we pitch it. We make the first game, and this isn't your standard escape room, because we actually rent out a huge property for half a year. We spend three months implementing everything and another three with the game opened. There's the room. Just one game. But there's other parts to the event. People with tickets get to play the game, and I think we make the game a little longer, two hours, maybe two and a half. Afterwards, they get refreshments, snacks, get a screening of one of your movies. Maybe you even have some secret vault deleted scenes we could tack on to make the screening extra special. We design everything based on your movies, but the games are totally, one hundred percent original Caleb Jones stories. Not only are we changing the landscape of escape rooms, but we are hyping your name in storytelling again.

"And we charge a fuck ton per ticket. Like, out of reach prices. Two hundred dollars a pop, maybe. We start by inviting only influencers and celebrities, then we go on social media and find the diehards, the reviewers, the people who already spend a fortune traveling the world playing these games. And we bring them in and let them tell the world about it. We make this thing so hyped up and talked about, when we pop open game number two in a different location, different part of the country, everyone is going fucking crazy. We charge more. Five hundred a pop."

Mr. Jones leaned back, resting his head on the leather. He still held his glass in hand. "What's the math on this?"

"Say we spend 150k to design the game and room otherwise. For the first time, we charge 200 a pop, run each game with six people in the room, and run it five times a day, seven days a week for three months. You're talking over half a million coming in. Obviously, that's minus the 150k room build, rent, electricity, staff. Probably 200k profit."

Mr. Jones shook his head. "Less than that. There's a lot you're not factoring in, but if that's the starting price for room one, and we price higher for room two, I see a lot of potential to turn this into a cash cow. And to be honest, I think 200 is a low ticket price, even for game one. We could start at 500 and go up from there."

Brian smiled. It was working.

"Just one question." Mr. Jones sipped his water.

Brian put his hands out, palms up. "Ask away."

"What's in it for you? Why are you pitching this to me? Are you asking to help design the games? What? You just want me to pay you for the concept?"

Brian tilted his head and furrowed his brow. "Oh, no, sir. I want to run it with you. I want to work with you on all of it. I've been studying this for a long time. I have notebooks filled with information on design, pitfalls within the industry. I know it all. I want to be a co-owner. Now, I know you'll be fronting all the investments, so I know my cut will come just from profit after cost, but that's fine with me."

Mr. Jones laughed. It was a loud, violent laugh, and it echoed through the cavernous room. Laughs like that punched, and Brian felt the strike on his jaw, but he wasn't ready to drop to the mat.

"Sir. I assure you. I will be an asset."

"No. Let me stop you right there. I don't doubt you'd be valuable. I'm sure you have a lot of knowledge and insight that would help if I went into this venture. First, that's a big *if*. I still don't know if I want to waste my time on this. But let's say I do. I wouldn't hire you to manage the staff, let alone run the place with me. And look, I know that sounds cruel. You seem like a nice guy, smart too. I don't doubt you could excel. But I see the thunderstorm of red in your eyes, the way your fucking fingers have been trembling throughout this conversation. You're a junkie. Your teeth are rotting out of your skull. What's that from? Meth?"

It wasn't from meth. It was simply from not brushing his teeth. Brian drank and popped pills all day, often fell asleep wherever he sat, and he sure as fuck didn't plan a nighttime routine. Sometimes he'd throw up and fall asleep right after, letting the acidic spew settle on his enamel. Four of his teeth were cracked, wiggling their way out of his skull, and he'd had more than a few infections. Luck-ily, antibiotics were easier to score than Vicodin or codeine.

"Sir, I assure you my past drug issues wouldn't be a—"

Mr. Jones put his finger up. "Let me stop you again. I don't care what you're on or what you were on. I don't care if you're cleaning up or if you plan to. I hope for your sake you do, but that's not my busi-ness. However, if I open this idea of yours, the escape room will be my business. And I don't know you, and I have no reason to trust you. I never will. You're not going to change my mind about that. Ever."

"I can prove it to you. I can do daily check-ins, go to rehab, piss in a cup, whatever you need me to show you that I'm clean before we get started."

"Kid. Never gonna happen. Never. Because if you show me you're clean, and I sign contracts with you, and then you fall off, it makes my life a living hell. You're not my brother, my close friend, nothing. I met you ten minutes ago, and I won't get involved with someone I don't know who is clearly a liability. There's no reason for it. I get nothing out of it. Your plan is smart, but it's still a risky plan, and it will cost me a lot of time and money. I don't need added worry. And I'm not going to spend the night arguing with you about this because it will never happen. You can't change my mind on this."

Brian's chest had filled up like a balloon with anxiety when he had first talked up his idea, but now Mr. Jones had tossed a dart at it, and *POP*. It deflated him. He could keep arguing, keep trying to convince Mr. Jones to trust him, but the man was right. He was a junkie, and couldn't run his own life, let alone a million-dollar busi-ness idea. A better version of Brian would offer to work from the bottom. *All right, Mr. Jones, just hire me on as an assistant, a contractor, a fucking janitor, and I'll prove to you how much you'll want me on your team until I work my way up to your partner.* But Brian wasn't a better man, didn't have any fight left in him, and frankly, was too tired.

He rubbed the back of his neck. "Do you mind if I use your restroom?"

Mr. Jones closed his eyes and sighed. "Sorry to disappoint you, kid. I wish you the best." He pointed toward a hallway. "Second door on the right."

Brian stood up. A rush of blood flowed through his skull, and the room spun around him. Slowly, he walked and slid down the hall with his shoulder pressed to the plaster for stability.

Inside the bathroom, he locked the door and with trembling hands, snapped open the Ziploc bag of pills he'd gotten from his jacket pocket. They were not the prescribed ones. He counted them. Seventeen. He moved them to behind the faucet and pulled out his cell phone. The time showed 10:30 p.m., too late to get in touch with Charlie. Probably not if he had his brother's cell phone number, but he didn't. He only had his aunt's house number, and he knew she had probably turned the ringer off and gone to bed around 9:00 p.m.

Brian called it anyway. On the second ring, it went to Auntie's answering machine.

"Hey, Charlie . . ." His voice cracked as tears streamed down his cheeks. He cleared his throat. "Hey, Charlie. Listen, I'm not gonna make the trip with you guys tomorrow. I just wanted to tell you something important. Not everyone is made to be a hero. Some of us don't have redemption arcs, you know what I mean? This isn't the movies, and some of us don't repair, don't come in at the last second and save the day. But you, Charlie. You are a fucking hero. I know you have anxiety and all this other bullshit fucking up your brain, so it's hard to see, but kid, you're a fucking badass. Take care of Chrissy and Angela. Y'all deserved better than me and Dad."

He hung up, turned the sink on, scooped a palm full of water into his mouth. Two at a time, he popped the pills until the bag was empty.

II

THE SECONDS BEFORE IMPACT

Chrissy tossed a bag onto the Volvo's back seat. Charlie handed her his bag, and she threw his on top. After she shut the door, she leaped forward and gave him a hug. "Thank you for doing this."

The screen door on the house cracked as it popped all the way open. They turned to see Angela on the top step with a bag in her hands. They all stared at each other for a second.

"Don't look at me like that. She was my sister too."

Charlie shook his head. "You can't come. No way."

Angela stormed down the steps, fire in her eyes. "I can. And I am. I'm sick of everyone pretending their problems are acceptable, but mine aren't."

Chrissy stepped forward, blocking Angela from the car. "It's not that. I would love for you to come with us. But you're too young."

"Seriously, get out of the way. What am I too young for? Do you think something is going to attack us? Have either of you ever fought anyone? Bit, kicked, punched? I've been in three fights, and I've beaten up two teachers. I win."

She maneuvered around Chrissy and opened the back door, plopping herself into the seat with her bag on her lap.

Charlie shrugged. "She's probably right, and honestly, she deserves answers as much as any of us."

"Fair enough."

As they drove, the grime of Tanner's Switch transformed into the tourist sections of Charlestown, the long stretches of motels dotting Route 1. Chrissy read a new book.

Angela kept to herself, resting her head back and letting the fall breeze tunnel in from the window.

When they reached Narragansett, driving down roads built entirely around clam shacks and tackle shops, they all stared out the window, a foreign world zooming by.

Tanner's Switch was twenty minutes away, but it could have been on a different planet, where oceans were ponds, beach houses were trailers, and adventure was a dream for a different tomorrow.

They parked and walked to the Point Judith terminal, where a few others were gathered. The breezy sea air made the chilly morning bitter. Chrissy crossed her arms, bringing both sides of her cardigan together. Angela stared off into the ocean, unbothered by the high wind.

The smell of fried fish from the surrounding restaurants and the salt from the ocean traveled with the breeze, and Charlie wished he had brought snacks.

They waited for fifteen minutes, cold and quiet. Charlie regretted the decision to follow through with this. The ferry boarded and would leave soon, but Brian remained a no-show. Charlie couldn't believe he fell for it, thinking his brother would change.

"Should we get on?" Chrissy asked.

"We'll give him five more minutes."

Each second was like watching your car move closer to a brick wall in slow motion. You knew you were going to hit it, but all you could do was count down the seconds until impact.

His brother wouldn't show up, and Charlie's heart would hurt for days. All he had left was a few more minutes to build up his hope.

Chrissy tapped his shoulder. "Come on. Let's go."

He gave one last glance to the parking area, hoping to see a car pulling in. He didn't even know what Brian drove, or if he drove at all. The car he got into yesterday was a brown sedan. Old. Shitty. He'd recognize it if he saw it.

He stepped backward and up the metal stairs. When they were on the boat, they stood at the back railing of the middle deck, Charlie checking the nearby lots from the improved vantage point.

Angela rubbed his arm. "He's not coming."

"I know," Charlie said and headed inside. The seats inside the ferry were more comfortable than those outside, but they had the air conditioning going for some stupid reason.

Angela and Chrissy sandwiched on each side of him. Chrissy tapped both feet on the ground. "This is going to be so fun."

Angela giggled. "Fun for you? I literally have no friends and do nothing but go to school and watch television. This is like the best day of my life."

Charlie's stomach dropped. He had always thought of Angela as a little pain in the ass, but the poor girl spent her life alone. He never considered how she handled the monster because she didn't talk about it the way everyone else did. Looking back, he regretted ever saying no to this trip and to giving Angela a hard time about coming.

This mattered.

He put his arm around her. "I'm glad you're here. I know you guys are on a mission, but we should also make sure we have some fun today."

Chrissy did an awkward dance reminiscent of Elaine on *Seinfeld*. "Heck yeah. Let's party."

"Charlie," a gruff voice said in a taunting tone.

They all turned around, hopeful to see their brother. Charlie couldn't believe his eyes. "Tiffany? Doug? What are you guys doing here?"

Tiffany and Doug scooted into the seats behind them. "You said you were going on an adventure to Block Island today, and we're big fans of adventures," Tiffany said.

A part of him was so happy his friends came. He had told them about the conversation with his brother but obviously left out the monster part. Instead, he'd just told them his sisters wanted to explore the island, and his brother made Charlie feel bad for saying no, so he decided he should do it. To Tiffany and Doug, this probably meant Charlie was going to have a boring day, and they were joining him to help make it more fun. It was a kindness, one he appreciated.

However, now that they were on the boat, Charlie realized he actually was looking forward to spending the day with his sisters, and Tiffany and Doug would only make Chrissy and Angela feel pushed to the side. He also couldn't fathom how he would explain to his new friends what they were really there for, so he'd have to separate from them at some point.

The boat made a mechanical sound and lurched forward with a jolt.

"I think it's time," Chrissy said.

Angela glanced out the window. "Fuck Brian. Better off without him."

Doug sniffed. "They're making hot dogs. I love ferry hot dogs."

Charlie turned back to Tiffany and Doug, who sat with smiles on their faces. He put his head forward, feeling a fresh wave of panic in his gut. They were returning to the place responsible for their nightmares, where four years ago, a monster chewed on their sister and destroyed their lives forever. His new friends sat behind him. His sisters on each side. He didn't know what they were moving toward or what the day would bring, but he felt in his guts: it was going to be a shitty day.

Chrissy giggled. "This is all very fucking awkward."

12
DON'T BELIEVE IN MONSTERS

The passengers marched down the metal staircase onto the shores of Block Island, the ramp clanging like a church bell under their feet. A whipping breeze welcomed them. Charlie hated the wind. It was like getting slapped in the face by Mother Nature. There wasn't a single type of weather or temperature Charlie couldn't handle if the wind wasn't involved.

After they navigated around the large groups of other people, Charlie and his friends met in a circle to discuss their plans.

"I think we should go get scooters," Doug said, causing a wide, devilish grin to ride up Angela's cheeks.

During the summer months, Block Island would teem with tourists on scooters. Charlie hated them more than the wind. In fact, riding on a scooter was just a way to invite wind into your life. He never understood people who bought convertibles or motorcycles. Why would you seek wind? It sucked.

Angela said, "My sister will want to hit up the bookstore, for sure."

Chrissy shook her head wildly. "Nope. They don't even have a horror section. I asked them to order a book for me once, and the lady straight up told me they don't carry horror if it isn't King or Koontz. Now, I love King and all, but if you can't respect the genre enough to carry more mid-list or indie books, then you don't get my business." Chrissy eyed Charlie. "There's an art studio I'd like to visit. Maybe we should split up and meet back later?"

Charlie fidgeted with his fingernails. "I like that idea. Tiff and Doug why don't you guys get some scooters, and I'll go with my sisters to the art studio. We can all meet back in an hour at The Flavorful Scoop."

Tiffany shook her head. "No way. We are all in this together. Let's go to the art studio. I'm gonna guess any art studio in Block Island is all seashells and 'Beach Life,' whereas I'm more of a Munch kind of gal, but whatever."

Chrissy's eyes perked up. "I love Munch. I don't think this lady is going to be Munch, but I think she's better than seashells and 'Beach Life.'"

They walked the semi-crowded streets of Block Island. Going in fall made it a little less full, but enough people were moving around to make Charlie push out into the street.

The shops were a combination of mini Victorians, saltboxes, and wood-shingled beach huts squished together, reaching out toward the road with waving American flags or hovering box eaves.

Clothing shops with racks of BLOCK ISLAND tees, sun hats, and sweatshirts. Ice cream shops and beach food. Boutiques, craft stores, home goods, and surf shops. If you took away the walls, you'd be at an arts and crafts fair.

Chrissy led the group, her plan well-researched.

Charlie and Tiffany fell behind, but Charlie monitored Angela, feeling bad about how ignored she'd been. Luckily, she seemed to hit it off with Doug. Hopefully she wasn't developing a crush. The dude was way too old for her.

"So, Charlie, do you want to tell me what's really going on today? And listen, I understand if you don't want to talk about it. I'll get Doug to hang back when we hit the art place. I know you have something going on. We jumped in today to let you know we have your back, but we aren't trying to intrude on something that's none of our business. To be honest, I was worried about your brother. He scared me a little, and I wanted to be here if he upset you. I didn't realize he wasn't coming."

Charlie looked down at his feet as they marched along the stone sideway. "Me neither, and in that way, he did upset me. I'm glad you came. It means a lot to me, but my family and I . . ."

He trailed off, looking ahead at Angela giggling as Doug mimicked a guy on a scooter driving by. He couldn't remember the last time he'd seen her smile, let alone laugh. Like Charlie, if his sisters could make some friends or find something to escape the prison of their past, they could be happy. He went all in on this adventure today, but after this, he wanted to give them both a better life—one where they could stop dwelling on the monster.

Tiffany nudged him with an elbow to his arm and a soft, warm smile. "I get it. You know I love to pry, but even I realize this isn't something to dig into. I need you to know something, Charlie, and I'm scared to tell you."

He turned to her and even without knowing what she had to say, understood the weight of it. His cheeks turned hot, and a nervous twitch developed in his hands. He almost forgot who he was. His confidence loosened lately, but he was still the same scared kid who grew flustered around humans. Sure, he'd found his tribe, but he still hadn't found himself. "What is it?"

She looked at him with droopy eyes. "If I had known, I wouldn't have done it. I promise."

Charlie stopped, letting the gap between him and his family grow. The imaginary line that connected them all grew more and more taut with each second. "You wouldn't have done what?"

"Looked you up."

He stepped back, water filling his eyes.

She shook her head. "I'm so sorry, Charlie. I just thought I was going to find something about you being a nerd in school, like some articles about spelling bees or some shit. I didn't know. I'm so sorry."

Tears trailed down his cheeks. "I don't know what to say."

She stepped forward, approaching like she wanted to pet a lion. "Say what you want."

His throat closed, and he was back to the old Charlie. His mouth turned to sand. "I feel naked."

He turned his head, watching his family disappear around a corner with Doug.

Tiffany's lip twitched. "Charlie, me knowing about this doesn't expose you. It gives you more armor. I'm your friend."

He pulled away from the curb and kept walking. "Yeah. I mean, you've proved that enough. You're here, and that means a lot to me, but if you read about it, you have questions in your head. I know you don't believe it. Who would? And which sources did you find? The ones mocking us or the ones obsessing over us?"

She put her hand on his arm, trying to stop him from walking away. "Charlie. Who the fuck am I to judge what did or didn't happen to you?"

He stopped, turned around, and said with a voice more aggressive than he meant, "My sister went to the library the other day and checked out a book about monsters on Block Island. Do you know what my biggest fear was?"

Tiffany tucked her arms around her belly. "What?"

"That they wrote it in the last four years. That we would be in there. The worst fucking night of our lives is a goddamn myth for assholes to lap up and tell around campfires. There's fucking YouTube videos. *Don't be near this family at 3:00 a.m.* Podcasts. Wannabe TikTokers. They call us all the time. Still."

"I'm sorry you have to deal with that. I just read a couple of legit news articles." Her voice softened to a near whisper.

"Is that why Doug invited me to hang out with you guys? So I could be your cool story to tell your friends about?"

She shook her head. "What? No. And Doug doesn't even know

about it. I didn't tell anyone. It's so easy to find out anything about anyone, but the thing is, most people aren't fucking weirdos like me, and they don't go Google searching their new friends. I can't possibly understand what you went through, but you're not a fucking circus act, Charlie. And you're not alone. Not everyone in the world wants to hurt you or use you."

He stepped forward, wiping tears from his cheeks. "I was stupid to think I could get by for as long as I did without people finding out. They always do. Everywhere we move. Lucky for us, my aunt is so unstable she moves us around a lot, so we don't have to deal with the bullshit for long. Just answer me one question, do you truly believe we saw something that night? You read the articles, and so have I. The implications oozed off those pages. We covered up my sister's murder. My father killed her. Maybe a stranger in a mask. The articles were never just about what happened. They always had to dive into shared psychosis or shared delusions, blah blah. So tell me. What do you believe based on what you read?"

She stood up straight, ready for this question. "My answer can't be based on what I read because I met you first in Charlestown, and I sensed something in you before any article could sway me. *You* sway me more than a newspaper. And you did that within ten minutes of knowing you. I trust you more than any words on a page.

"I don't believe in monsters, but I'm aware I know nothing, that I can't possibly gather even a small fragment of the information from the story you lived through. I don't believe in supernatural shit, but I've only known you for a little while now, and I knew from the moment I met you on the beach that I believe in you. Charlie, I trust you. I've never made a friend so quickly, been so relaxed around a new person as I am with you. So if you tell me you saw a fucking monster that night, then I believe you saw a monster."

Charlie said nothing, just stared down at his shoes. "Chrissy found out about a woman who paints monsters that look just like ours. We're here to talk to her, to find some kind of answer. We never got closure. I want to stop thinking about that night. I need to move on. So do my sisters. They were really fucking little when it happened. I have to help them."

Tiffany nodded. "When I was seven years old, my uncle kidnapped me. He was a drug addict, and he lived with us, but my mother and father kicked him out when they saw how bad he was getting. They didn't want him near me and Doug. He came back to get his shit, and Doug and I were home alone. Doug was babysitting. My uncle stole me, just wrapped his fucking arms around me like I was a suitcase and dragged me to his car. I was too scared to fight back. He didn't do anything to me, nothing gross. But he drove with me for three days. Three days. We went all the way to Florida, staying at motels, eating McDonald's. I was terrified the entire time. Shaken to my core. I didn't want to breathe, worried I'd send him over the edge. Anyone who kidnaps a child will do scary shit.

"There was this huge manhunt for me. National news kind of thing. When they found me, the police busted down the door of the motel we were staying at, guns drawn, everyone screaming. My uncle pulled out a knife and waved it at them. I was as scared of the police as I was of my uncle. All of it terrified me.

"When the police arrested my uncle, they told me he'd been blackmailing my parents for money. I was still terrified, sitting in a police station, waiting to find out how I'd get home. It never ended. Even once I was home, safe in my bed at night, I couldn't close my eyes. I couldn't concentrate. I couldn't play. Every stupid fucking thought came back to, *What if he gets out again? What if someone else steals me? When will I ever be safe?*"

Charlie stared, unsure of what to say.

"For a long time, I felt like a prisoner. I still have nightmares, still get nervous around crowds. But do you know what made me finally feel a little freer?"

"What?"

"The internet. Being able to look up where my uncle was. Seeing he was still in jail. Eventually, he died, and I felt a fuck ton better. But before then, I checked every day to see if he got out. As long as I knew where he was, I knew I was okay. That's why I looked you up, and why I look up every person I meet. I enjoy being the outgoing person who randomly walks up to cool kids at the beach, but I need some security. I'm sorry I checked you out, but I am not sorry for why."

Charlie's heart sank. "I understand. I'm sorry you had to go through that. And I'm sorry I got weird. It's just tough for me."

She shook her head. "You don't need to be sorry for being guarded. It's your reaction to everything you've been through. You can be free knowing why it's there and why you need it. I had a point to my story. Maybe you think you found a new freedom because you're trying to forget what happened that night, but for your sisters, they need to find their freedom by knowing they're safe. And they won't know that until they can define it. I told you, I don't believe in monsters, but something happened to you that night. And if you don't find out how to understand it, it will always own you."

She reached out and held his hand. "I'm with you. Maybe that helps, or maybe it doesn't, but I need you to know I'm with you. I have my own monsters. And I can describe my uncle to you, but you'll never fully be able to see what it was like in those motel rooms, alone, scared, watching him move around erratically and out of his marbles. And I'll never be able to see in your sister's room, no matter how well you describe it. But I believe in you. I will always believe what you say, even if I don't believe in the characters, because I'm your friend, Charlie. A real friend who wants nothing from you but your happiness."

"Okay," he said.

"Now, let's go fuck with some monsters."

13
WE'RE GONNA GET YOU

Tiffany and Charlie caught up to the rest of the gang just as they reached the front of the art studio. It was a square wooden building with a short concrete ramp leading to the front door. The blue paint on the wood had flecked off or peeled up, giving it the shore-worn look Block Island tourists loved to see.

In the window, paintings of seashells and foamy surfs stood on displays. Tiffany and Chrissy snickered at the sight.

Angela turned to her brother with wide eyes exploding with anxiety and excitement. "You ready for this?"

Charlie glanced at Tiffany. "Ready."

Chrissy took a deep breath and opened the door. A bell dinged as the screen door shot open. Charlie followed with Angela at his side.

Behind him, Tiffany said, "Stay out here with me, Doug."

As Doug protested, Charlie walked into the incense-filled studio. All the paintings on display were as Tiffany joked they'd be. Seashells and "Beach Life." Lighthouses, shores, shorebirds, waves.

A woman sat behind a glass counter, playing on her phone. She was cute. Her hair was frazzled, and she wore glasses with thick black frames, the dorky-chic kind. She put her phone down and stood, revealing her loose floral dress.

"How are you guys today?" She smiled.

Chrissy smiled back and nodded while Charlie examined the objects on the glass counter: painted shells, pins, buttons, stickers.

He rubbed his hand along the counter's edge. "Are you the artist?"

She smiled. "Yep. I did all these."

Charlie had imagined the woman would be older, but this lady was in her early twenties.

Chrissy feigned interest in the beach paintings, strolling the perimeter, rubbing her chin as she checked them out. "Is this all you have?"

The artist lady stood on tiptoe to talk to Charlie. "Everything I have for sale."

Angela, lacking subtlety, approached the counter and tapped her fingers on the glass. "We were looking for paintings of monsters."

The artist maintained her cordial smile, but her eyes flickered. "Ah, so you've read the Block Island folklore book?"

Chrissy found her way to the counter, and Charlie stepped back, figuring it best not to crowd her as they interrogated.

"Yeah, we wanted to know where you got the inspiration for that creature," Chrissy said.

The artist stared, thinking of how to answer. Chrissy made a smile where she hid her lips, and her cheeks offered big dimples. She put her hand out. "I'm sorry. I'm Chrissy. I was just a big fan of the artwork. I'm a huge horror nerd."

The artist took her hand. "Milicent. I'm also a horror nerd. I think the inspiration was just based on seeing lots of horror movies."

There was a lie there, a very obvious change in pitch when she said those last words.

Charlie stepped in. As he reapproached the counter, his nerves kicked up a notch, his pulse throbbing in his neck. He cleared his throat, unwilling to allow his social awkwardness to ruin his opportunity for answers. "Listen, my sister is lying. I mean, she is a big horror nerd, but that's not why we're here."

Milicent's eyes grew to the size of silver dollars. "Oh my god. I know who you are. I can't believe I didn't recognize you immediately."

Chrissy and Charlie lowered their faces toward their chests. Angela didn't seem to mind.

"I've always wanted to talk to you guys."

Chrissy perked up, but her eyes turned to thin slits. "Why?"

Milicent came around the corner. "Come with me."

They followed her into a back room. It was a kitchen area with a small bathroom. She waved her hand, telling them to sit at the long picnic table in the center of the room. While they all got seated, she fished for something in a cabinet.

Chrissy leaned into Charlie. "Do you think she got the picture ideas from us? Was this all just her drawing what she read about in the papers?"

"Maybe we came all this way just to meet a stupid fan. Some kind of weirdo who read about us and became obsessed with the story?" Charlie whispered.

Without turning from the cabinets, Milicent said. "Have any of you heard of Molly Mix?"

They all looked at each other to see if any of them had. Chrissy shook her head. Angela frowned. Charlie said, "No. Never heard of her."

She dropped the binder on the table with a thud. "Pretty much what I suspected. If you had, and if you knew the entire story, you'd know why your monster story isn't much of a stretch."

She pried the book open, her fingers moving erratically. Flip, Flip, Flip. Pages of newspaper articles, book pages ripped from the spine, printed documents from the internet. "I don't have any of the monster paintings here. I keep those at home. But I have some photos of my artwork along with some other drawings people on the island made. But I want to show you something else first."

She landed on a news article. The headline read, "Block Island Teen Disappears in the Middle of the Night."

Chrissy snatched it, eyes darting left to right as she devoured the article. Luckily for Charlie, Milicent dictated the highlights for him.

"Molly was my best friend in elementary school and junior high. I mean, we did everything together. Block Island is small, and the folks who opt to live here in the fall and winter are few and far between."

"And rich," Angela added.

Milicent nodded reluctantly, as if she weren't proud to have money. "And that, yeah. Not all, by the way, but a lot of them, sure. Molly and I both had well-off families, but that's beside the point. Here's the thing: Molly started getting terrible headaches when we were in junior high. They were so bad she'd bend over in pain and sometimes scream like someone was stabbing her. It was intense.

"They sent her for brain scans, worried it could be a symptom of aneurisms or something. I'm not sure. I don't know medical stuff, but the headaches were more than just migraines, is all I'm saying. Then, she started having these weird dreams at night. She'd call me and leave these voicemails where I could hear the raw fear in her voice. She'd ramble on about shorebirds. Always shorebirds. She said in the dreams, she'd be lying on the sand, frozen, unable to move, and the birds would peck at her. Nibble her flesh. Poke her eyes. She'd go into detail about them cutting through her flesh, ripping out muscles. She'd describe little thin strands of gore hanging from their beaks. I remember her telling me one time, in the dream, they plucked out both her eyes, and she couldn't see the world turning deep white, but she could picture the birds chewing on them."

"Jesus," Charlie said, pretending not to lose patience but hoping she'd hurry and explain the connection.

Milicent pulled her phone from her pocket and tapped the screen a few times. "So anyway, one day we're walking down the hall from one class to another, and Molly just drops to the floor and has a seizure."

All eyes went to Milicent's face. Chrissy dropped the article. But no one said anything, too eager for the story to continue.

Milicent didn't notice the attention she'd drawn because she scrolled through her phone, talking while she searched for something. "I freaked out. I'd never seen someone have a seizure before. It scared the shit out of me. Teachers ran over, and someone called an ambulance. She stayed home from school for three days.

"When she came back, she looked like a different person. Her eyes were all glossy, her hair frazzled. She'd jolt in fear over every little sound. When I came up to her to talk to her, she just stared at me for a minute, like it took that long to remember who I was. Once she did, she got all weird and rambled to me about how she kept having seizures, and while she was having them, she saw a monster, and he kept getting closer and closer to her.

"Because she knew I liked to draw, she asked me to make a sketch."

Milicent placed the phone down on the table and slid it to Charlie. On the screen was a crudely drawn version of the monster. Their monster. It didn't scare him, not this particular drawing. In fact, it made him excited. Someone else had seen it. It wasn't just a creature that *looked* like the one they'd seen, it was the same exact monster. And not just that, but the girl had seizures, just like Wreath did as a child. There were connections, ones written in bold lettering. **Seizures. Block Island. Monsters.**

Chrissy and Angela stared at the drawing. Angela's eyes filled with water. "That's it."

Milicent nodded. "A few months later, Molly looked like she was wilting away. She wasn't eating or sleeping. She told me it was getting closer and closer. And then one day, she disappeared."

Chrissy sat forward. "Disappeared in what way? Where was she last seen?"

Milicent took her phone back and scrolled some more. "Depends on who you ask. Her father said she was last seen getting ready for school. I had last seen her the day before in class. But her brother, well, he said on the way to school, it was super foggy and out of nowhere, he heard his sister scream. When he ran toward her cries, within the dense fog, he glimpsed a monster chewing on Molly. Then, poof, the monster and Molly were gone."

Charlie eyed Chrissy to gauge her reaction. He trusted her to make sense of this story more than he could. Chrissy opened her mouth to say something, but before she could, Milicent said, "Of course everyone thought he was nuts, but I asked him what the monster looked like, and I drew it how he described it."

She slid the phone back again, and landing right in front of Charlie was another drawing of the monster, this one with more detail. His black swirls for eyes, red lightning streaks bolting away from the dark pools. The long, slender claws. The pale, gray skin tightened like shrink wrap around the bones. Daggers for teeth. There were other details, too, ones he hadn't remembered. Its ears were crooked, the left one higher than the right, and they triangled out like little arrows moving away from the face. Its chest was covered in red lines, which Charlie couldn't be sure from the drawing whether they were cuts or part of the thing's features.

"I went to the police and showed them the comparisons between what Molly said she saw in her dream and what her brother described seeing. They didn't seem to care much, but they brought her brother in for questioning. My guess is they thought maybe someone kidnapped Molly, and her brother witnessed it. Maybe some psychopath wearing a mask. I don't know. But Molly never came back. And once I read your story, I went to the police again, just to remind them that you weren't the first people to make claims a monster went after a teenage girl. They again, ignored the shit out of me. But I'm guessing since that Block Island book brought you here, we're looking at the same monster."

Charlie nodded. Chrissy said, "Yeah, exactly the same. And our sister had seizures when she was young. I don't know how that connection works yet because she didn't have them when she got older, and she never mentioned anything about seeing a monster, but I'm sure the connection matters somehow. It's too similar."

Angela put her hand on Milicent's arm. "Can we speak to him? Molly's brother?"

Milicent frowned. "No. He disappeared too. About six months later. He became obsessed with finding Molly and proving he wasn't crazy. One night, he went out and never came back. Most people around here think he killed himself. George Stephens saw him last. He's kind of a local myth himself. A weird dude. Anyway, he said he saw Molly's brother wandering the woods, rambling to himself."

14

SOMEONE ELSE'S
HORROR SHOW

Tiffany leaned on an outdoor table full of Block Island sweatshirts while Doug played hacky sack with himself. She eyed the artist's studio across the street, hoping Charlie would come out soon, partially because she was bored but mainly because she was worried about him. The kid was a weathered and leaning gravestone, stuck in the place where his sister lay and ready to crumble from a gentle breeze.

Doug kicked the hacky sack all the way across the street, onto a small pocket of grass in front of the artist's studio. She came with him to retrieve it. As Doug scooped it up, Tiffany eyed the door, which Charlie had left slightly ajar.

She looked in both directions, as if someone outside would get mad at her for contemplating going inside an open business. A man crossed the road, not even looking in their direction, and even if he were, he was a salmon pantser, so no one worth worrying about.

Tiffany scrunched her brow and tilted her chin toward the door. Doug caught her drift. "You sure?"

"It's been a while. Maybe just a look-see."

Doug peeked in through the glass. After a few seconds, he turned to Tiffany and whispered, "I don't see anyone in there. Is there a back room or something?"

Tiffany screwed up her face. "How the fuck would I know? Let's sneak in."

"Oh sure, when I said we should do that, you said it was spying. Now, suddenly, it's your idea, and it's awesome?"

She rolled her eyes. "Get the fuck over it. Let's go." She slid past him and gently pressed the door open. Once she was inside, Doug crept in behind her and reached up, holding the clapper of the bell in place. Tiffany gripped the door handle and closed it slowly. She didn't know why she sneaked instead of just announcing her presence. Probably because she wanted to overhear something before it could be censored.

Voices came from a side room. Doug crept in front of her and peeked around the corner.

"Door is closed," he whispered.

She rolled her eyes again. "Thanks, James Bond."

He shrugged. "What? What kind of businessperson hides out in the back room and leaves the front door unlocked?"

Tiffany scanned the walls. "One with cameras."

Doug straightened and joined her in scanning the walls. "I don't see anything. I think she just sucks at her job."

She nudged him with her elbow. "I don't think there's a lot of worry for anyone to steal this shit."

He smiled but held in his chuckle.

She knew Charlie would feel betrayed if he caught her spying, but something itched at her brain, sending her on high alert, and she felt a need to check on him.

She took slow steps down the thin hall and leaned her ear toward the door. Angela was speaking, but Tiffany couldn't make out the words.

An unfamiliar voice came in, a female, probably the artist lady. "I've sketched it about a thousand times now. It's like a mini obsession."

Tiffany leaned in a little closer, and when her hand touched the door, it creaked open an inch. She hadn't realized it wasn't clicked shut. Her face turned hot with embarrassment.

"Idiot," Doug whispered. "I got you."

He pushed her out of the way and pulled the door open. Everyone looked at them at the threshold. "Uh, sorry to bother you all. Tiffany and I are going to Ben and Jerry's, and we just wanted to give you a heads-up so you didn't think you lost us.

Tiffany knew nothing about seizures, but from having seen them on television, she just assumed a person was unaware when it was happening, but at that moment, she knew. She knew she was having a seizure, or at least knew it came on. A weird pressure drove from belly to throat, and at the same time, a wave of dizziness, numbness in her limbs, and tingling washed over her. Then, she was falling, and as she drove toward the floor, she caught one last thing before she succumbed to the seizure. Everyone else was experiencing the same thing. All of them. They were all having a seizure. Was that possible? Had that ever happened in the history of the world? A room full of people all having simultaneous seizures?

Her surroundings turned foggy, but not the dreamscape sort of blurred lines, more like an actual fog crawling toward her.

As the mist circled around her head, she smelled it. It reeked like sulfur, which made her think it was more smoke than mist, but it also had a briny scent to it. Sea water. And not the good kind. More like dead fish, as if the mist carried with it a spoiled ocean.

I'm going to die, she thought. A newfound love of life making her regret every poor decision she had made up to this point. One last gulp of clean air. She sucked it in and spit it out before the mist swallowed her whole.

Silence.

Emptiness.

She no longer heard the cacophony of panic from her friends. Her brother's hand left her arm, leaving a cold spot where his fingers once gripped. She lost all sensory capabilities. Instead, she hovered in the darkness.

Nothingness. Floating.

Her vision returned first, revealing a pale white world.

Her hearing came next. Someone giggled.

She spun. It was herself.

Her as a child.

Was this Heaven? she thought with zero belief in such a thing. The kid version of herself came into view, crossing a clearing like a shadow through a blinding light. Young Tiffany skipped and giggled toward her, coming closer. Another shadowy figure passed through the invisible threshold. Tiffany blinked, tears bubbling on the surface because she knew before the figure fully materialized who it would be. Because this wasn't Heaven. It was Hell. It had to be.

Her uncle.

The fear of it all, the mist, losing her senses, the idea she might be dead, and that her brother and friends were granted the same fate, none of it scared her down to the marrow of her bones quite like the sight of her uncle approaching the child version of herself. She needed to save the little girl. She ran, her feet touching nothing but still bending at the arch enough to propel herself forward.

"Look out!" she yelled.

Her younger version ignored her warnings.

Her uncle crept up behind young Tiffany, wrapping his arms around her, and with a swift upward motion, lifted her to his chest.

"No!" Tiffany charged forward, ready to connect, ready to smash, ready to let her bones snap in the name of destroying not only her uncle, but any memory of him. She wanted to pulverize him out of existence.

As she neared her uncle, he squeezed the little girl until she evaporated into a puff of mist. Tiffany tried to stop herself at that point, suddenly recognizing her stupidity, that she was trying to accomplish something with human actions in a world that defied the natural order of things.

Her uncle peered up at her, a crooked smile sliding up one side of his face.

She tried her hardest to stop, to even slow down, but her fucking feet kept running forward. The closer she came, the more her uncle changed. His stubbly chin smoothed out. His skin turned gray and leathery. His mouth ripped at the corners, spreading, and growing. His teeth sharpened and elongated. And her stupid fucking feet ran on.

The bones in her uncle's body cracked, expanded. His flesh too. He grew abnormally tall, and his chubby shape caved in, skin wrapping taut around the bone.

As the transformation unfolded, Tiffany knew where it was headed. Her uncle was turning into Charlie's monster.

"Please, fucking stop," she yelled to herself, tears barreling down her cheeks. "Please."

The monster's arms extended, catching Tiffany in mid-run and lifting her body in the air. For a moment, her feet kept running, just two legs flailing back and forth. The monster's arms were too long for her to use that momentum to kick the fucker in the teeth.

God, she had been so wrong, assuming nothing could be more terrifying than her uncle. She closed her eyes, slammed them shut, unable to look at the monster. Jesus, if Charlie and his siblings had to witness this as children, she couldn't imagine the PTSD they must have. Its hot breath smacked her cheeks as it pulled her closer. She punched and kicked, finding purchase with various parts of the creature but doing zero damage. Its lack of reaction didn't stop her from attacking, but it stole the oomph from her shots.

Its breath smelled like the mist, a sulfuric ocean graveyard.

When it spoke, two voices spewed from its throat. One female, one male. What it said broke her. The wind of the words ripped her body from its roots, pulled her from the soil, and slammed her spirit right back into the dirt. The sentence echoed in her skull, rattling like an unanswered cell phone on an end table. A phrase vibrated through her bones, bobbed, and made waves in the marrow, plucked her veins with discordant notes.

"Wash up, Scumbag."

Scumbag. Her uncle's nickname for her. Scumbag. There was a time before he had kidnapped her when the name was endearing, a cute, jokey name for her. Meant as a ribbing, not sincerely. But when he dragged her across the East Coast, it came to her that a person who can't be nice without being cruel was a bad person. The kind of person who had to diminish everyone, hiding behind "it's just a joke" to get there, was both lacking in self-esteem and courage. Weak. A weak fucking villain, who despite his pathetic nature still sent a tremor of panic through her limbs, because even the weak could evoke horror. In fact, they usually did.

Whenever he had dragged her into a new motel, he'd push her on the shoulder and say, "Wash up, Scumbag," with a shitty smile on his face, as if he were trying to make her laugh. But his playful mannerisms had turned to poison by then, and she'd found nothing endearing about it.

She'd been too young to recognize the man's compulsion for insult. She thought when he told her to wash up, that he just wanted to act like a parent, but it was really another way to make her feel gross, lesser. Always a dig with him.

She still woke up some nights, sweat dripping down her back, and those three fucking words ping-ponging in her mind. When he said those words to her during their cross-country trek, they seemed so unimportant in the scope of things, but after it ended, that three-word mantra stayed with her, a tattoo branded deeper than flesh, seared into the sinew under her skin. They were the motto for the worst time in her life, the whole story wrapped in a horrific, nightmarish bow. *Wash up, Scumbag.*

Tiffany dropped from the memories, literally plummeted as the creature's grip left her throat. Her stomach lurched into her lungs. Free falling.

She never landed, just reappeared in her body on Earth, right where she had left it in the art studio. The mist had vanished. Doug stared at her, trails of tears drying on his cheeks. She slowly turned toward the back room. Chrissy, Angela, and the artist lady all stared off, complete and utter terror drenching their faces. She understood. They'd all just received the same warning, and she wondered what words the beast whispered to each of them. What sentence haunted their lives, or was it more than a few words? Maybe other people needed more than one expression to summarize their worst nightmare.

The next few moments were a blur of action. People were brushing past her, bumping into her as they ran into the shop. Chrissy pulled Angela. She had her fists clenched and her teeth gritted.

Doug put his face in front of his sister, horror in his wide eyes, the always stoic and strong brother, bleeding panic from his facial features. He grabbed Tiffany, and the world came back. She heard the screams, and horror.

Chrissy shouted, "We have to go! We have to go!"

The artist ran to Chrissy. "You need to get out of here. Run. Go home."

"What is even happening?" Angela asked, covering her face with his hands.

"You don't get it, do you? That was it telling you to back the fuck off. All of us. Go home and never think of that thing again. Never. I'm going to do the same thing. Don't call me. Don't talk to me. Get out. I'm sorry," the artist lady shouted.

The next thing Tiffany knew, she was running down the road with Doug, following Angela and Chrissy.

Angela ran with her arms clutched around her torso, mumbling to herself. Her face was pale and her lips, blue. She looked destroyed, but she was alive, and all things considered, that was the best one could hope for.

The world kept fading out for Tiffany; one moment, she was there, her heart pounding, her mind racing, trying to piece together everything she'd just witnessed, and the next, it was a blurred landscape in front of her, her mind homing in on ridiculous things like the bell on the door of the artist's studio, and the Block Island sweatshirts on the table.

The world no longer made sense, and her mind refused to settle on that fact, unwilling to accept it.

They reached the ferry, and everyone went into hysterics, Chrissy a frazzled mess, Angela literally pulling at her hair, still mumbling to herself, and Doug nearly hyperventilating.

"What the fuck?! What the fucking fuck?!" he shouted.

Angela wiped the snot from her nose. "What the hell do we do now?"

Chrissy screwed up her face. "We go home. We do exactly what Milicent said. We try to move on and forget it."

Tiffany looked up. Her eyes burned, but she didn't cry. She probably would tonight when her mind worked again. "We can never forget this."

"What other choice do we have?" Chrissy asked

"Exactly. We have no choice. Forgetting it is impossible," Tiffany said.

A few years back, Tiffany had a phase where she read a lot of true crime books. In one of them, she read a story about a man who witnessed a mob hit. Eventually, they found him and killed him. She wasn't bothered about the witness dying. It was the chapters in between that haunted her. When the man couldn't sleep, couldn't close his eyes, because he knew once he crossed the threshold into the darkness, he was a prisoner there. He'd stumbled into the wrong world, and once he entered, the only escape was death.

Tiffany, having been kidnapped as a child and knowing very well the feeling of being prisoner to someone else's horror show, read those chapters with a tight chest and a wind stuck in her lungs. And as someone who had lived as a prisoner, she also knew when that threshold had been crossed, when a person was trapped in a horror they couldn't escape.

She was there now. So was Doug. Her heart raced again. She could feel it in her temples.

And then she remembered another book about a prisoner. Bobby Sands, a member of the provisional Irish Republican Army, who died in prison during a hunger strike after sixty-six days of not eating. While in prison, he wrote a diary, and he, too, knew his only escape would come from death. He wrote, "I am standing on the threshold of another trembling world. May God have mercy on my soul."

Tiffany didn't believe in God, but her world was trembling, and her soul was about to leave Block Island on a ferry toward Tanner's Switch, where she knew it would never rest again until a monster clawed it from her fucking body.

Then Chrissy asked, "Wait. Where's Charlie?"

15
CHOKECHERRIES

Charlie watched as his siblings and friends fell, convulsed on the floor, and he, too, fell into a seizure of some sort. A strange mist surrounded him, wrapped itself around him, and pulled tightly, squeezing the air from his lungs. His world turned to bright white and then fizzled back, and he was there on the ground, watching his friends and family continue their horrifying seizures.

He stood up, terrified, unsure what to do. But his feet reacted without his mind, and they moved him forward, yanking him past the people he needed to help. His mouth opened, and a gentle whisper dripped from his mouth, "No. Wait." But his body did not wait.

He left.

As he exited the studio, he scanned the waving flags draped in front of the shops, and each felt like fingers drawing near, ready to gouge his eyes out. The people, too, moving from storefront to storefront, all eyed him, and Charlie wondered if the creature used their sight as his own. The wind was the devil's breath, hitting his face like hot exhales.

His throat closed up, and his ribs pressed in.

When was the next ferry out of here? Would his loved ones awaken in time to flee the island before the night approached?

He wrapped his arms around his torso and turned back to the art shop, staring at the front façade. It looked unchanged, the pastel oceans and colorful boats on canvas hanging in the windows were a faux smiley face, hiding the trauma and horror quaking within.

Charlie battled with himself, screamed internally to go back in, to save the people he loved. But he marched away despite himself, slowly at first, almost floating. And his feet argued with his brain, pushing a little faster, a little faster, until he was speed walking down a long winding road to God knows where. He followed it past beautiful houses, vast empty spaces, and untouched woods between them.

Where the fuck was he and why was he going this way? He didn't know, but he kept walking. A man possessed, he marched down neighborhood streets, houses unfamiliar to him, even from his short time living on the island. Not that he had a lot of time to see the other habitats, but still, his internal GPS was spinning in circles, drunk and confused. His mother's voice echoed in his skull, *Keep marching.* The fear left him, dripped from his pores like sweat. Everything would be okay. This was supposed to happen. No more battling an internal monologue that fought against action. The old Charlie would go back, shake his family free from their prison, and run them to the docks. Away from the terror. Forever.

But the new Charlie, the brave Charlie, the one with his mother's spirit inside him, knew his friends and family were okay, that they'd wake up like he had, and they'd go to the boats and go home, and when Charlie finished this journey, he'd learn something new, something to help them all move on. His mother guided him. And she never steered him wrong.

With no sidewalks, Charlie had to keep hopping on lawns or into the woods to avoid fast-moving cars unconcerned about the bends. After a while, the roads looked the same, the houses too. Old Town

Road, Center Road, Cooneymus, Lewis Farm. They were all named, marked as different from one another, but to Charlie, they were one and the same, a bizarre melding of slithering worms, intertwining, wrapping around the island, suffocating, choking the heart, squeezing.

Or maybe he had it wrong. Maybe it was a bloodstream, the island's lifeblood, and Charlie was a free radical, a rogue cell coursing through and clogging it.

He didn't know, wasn't even sure whether he was awake or dreaming all of this as he shook uncontrollably on the floor of the studio. All he knew was that a ghost spoke to him, and his feet followed a plan. But most importantly, he knew to obey because the spirit was his mother, and she led him from the darkness toward the truth, toward hope.

He'd left the comfort of the wide asphalt streets a while ago, traveling on uneven dirt roads. The houses were still regular, but the spaces between were thicker with woods, more ominous.

His legs ached, not used to this level of walking, but his will to proceed, to see this through, kept his feet moving. But where the fuck was he going?

He shooed thoughts of the monster from his mind, not wanting it to scare him from whatever it was his feet forced him into. This trek, like going to the island in the first place, was necessary, a fate assigned to him that he tried to fight against until he knew better.

Still, when he hit those isolated stretches of road, his heart punched his ribs, and he winced at the idea of the monster storming from the white oaks.

He escaped the roads, down a thin stretch of dirt made just for walking. The trees around the path bent over, their branches hovering like hands in supplication. Charlie's palm stung, and he gasped as he saw red dripping through the cracks between his fingers. He flipped his hand and opened it. Chokecherries. Their bodies mushed and gunked, and the juices flowed down his fingers and wrist. He had no memory of picking them, no idea how they ended up in his grasp.

Suddenly, the journey felt wrong, poisoned. A shroud of safety had hovered over him, as if Charlie operated under the influence of a higher power—his mother guiding him. He'd been entranced, like when an athlete claimed to be in the zone. But the chokecherries violently shook him from his hypnosis, awakening him to his surroundings. He was nowhere, and he was alone.

He took his phone out of his pocket and checked the time. It was 7:15 p.m. He'd been walking for hours. Jesus. Seven of them? It seemed impossible. The walk felt like an hour, tops. Hell, a walk around the shore, covering the entire island probably wouldn't take seven hours. If the timing was accurate somehow, he wouldn't be back to the studio until two in the morning. But he believed that was wrong, maybe he'd been unconscious for hours and only walking for an hour or two? Nothing made sense. Panic set in. The sun hung low on the horizon, threatening to vanish. He had minutes to burn before it left him alone in the dark.

He clammed up, rooted to his spot, unwilling to step forward, too far gone to return to where he had started. Had the monster lulled him off into isolated territory?

Something had to give, a move to be made. The world fell silent, and Charlie heard the blood coursing through his veins, and his heart—an obedient workhorse—pumped it through, but it knocked hard on the door. "Hey, I need a break here. I need a fucking break," it told Charlie.

"Going to the graves?" a voice asked through a throat full of marbles.

Charlie jumped and let out a childlike screech. He turned to see a man with a yellow-stained beard smiling at him. The man had no shoes on, and his pants were worn thin, barely holding on to their stitching. But his shirt was a clean, crisp, blue button-down.

"The *Palatine*? Going to their graves?"

Charlie shook his head. His mouth turned to chalk and speaking felt like coughing up dust, "No."

The man let a smile crawl up one cheek. "Then what the hell you doing out here?"

Charlie snapped out of it, now as equally concerned about murderous humans as monsters. "No. I mean, yes. I am. I guess. I think I got kind of lost."

The man's eyes turned to slits. "Uh-huh. You're going the right way." He pointed toward a thin, unkempt path shrouded by long blades of grass with towering oaks flanking both sides. "It's right there. Not more than about ten minutes down that path."

Charlie stared, unsure what to say. He didn't want to proceed down the dark path without seeing the man go in the other direction. Hell, he didn't want to go down the dark path at all, but he knew he would, knew he was called here for some reason. If he were being honest with himself, this whole trip to Block Island was more than just for his sisters, bigger than a talk from his older brother, it was an invisible force pulling his puppet strings, urging him back. He argued as well as he could, but he knew his destiny beckoned with a louder voice than his own could speak. His only concern now was figuring out if the entity pulling the strings was on his side or luring him toward death.

The man gave up waiting for Charlie to respond. "The *Palatine Light* is chock full of bullshit, though. Ship didn't even sink around here. It went to Pennsylvania or some shit. I don't know what you're hoping to find at those graves, especially this late in the evening. They ain't anything special to look at."

Charlie moved his tongue around, hoping to bring some saliva to his mouth. "Yeah, maybe I'll just turn around."

The man tilted his head, staring with blatant suspicion in his eyes. "You on something, kid?"

Charlie felt guilty for a crime he hadn't committed. *Why yes, sir, I am currently drugged up by either a monster or a ghost, and they happen to be very much in control right now. Better watch out. They might eat you for getting in the way.*

Charlie wiped his sweaty palms on his pants. "No, sir."

The man's stony face altered, and the tides turned. Suddenly, he looked terrified of Charlie instead of the other way around. It was as if he read Charlie's thoughts, or worse, saw whatever haunted Charlie.

"Be on your way then," the man said, turned around, and walked away.

What had he seen? What had scared him?

And suddenly Charlie didn't want the man to leave because it meant he'd be alone. He opened his mouth to shout, to beg the man to stay with him, but what good would it do? The man wouldn't listen, and even if he did, could that gentleman save him from a monster?

Charlie's feet moved again, not toward houses, or the man, or town, but into the thick woods where the man told him the *Palatine* graves were. A thought occurred to him that gave him a sliver of relief. If the monster wanted him dead, it could have slipped into the art studio and eaten him in front of everyone with no repercussions. Charlie knew this because it had done just that with his sister at their old house on the island. This wasn't the monster calling him. It was his mother. It had to be. The man said Charlie neared the *Palatine* graves, and Chrissy had told him the story of the *Palatine* ship when she ranted about all she'd learned at the library. It was all connected.

He headed toward answers. And maybe that meant the monster was scared, angry, and maybe it was hovering around, wanting to attack, but it hadn't yet, which Charlie thought meant maybe it couldn't. Maybe Charlie's mother protected him.

It wasn't enough to strip him of his fear, but it tempered it. The path opened to a small field, and there stood the *Palatine* graves. The weird man had spoken the truth. They weren't much to look at. As unassuming as Charlie in a school hallway. One large rectangular stone had *Palatine Graves* etched in it and drove up from the earth like a tree root. There were no other graves, just a plot of land where Charlie supposed the few sick passengers who passed away on the island were buried. There was another small path moving away from the gravesite and spilling into the yard of a large property with a massive house looming in the center of it. It would have made Charlie more settled, knowing people were around, but all of the house lights were off, and the yard was nearly charcoal in the evening light.

"What now?" he asked the ghost. His mother. The monster. An angel or a devil. It didn't matter anymore. Here he was, a prisoner of his own fate. The concept of the next few minutes terrified him, an ethereal aura of possibility. An endless expanse of prospect or danger hovered over time itself. He could learn the secrets of the world, magically transport back to the studio with only mere minutes having passed, or he could find the teeth of a rabid creature.

The trees around him shook.

Charlie turned back to the dark path, and as his eyes landed on it, noises broke through the woody maw. At first, it sounded like choral birds, but as the noises came together, conforming with each other to produce a melody, he understood what he was hearing. Laughing. The woods laughed at him.

Dread filled his soul. "No," he said. "No."

"Welcome home," it said from behind the thicket. Both voices conjoined, so screechy and painful. It dribbled down his spine like ice water.

He turned to see the creature coming through the tree line. Tears filled Charlie's eyes. Horror. He hadn't experienced horror like this since he witnessed this monster in his house four years ago.

"Welcome home," came the song from behind him. He shot around to see another monster, exactly the same. Two times his size, it bent low to clear the tree branches.

"Welcome home," a third voice sang out from his side.

They crept toward him in three directions. They sang with their double voices, "Welcome home."

"No!" Charlie screamed. "It's not fair."

One of the things gripped Charlie's upper arm, digging its sharp claws into his muscle. He screamed again, "Please!"

The one in front of him dropped to its knees and crawled to him, head tilted. A grotesque smile fissured up its cheeks.

"Please. I finally made friends. My sisters and I just reconnected. I need them. They need me. Please."

The one on Charlie's side drove its talon through Charlie's stomach. The foreign object grinded into his insides. It burned, searing his lungs.

"Please!" he yelled into the hollow night air, then whispered, "I finally have friends."

The creature in front of him leaned in and licked his cheek.

With its touch, Charlie's mind jolted to half a dozen places at once, as if the creature was showing him what it envisioned.

A dense fog traveling from Block Island to the coast.

Gore splashing the street signs.

Charlie's sisters running through what looked like a hallway.

Tiffany barricaded in a closet.

Dead people everywhere.

The creature's tongue left his skin, and it opened its mouth. Hot air hit Charlie's ear.

"Please. Let me see my sisters. I need them. I need them. I don't want to be alone anymore."

The monster bit into his neck. From behind, the other bit into his shoulder. The third dropped to the ground and dug into the meaty portion of his calf.

"I don't want to die. I'm not ready for this. Please. I finally have people."

The bites came more ferociously. Burning, ripping, tearing. Pain went from localized to one central agonizing beat flowing through his entire body, increasing as if he sat in a frying pan and someone cranked the heat.

The monster in front of him pulled away, strands of gore dangling from its mouth, crimson dripping off its chin, and he snarled. "Welcome home," it screeched before opening its mouth so wide it covered Charlie's face. He felt the daggers digging into the space between his chin and neck and the top of his head. And then it all faded away.

16

ALL IS LOST

The ferry had already boarded, and it would depart in about ten minutes. Chrissy panicked. She tried to keep it together but knew when she spoke, she yelled, the words unable to come out any softer than the ferry's horn.

"We have to go back and find him," she said.

Doug stood behind Tiffany, wild-eyed and bursting with energy. "The ferry's about to leave. It's the last one for the night. How long were we out?" He turned toward the boat and slammed his foot down. "What the fuck is going on?"

Chrissy realized as crazy as the preceding events were for her and Angela, they must have been ten times as nuts for Tiffany and Doug, who hadn't the faintest idea what any of this meant. Of course, knowing might have only made it worse.

Tiffany grabbed Chrissy's arm. "I love Charlie, but we lost like seven hours of time, and this shit is terrifying. He'll be okay. Maybe he's already on the boat. We know how he is. He gets scared and retreats."

Tiffany lecturing about Chrissy's own brother made Chrissy furious. "Are you seriously fucking Charlie-splaining to me? I know my brother. No matter how scared he was, he wouldn't leave us behind. Never."

Tiffany pulled her hair back. "I know. You're right. But as much as I adore Charlie, I can't stay here. I can't. I have a family too."

Angela came between them. "No one expects you to stay, but you can't expect us to leave. You and Doug go back. Chrissy and I are going to find him."

Doug grabbed his sister's shoulder, trying to pull her toward the boat. "Come on. Let's go."

Tiffany yanked her arm away. "Wait. I have to leave, but I really don't like the idea of just letting you guys go. Whatever we just saw, it was fucking real. I know it was. And it's here. On this island. And it's nighttime. Even if you find Charlie, none of you will have a place to stay, nowhere to go."

Chrissy shook her head. "I'll call my dad and force him to pay for a room for us at a hotel."

"I thought you didn't talk to your dad? And Charlie said he was broke."

Chrissy stepped back. "Yeah. That's not entirely accurate. Now get on the boat."

Tiffany's lips quivered. "I really don't like the idea of leaving you on the island with that thing."

Angela pushed Chrissy back toward the main road. "You don't have a choice."

As soon as Chrissy's feet left the curb into the now desolate road, the strands between her and Tiffany broke. She liked Charlie's new friends and thought they had his best interests at heart, and she also didn't blame them for leaving. Friendship is powerful, but so is perseverance, and they had their own bonds, not unlike Charlie and Chrissy's, and those bonds needed protecting too. But every second Chrissy waited was a second Charlie could be moving farther away, and she didn't have time to argue.

"Take my number. Call me if he's on there."

Tiffany handed Chrissy her phone and she quickly plugged her number in.

With Angela at her side, they ran away from the boarding station, crossed the road, and charged down Main Street back toward Milicent's studio. With the last ferry shipping out, most of the tourists had cleared, and it being fall meant there weren't many to begin with. Half of the businesses had already closed down for the night.

A bottomless pit of dread filled Chrissy's guts. Anxiety swirled with regret. How could she have traveled from the studio to the docks without recognizing her brother's absence? He never would have left without her, would have noticed instantly if she weren't there.

They turned the corner by the studio as Milicent stood at the stoop, locking the front door. Panic streaked her face.

"Milicent!" Angela yelled.

The woman startled and jerked her head toward them. Her face dropped as if it had turned to stone. "I told you to get away from here."

"It's Charlie. Have you seen him? We ran in a panic and realized he wasn't with us," Chrissy said. She hoped she kept her voice even, not trying to freak Milicent out even more.

"Shit. I don't remember seeing him either. It's like he had already left the room before I snapped out of it." She shook her head violently. "I'm sorry. I can't help you. Go to the police, but please leave me alone."

She stormed off in the opposite direction, squeezing her arms around her chest.

Chrissy and Angela stood there, dumbfounded.

"What do we do now?" Angela asked.

Chrissy put her head down, hopelessness wetting her eyes. She wanted to scream, but she had to keep her head straight. "We have no other option. We go to the police station."

Angela gave a look like she chewed on a lemon, but she didn't argue. What other choice did they have?

The police department was less than a ten-minute walk, just a straight shot down Ocean Avenue, before one right turn onto Beach Avenue. The small building looked more like a summer cottage than a police station. It sat next door to the local volunteer fire department station.

Chrissy slammed through the door, surprising the middle-aged woman behind the desk. "I need to speak to Officer Duplass."

Even as a child, when her family had called the police after the attack on Wreath, Chrissy knew no one would believe them. Who would? What happened to them was insanity personified, or monsterfied, rather. She didn't blame the police the way her family did for looking toward alternative answers, for questioning her father, her, and her siblings until they were blue in the face.

These weren't yokel police officers, and the state detectives they brought in were thorough and helpful.

But Officer Duplass stood out because he *did* take their stories seriously. Sure, not seriously enough that he dropped his concerns over their father or the possibility of an intruder, but he entertained them, showed concern and care.

The woman said, "Duplass isn't on tonight."

Chrissy shouted, "Call him!"

The door behind the woman opened, and an officer in his forties stepped into the room. "What's going on out—" He stared at the two girls standing in the doorway. "Chrissy and Angela Keating?"

Four years. It had been four years since they'd seen or talked to anyone in this department, yet this officer remembered them, recognized them through all the changes they'd gone through during that time. And Chrissy recognized him back. "Officer Carmen!"

Words spewed from her mouth, and at the same time, Angela ranted too. They both explained what happened with different tones: Chrissy pleading and Angela hostile.

Officer Carmen put his hand up to stop them. "Hold on. Hold on.

We can get to the other stuff later. Your brother being gone is the important part. Are you sure he didn't get on the boat?"

"Our friend got on and said she'd call us, but I'll call her just in case," Chrissy said.

As she dialed, Officer Carmen said to Angela, "And have you called him? See if he just decided to take a stroll and lost track of time?"

Angela huffed, but her eyes gave away her embarrassment that through all of this, she hadn't considered just calling her brother. She took her cell out and dialed.

Chrissy hung up on Tiffany. All she needed to hear were the words, "He's not here." Tiffany had kept talking, apologizing again for leaving, but Chrissy didn't have time for it.

"He's not on the boat."

They all turned to Angela, who clicked the phone off. "Voicemail after one ring."

Officer Carmen's face dropped, realizing his night wouldn't go as calmly as planned. "Okay, come here. You two sit in the back office."

"You have to do something!" Angela shouted.

Carmen's voice rose, but not in a way where he was yelling. "I am going to do something. We're gonna find your brother, but for now, I need you out of the way while I make some calls."

He ushered them into the back room, a room they'd both sat in before. It had a few round tables, a snack machine, a water cooler, and a coffee pot.

Chrissy and Angela sat across from one another, neither saying anything but both becoming balls of energy. Chrissy's feet tapped and Angela rolled her neck around, checking out every inch of the room.

"Why are you always looking in the corners? I see you doing that all the time," Chrissy said, distracting herself.

"Well, maybe you should have asked me about it."

"I just did."

"I know. Now that our little boat trip turned us into best pals, right?" She rolled her eyes and looked away.

"Never mind then. I forgot how much of an asshole you can be."

"Go read a book, bitch."

"I'd tell you to do the same, but I'm not sure you know how."

"And there's the Chrissy I know, always better than everyone else just because she likes shitty books."

"I don't think I'm better than anyone, other than you, and it has nothing to do with reading books, and everything to do with how incredibly cruel you are to everyone you meet."

Angela pounded her fist on the table. "I stare at the corners because that's where I see it. It hovers there. All the time. It's just fucking mocking me. I've seen it every single day since Wreath died. Oh, and by the way, Wreath was my sister, too, and Mom was my mom. And I sat through so many bullshit days where you and Charlie hung out and tried to understand each other, and you talked about your problems and acted like a bunch of douchey sad losers. And the entire time you were talking, there was a monster hovering in the corner above you both, licking its lips.

"You want to know the truth? If anything happened to Charlie, I'll be devastated, but it doesn't change the fact that I don't really like him, and I don't really like you either. Why should I? You both might as well have been two more monsters in the room."

She crossed her arms. "In other words—" She slowly lifted her middle finger.

17

SPILL IT

After Tiffany scoured the ferry for Charlie, she went to the top deck and stared out at Block Island as it shrunk into the distance. Doug tailed her the whole time, and now that she'd stopped running from seating section to seating section, he settled in behind her. Tiffany's hands shook, from the foggy nightmare she'd experienced, and the worry over Charlie, and now the freezing cold breeze from the ferry's trek.

She pulled out her phone to text Chrissy and let her know she hadn't seen Charlie, but before she could dial, Doug put his hand on her shoulder. All he said was, "Spill it."

It was all he needed to say.

She turned to him and huffed. She wanted to tell him everything, but the nerves firing through her made it difficult to speak, let alone rant.

"When I first met Charlie, I wondered about him. He seemed cool, but he seemed, I don't know, messed up. So, I looked him up. Remember how I got all of his information when he passed out in Beth's car? Anyway, I found out a lot."

Doug's eyes softened, but a nervous curiosity twitched his top lip. "What did you find?"

"When he was little, like four years ago, his family lived on Block Island. He had an older sister and she disappeared in their house when they were all there. The police found no trace of her. Just gone. And never found again."

"Jeez. That sucks, but what does it have to do with what's happening?"

"The police questioned Charlie's father, and seemed to think he had something to do with it. But the family, all of them, right down to Angela who was super little at the time, all held on to the same story. And that's true to this day."

Now an undercurrent of fear flooded his eyes. "What was their story?"

Tiffany glanced back at the island, worried to say this part, thinking of how ludicrous it would sound even to someone who probably just envisioned the same entity she had when they collapsed at the art studio. "That they were all playing a game when they heard their sister making horrible noises in her room. When they bashed her door in, they saw—"

Doug shook his head. "What?"

"—A monster eating her." She stood up firm, not feeling as weird about it as she thought she would. "They all say they saw a monster eating their sister."

Doug put his hands over his face and rubbed hard at it, as if he wanted to scrub his damned face off. When he pulled his hands away, his eyes were bloodshot, fiery little storms. "And I'm assuming that's what I saw in my little fucked-up foggy dream?"

She shrugged. "I assume. It's what I saw."

"What happened in yours?" he asked.

"Uncle Billy."

He nodded. "I'm sorry."

"Which turned into a giant weird-ass monster. What about you?"

114

"You getting dragged out of the house by Uncle Billy. This time, I chased after you, but when Uncle Billy turned around—"

"—He was the monster?" she finished for him.

"Yeah."

"Yeah."

They both stared off in different directions, Tiffany toward the island and Doug into the sea. Eventually, Doug broke the silence. "So, I still don't get it. Was the monster thing the reason we came here? Why didn't you tell me?"

"I didn't know," she said. "I mean, I assumed their trip here had something to do with it, but I didn't know what. It's not like I believed there was a fucking monster on the island. I just assumed they were coming here for some sort of closure. Maybe to talk to a friend or relative about it. I'm still not sure what they were doing. I mean, I know they were going to see the artist lady because she paints pictures of it or something, but that's all I know, and I just found that out five minutes before we got there."

Doug gripped the railing hard, his fingers turning ghostly white with the pressure. "So, do you believe there really was a monster?"

She looked away from him and bit hard on her lip. "I do now. Yeah. You?"

"Yeah," he said softly. "Yeah, I do. So what now? Where do you think Charlie went?"

She shook her head. "No idea. To either question."

"Because if the monster did something to him, we never should have left."

"I know," Tiffany said more sternly than she meant to. "I know we shouldn't have left. But I was scared."

"I'm still scared," Doug said.

Tiffany saw something from the far side of the island, away from the docks they'd pulled out of. "What's that?" She pointed.

"Doug leaned forward, squinting his eyes. "What is that?"

It looked like a light fog, thin and hollow, at the bottom, but as it rose up, it grew thicker, like the raging smoke of a fire.

Tiffany turned away, unable to keep staring at it, thinking of only horrors. "Jesus, I hope they're all okay."

She turned and went inside, Doug following. They sat in silence inside the boat for the remainder of the trip. Chrissy called to ask if Tiffany had seen Charlie on board. She said she hadn't. Before she could finish apologizing for leaving, Chrissy hung up on her, which only exacerbated Tiffany's guilt. When they landed in Point Judith, they hurried to the stairs and exited as quickly as possible, as if the boat contained the noxious odors of their day, the poisonous air of all they'd just witnessed.

As they came out into the square parking lot, a figure ran toward them. Tiffany flinched, seeing creatures in everything, but as the figure closed in, she recognized Beth. Her girlfriend. Beth wrapped herself around Tiffany and kissed her cheek.

"You're back!"

Tiffany furrowed her brow. "What are you doing here?"

"Sorry, I just missed you today and wanted to surprise you."

"Color me surprised," Tiffany said, pushing past her girlfriend, heading toward the parking lot down the road where Doug parked their car. "How did you know which boat I was taking?"

Beth put her head down, following on Tiffany's side. Her cheeks turned speckled with pink. "I may have been waiting here for a few hours."

Tiffany gave her a double take, not slowing down in her walk. "That's a little weird, isn't it?"

Beth's mouth curved down and hurt flashed in her eyes. "I know. But I missed you."

Tiffany stopped in her tracks and faced Beth. She noticed Doug lagging behind, smart enough to stay away from this conversation. "It's weird. It's too much. I just wanted a fucking day with my brother and friends. This is too much. All of it." She didn't mean it. Sure, it was a bit much, but on a normal day, she wouldn't have held it against Beth, would have maybe cracked a joke and smiled, because the gesture was nice.

"What? I'm sorry. I didn't mean to like, invade on your shit. I thought it would be cute and make you happy."

"Well it didn't. I think you should leave."

"I'm sorry," Beth's voice cracked a little.

"Just go the fuck home, Beth," she yelled the words so loudly a couple across the street stopped and turned to see the commotion. Beth's pink-speckled cheeks turned to beets. She opened her mouth like she wanted to respond, but nothing came out of her other than a thin wisp of air. Not even loud enough to be a squeak.

Tiffany wanted to apologize right then and there, wanted to hug the poor girl, but she had no strength for it. She was ugly and mean, and she knew it, but she couldn't stop now. All of these horrible emotions were bubbling inside her, and she felt so weak, but yelling and being angry and kicking at whatever stood in front of her took some of that away, made her feel in control again. Jesus, she was her own monster. A villain. And worse than most, because she KNEW she was one, had the self-awareness to know how she acted really sucked. But she carried on anyway.

"Leave. Go home. Stop embarrassing yourself."

Tiffany stormed off, unwilling to witness the damage she'd created on her girlfriend's face. When she reached Doug's car, she finally turned back again. Beth was nowhere in sight. Doug reached the car a few seconds later and said nothing as he started the Camry and drove them home, but his eyes showed worry for Tiffany. He wouldn't lecture her, wouldn't pass judgment, but those eyes. Those eyes showed concern.

18
LANGBLASS NEBELBEWOHNER

C hrissy and Angela sat up straight as Officer Carmen stepped in. He sighed and pulled up a chair at their table, sitting on it backward.

"All right, here's what's going to happen. We have state police coming in, and we're going to turn this island upside down trying to find your brother. We already have every officer on the island awake and preparing for the search. In the meantime, I suggest you keep trying his cell. We will too. The Coast Guard is sending some guys to pick you both up and bring you back to the mainland."

"What?" Chrissy asked.

"No, they fucking aren't," Angela said.

Officer Carmen put his hand up to stop them. "It's not a conversation. I know you've both been through a lot, and I know you're worried about your brother, but there's nothing you can do here but be in the way. Listen, normally if a teenager didn't show up to meet his family at the docks, we wouldn't have state police rolling in to begin a search. This is different because of . . . Well, you know. But that means YOU two need to be safe and sound too. At your home. With your family. I'm sure you both have schoolwork to get to this weekend, and I know your dad will be worried sick if you don't get back."

Chrissy prepared to let the comment go, unlike her sister, who broke out into laughter.

"Our dad has no clue where we are and hasn't for years."

Officer Carmen pursed his lips. "Then who do you live with?"

Again, Chrissy saw no point in indulging this conversation. It didn't matter. Charlie mattered. But again, Angela had a different mindset.

"We live with our aunt. My father's sister. She also doesn't give much of a shit about us, but she at least feeds us and gives us a place to sleep, although that place usually changes on the regular." She leaned forward. "See, after you all berated him for months on end and made this entire island think he was some kind of murderer, he sort of snapped, gave away all of our money. Literally! He gave it away. Didn't consider giving it to us! He gave it to charity. Then he pushed us on his sister, moved into a little shitty house in Westerly, and spends his days drinking and sobbing like a little bitch."

Officer Carmen slumped. "I'm sorry to hear that."

"Yeah, well, maybe it wouldn't have happened if the police decided to look into everything we *told* them happened instead of going with their gut. And Milicent even came to you *before* we told you pretty much the same thing. Two different families, two different times, both with the same story, and you just fucking ignored us."

Officer Carmen grinned. Chrissy saw the way he held in his anger, how he tried to smile and take it all, but it ate at him. He leaned in, keeping his voice calm. "You think we didn't look into your story? You think we didn't take it seriously? You have no idea. Yes, we checked out your father. We also looked at some neighbors. I'm sorry it bothers you that we were thorough." He sat up now, confidence kicking into his voice. "And for what it's worth, no, I don't believe you saw a monster that night, but I do believe you saw something that resembled one. Someone in a mask, a distortion of some sort. I don't know. And yes, Milicent came to us about her friend Molly and Molly's brother. And yes, when you all described the monster to us, we put all of that together, and we've operated ever since—which, by the way, means to this day—under the assumption we are dealing with some kind of serial killer. But we don't just bring that information to the local newspapers unless we have something really strong to show them."

Chrissy put her hand on top of his, her forehead wrinkling. She wasn't Angela and had no interest in antagonistic approaches, but what Officer Carmen said offended her on a deep level, words like shovels digging through her bones. "But we didn't see someone in a mask. I know you're trying to rationalize it, and I get that, but what we saw was a giant monster. It was ridiculously tall, and its body shape, the way it moved, the way it spoke, those weren't things humans can just do. And we watched it eat our sister. It ate her. Not like a cannibal, but it chewed on her until she was gone.

"And we saw it again tonight. Not in person, but it infiltrated all of our minds at the same time. We all fell to the ground like we were having a seizure. All of us. At the same time. That isn't normal, and you can't explain it away. I need you to understand this because Charlie—" Her voice broke, and a rush of sadness sloshed in her throat. "Charlie is gone, and I need you, absolutely *need* you to believe us. He didn't just skip off for ice cream. He didn't go for a leisurely walk. He disappeared while we all, simultaneously, lost control of ourselves and fell into a nightmare."

Angela's eyes darted back and forth between Chrissy and Officer Carmen. He pushed his head forward, closer to Chrissy. "And I need you to understand it's possible for me to not believe in monsters, but to fully believe you. I, and the state police, are not going to dismiss anything. That means we'll follow through as if a damned demon stole your brother, and we'll operate as if it's possible your brother decided things got too heavy and he needed a scoop of Ben and Jerry's. Checking into one doesn't dismiss another. We'll check on everything."

The door to the back room opened, and Officer Duplass stepped in. He had bags under his eyes and a few more grays than the last time they'd seen him. He wore sweatpants and a hoodie, and Chrissy guessed he'd just rolled out of bed, probably awoken by a phone call from the woman out front. What surprised Chrissy, though, was that an elderly woman came in right behind him.

Officer Carmen turned to the sound and gave a brief smile at his fellow officer. "Mark," Officer Carmen said.

Duplass nodded. "John. You mind if I talk to them?"

Officer Carmen stood up and shook Duplass's hand. "Go for it. I need to head to the docks and meet up with the state police when they get here. We got the rest of the gang dividing up the island and preparing search party routes. When you finish up with them, drive them down to the docks to meet with the Coast Guard. Don't let them out of your sight. We don't need them running out there, making us have to search for more kids."

As Officer Carmen exited the room, Duplass spun the chair around so he could sit on it the correct way. The old woman sat across from him.

Officer Duplass wasted no time cutting to the chase. "Just want to make sure I heard all this correctly. You two, Charlie, and a couple of friends went to Milicent's shop because you saw her drawings of your monster. Then, you all collapsed, somehow lost track of time, woke up, and fled to the docks only to realize Charlie was missing. Do I have that all right?"

Chrissy and Angela nodded.

"And why do you believe this has to do with your monster?"

Angela chimed in, an impatient frustration guiding her, "Because we all had a seizure at the same time, and I guess I don't know what everyone envisioned, but I saw the monster chewing on Wreath, and then it whispered a secret in my ear."

Chrissy jumped in, realizing they hadn't shared their nightmares with each other, they only assumed each of them saw the creature. "I also saw the monster, but it was crawling out from a book, lying on my bedroom floor. And it screamed at me. It said, 'Welcome home,' which is what it always says, but this time it pointed out the window to the street, and when I looked out the window, it was the street in front of our house. The one we live in now. What secret did it tell you, Angela?"

"It told me that it had all the blood it needed to be free. Whatever that means."

Everyone turned quiet for a moment until Chrissy looked at Officer Duplass. "I think it was all a threat. Look, I'm not stupid, I know you don't believe any of this. But it's true. I swear. And I know you know there's more to our story. Milicent told me how she came to you guys with the pictures from Molly and her brother."

The old woman took a cell phone from her pocket. "Hi. I'm sorry to interrupt. My name is Cathy Bogner, and I work for the historical society. It's nice to meet you both. I wanted to ask you a question." She opened her phone with a few finger swipes and placed it down on the table. Her finger clicked the photos app, and a picture opened up. Chrissy didn't see it at first, too busy eyeing her sister to see if she was as confused as Chrissy over why a member of the Block Island Historical Society would be there.

"Does this resemble your monster?"

Angela's eyes widened. Chrissy looked down. It was a crude drawing, old fashioned, and without detail, just an outline of the creature's shape. It was on a yellowed background, as if it came from an old book.

"That looks like it, yes. What is that?"

Dimples appeared on the woman's cheeks as she gave a pleasant smile. "This is Langblass Nebelbewohner. Silly name for such a frightening creature, I know. The picture comes from a book on German lore."

Chrissy was tired, too tired to hear about German lore, even if it was closely related to her own nightmares. What did it matter? She just wanted her brother back.

"What's a Langblass Whatchacallit?" Angela asked.

Officer Duplass rubbed his hand over his mouth and turned around, checking the door. "Look, I brought Cathy here because she's been following your case for a long time. Along with Molly Mix's. She provided us with a lot of information that, sadly, our police department didn't have. Stuff from before computers stored everything.

"For the record, and I'm not saying this to be a jerk, but I want you to understand where I'm at: I don't believe in monsters. But all the stuff Cathy's gathered paints a pretty crazy picture. And I think it's a picture you deserve to understand. It's a lot of folklore and weird stuff, but somehow it all correlates to what happened to your family. How? Why? That's what we're trying to figure out."

They all stared at him, waiting for his speech to end. Chrissy felt a small wave of relief. Sure, they didn't believe the monster stories, but they had investigated it and in some way, knew it all played into something more than a family going crazy together. If only the newspapers had the information the police did.

Cathy took her phone back and put it in her pocket. "Langblasses were tall, pale beasts that lived in the Black Forest in Germany. It was believed that they infected people's minds, showing them their worst nightmares before devouring them. I never found anything that mentioned seizures like you said you had today, but I did find a story from 1837 where a man talked about his family 'falling into a spell' in the Black Forest, and when he awoke, his children were gone, and a Langblass was eating his wife. You can find tons of silly stories about them on the internet. And they are all so wildly different from one another that it's hard to parse what's real and what's nonsense. Assuming any of it is real, of course. But there are commonalities. Having a foggy brain, seeing visions of the beasts, that sort of thing. Now, that's what I found researching Langblasses, but there was another story that *did* involve a seizure and a monster."

Chrissy sat back and pinched her nose. A headache was building in her skull. She already knew the Vanderline story and didn't need this woman reiterating it. "This is all really interesting, and I especially love research and wanting to know more about things, but I'm so tired, and my mind just keeps going back to my brother, so I just don't know that I have the patience for this right now. I'm not trying to be mean. I truly need to know all of this stuff, but I just can't process it right now."

Cathy put her arms up in defeat. "I understand, dear. Let me cut to the chase. Do you know anything about the *Palatine*?"

Chrissy nodded, still pinching her nose with her eyes shut tight. "Yes. I just read all about it."

"Well, if you did your research, I'm sure you've heard the conflicting accounts where some believe Block Islanders raided the ship, killed the immigrants on board, and robbed them blind, and the other account where they kindly housed the ailing passengers until they left for Pennsylvania."

Chrissy opened her eyes. "Yes."

Cathy smiled again, a polite little stream drawing up her cheeks. "Well, there's another account, and it's a juicy one. So juicy in fact, when I brought the letters to numerous historians, I was dismissed and mocked. Most believe I forged the documents. In these letters, all from the first mate on the *Palatine*, he claims the boat only housed two immigrants. A couple. And the trip wasn't to bring them to America. The crew and the immigrants were working together to bring something else to Block Island specifically."

Chrissy sat up, getting it. Angela looked at her sister. "What? I don't get it."

"They had captured three Langblasses from the Black Forest and were bringing them to Block Island for examination by a demonologist who promised she and her husband knew how to contain the creatures."

Chrissy's eyes filled with tears. Beads of excitement. "Apparently, they failed?"

Cathy frowned. "I'm not so sure. Well, surely the beasts aren't locked in a cellar somewhere, but they seem to only appear on this island, as if they can't leave it. And they aren't marching around killing people left and right. There must be something stopping them from that, from turning this place into their new Black Forest."

Angela was nearly hyperventilating. "So, you think it's real? You think it took Charlie?"

Cathy raised a hand. "There's one interesting thing, and that thing pokes a big hole in the theory that Langblasses had anything to do with what happened to your family."

"What?" Chrissy asked.

"The demonologists, their surname was Mix. And the immigrants, they were the Vanderlines, sometimes spelled as all one word, sometimes separated after the *N* and *R*. Van. Der. Line."

"I don't get it. I mean, I understand Molly Mix. There's a connection there, probably some distant relative. But what does that mean?" Chrissy asked.

"Molly Mix wasn't the first Mix to disappear mysteriously. In fact, it happened quite regularly in their family. Once a generation. Always to the oldest child. Whether or not that happened with *every* generation, I couldn't confirm, but it happened to Molly, and it happened at least three other times in their family line."

Chrissy's shoulders slumped. "And it happened to the Vanderline family too. I read about Mary Vanderline who had a seizure in her uncle's bathroom."

Cathy nodded. "Indeed. Outside of your sister's story, it's the only time I've heard a direct mention of seizures in relation to the monster. But so far as I can tell, the Vanderline family tree ended there."

Chrissy had drawn herself into the mystery, growing more and more interested as the dots connected closer to her sister's death, but now it all pulled apart again. "Still, there's clearly something there."

Officer Duplass sat forward. "Yes. Obviously. What that something is, we don't know."

Cathy tsk-tsked. "Oh, I think we do, even if we don't know how to connect them yet."

Duplass rolled his eyes. "Okay, yes, we know it has something to do with what you saw. While Cathy may be more willing to believe in old German folk tales, I am not. But clearly there are a lot of similarities and happenstances here. And we aren't ignoring that."

His phone buzzed. "Duplass. Go ahead." He nodded as if the person on the other end could see him. "Got it."

He stood up. "Come on. Your boat awaits."

OFFICER DUPLASS DROVE them to the docks, and the Coast Guard helped them onto the boat, handing them life vests. As Chrissy put hers on, she looked to Duplass, who stood by the boat, watching them get aboard and to safety. "Thank you for having Cathy explain all that to us. It doesn't really help, but it also kind of helps a lot. It at least makes us feel like we've been taken seriously."

Duplass nodded. "You have."

"I don't care if it's three in the morning. Please call me when you find anything out."

Duplass nodded again. "I'm going to call your aunt and father too. And just so you're prepared, I'm pretty sure Officer Carmen already has."

Angela frowned. "Doesn't matter. They won't answer. They won't care."

The small boat took off, engine buzzing. Unlike the large ferry, Chrissy could feel the bouncing of the boat against the sea. It made her already upset stomach turn. Despite the tragedies she'd lived through, her mother, her sister, her drunken father, she couldn't accept a doomed fate, couldn't help but think Charlie was safe out there somewhere, that he'd return home soon. While she still battled the nervousness, that hope clung to her and kept her from losing it. If

Duplass called her with a somber tone later that night, she didn't know what would happen to her, if she could survive it. Charlie was the one thing in her life that felt unbreakable. Ironic, considering how fragile he was.

As the boat reached the midway point to the mainland, nearing the rock wall that arched around the docks at Point Judith, Chrissy turned back to the island. "What the hell is that?"

Angela and a coastguardsman turned to see what she noticed.

"Looks like fog," the guardsman said, but he squinted to get a better view, unsure of his own answer.

"Why does it look like smoke?" Angela asked. "It's all super thick at the top."

The fog or smoke or whatever it was wrapped around the far side of the island, away from the places they'd visited for the day. The way it moved, slithered, crept, had an eerie lifelike quality to it, not a product of nature, but something guided and maneuvered like a marionette. Thin and scrim on the bottom, but it puffed up and bloated at the top. A mushroom. And it crept along the shore, enveloping one side of the island.

Chrissy tried to make sense of it, to see it as something she could understand, and when she placed it, she had to sit down, too overwhelmed by the strong sensations at play. Something was wrong. Something bad was happening.

The fog was a mouth, and it was swallowing the island. Worse, it spread in their direction, chomping slowly away at the ocean.

19

ON A CLEAR NIGHT

Jackson woke with a start. Something had pulled him from his dreams, but he was too out of sorts to figure it out. He spent a minute gathering himself. His head felt okay. Usually, he woke with a splitting headache from grinding his teeth all night. His chest, too, didn't ache the way it normally did, where he felt sharp pains and a thrumming heart. Some nights were luckier than others, where he woke up without the hardcore detoxing symptoms. Was detoxing the right word? It had certainly moved beyond hangovers.

He sat up and looked at the clock, which read 11:27 p.m. Oh fuck. Well, that explained the lack of symptoms. He had only been asleep for an hour and a half, which meant he was pretty much still drunk. Dragging his feet, he went to the fridge and cracked open a beer. He wanted something harder, but his head was swimming enough already. He just needed something to soften the inevitable pain.

Sipping off the can, he slid back to the bedroom and noticed his phone had two missed calls. The vibrating was probably what woke him up.

The same number had called both times. He played the only message.

"Hello, Mr. Keating. My name is Officer Carmen of the New Shoreham Police Department. Could you give me a call at—"

Jackson quickly opened the nightstand drawer and pulled out a piece of paper and a pen. He jotted the number down.

"—It's in regard to your son, Charlie, and your daughters, Chrissy and Angela."

Jesus. New Shoreham? Why were the kids anywhere near that fucking place? And all three of them? His stomach dropped. A hysterical, helpless cry bubbled in his throat and filled his eyes before he even heard what had happened. For all he knew the kids just got in trouble. Had a fight with some locals. Stole something.

As he went to dial, a gentle knock came from the front door. Despite the soft nature, Jackson nearly fell off the bed. He rushed to answer it, shoulders bumping into the walls as he went. He could hardly stand up straight. He really wanted a long pull on his drink before opening the door, but he'd forgotten the can on the end table.

When he saw the somber police officer on the doorstep, he cried, unleashing those tears that had built in his gut.

The officer had his hands at his chest, holding his hat, and he stood tall. A man and a woman stood behind him, a step down. The officer in front wore a state uniform, and the woman had what looked like a Westerly Police Department uniform. The man in the back wore civilian clothes.

"Sorry to bother you, sir. Are you Mr. Keating?" the statie asked.

Jackson nodded.

"I'm Officer Barrett. May we come in for a moment?"

Jackson floated. Just as he had when he found his mother dead as a child, and when he received the call about his wife. He hovered above the scene, watching the actors play out their roles, watching himself, too, seeing himself open the door for the group, guiding them to the couch, and sitting next to them in an armchair.

The female cop stopped before sitting and shook his hand. "I'm Officer Burns. Or you can just call me Meghan."

Too many names. Cops on the phone. Cops at the door. It was too much.

"We have some bad news," Officer Barrett said, and just like that, Jackson was sucked back into his body, no longer floating. In fact, he hardly had the strength to sit. If he could flop over and die, he would.

"Your son, Brian, died earlier this evening from a drug overdose."

Jackson never questioned whether he was a bad parent or not. He knew he sucked. But his thoughts in the first few seconds after he heard the officer's words solidified it. Because after hearing the voicemail about Charlie, Chrissy, and Angela and then seeing these officers, he assumed something had happened to one or all of them. When he discovered it was Brian, his immediate thought was, *Phew.*

But then memories of Brian as a child, teaching Charlie to play *Mario Kart*, laughing with Jackson while watching *The Princess Bride*, all of those happy little glimmers came back. Memory was a lie, though, because most of their lives they butted heads, and those happy moments were so fleeting and desperate that they only acted as a mirage, something to cling to, something to break Jackson's heart at the end.

Brian was such a good kid, so caring about his family, so overprotective. He loved his siblings more than he loved anything, even his parents. When Jackson had to yell at Angela for coloring on the walls, Brian stood between them, talking Jackson down, reminding him how little kids behave and of the beauty in their creativity.

Jackson continuously saw Brian as himself, which made their relationship hard because the boy reflected the worst aspects of his father, projecting them for all to see. When he'd left home, dropped out of school, became a drug addict, disappeared, yelled and shouted, it was all Jackson. Jackson's Frankenstein. But worse, because he'd built this monster from his own parts. He fostered it, practically driving the boy to those dark corners. He'd failed on every front, and now Brian died so young, too fucking young. And Jackson only had himself to blame.

He bent over, head to his knees, and bawled. Sounds of anguish flew out of him—pained groans, yells, grunts.

The officers sat there, still and calm.

"Was he alone? That's all I want to know."

The man in plain clothes sat forward. "Hello, Mr. Keating. I'm Officer Long of the Providence Police. I'm the one who responded to the call and found your son. He was at someone's house, and he had a friend there with him. But he asked to use the restroom, where he proceeded to take a large amount of pills."

Jackson cocked his head. "You mean it was on purpose? Suicide?"

Officer Long nodded his head. "It appears that way. Yes."

Jackson stood up. "Oh my god. Just before you got here, I had a message from the New Shoreham police about my other children. I need to call them."

He ran into his bedroom and grabbed his cell phone and the unfinished beer. When he came into the living room, all three officers were still sitting on the couch. As he dialed the number he'd written down, none of them said anything. Probably not trained to handle a situation where a man just lost his son and also needed to call a different police department about his other three children.

The officer he dialed picked up. "Officer Carmen."

"Hello, this is Jackson Keating. You left me a message?"

There was silence on the other end. Jackson glanced at the officers on the couch, all staring up at him, and he turned toward the kitchen. As the officer on the other end spoke, Jackson made his way out the side door into his yard. The cool, fresh air hit his dry lungs. He killed the rest of his beer and tossed the can on the lawn.

"Hey, I would much rather have this conversation in person, but we're running thin here. Your children came to the island today, Chrissy, Angela, and Charlie. Apparently, they're all claiming they had a group episode—"

Jackson's heart banged hard. He stared off beyond his yard, where the ocean lapped against the shore. "A group episode? What does that mean?"

"Well, according to them it means they, and a group of their friends, all fell into a seizure. And they lost a good chunk of time. They say around seven hours."

Jackson shook his head. "They say" were good words to hear. It meant they were okay now. "I'm not sure I'm understanding. They said they ALL had a seizure for seven hours?" He held in a scream of frustration. "That doesn't make sense. Are they okay? Just tell me my fucking kids are okay."

Even having seen what he'd witnessed, Jackson couldn't comprehend a group of kids having a seizure at the same time, and worse, for it to last for such an absurd amount of time. It would have destroyed their brain, right?

He continued to stare out at the ocean, and then he noticed something he'd never seen before. To be fair, he almost never went in the yard. But now he noticed a series of blinking lights in the distance. It was Block Island. He had no idea he could see it from here.

"Yes." Officer Carmen gave a big sigh as if dreading the words to come. "They said they saw the monster. In a vision. All of them. But Mr. Keating, that's not why I'm calling. When they woke up, Charlie was missing."

"What?" Slowly the blinking lights dimmed as if something covered them. "Did you find him?"

"We have the state police here, and we're currently operating a full search of the island. Meanwhile, the Coast Guard took your daughters back to the mainland, and a Narragansett officer is driving them home to your sister's house."

"So, you haven't found Charlie? Do you have anything to go on? Any idea where he could have gone?" His knees buckled under him, head swimming. He leaned against a tree. The dimmed blinking lights vanished altogether.

"We don't have much to go on outside of where he was at the time they last saw him, but I assure you we have teams of folks here helping us search for your son, and we won't rest until we find him."

"Really? You have a full team? Seems like half the team is in my living room right now."

"Huh?"

The last blinking light visible faded as something covered it. The phone made a screeching sound, horribly high-pitched, and then the call went silent.

"Officer? Are you there? What's happening?"

The side door slapped against the wooden rail as the three officers came out into the yard. "Everything all right, Mr. Keating?" one of them asked.

Jackson fell to his knees. It was hard to breathe. "I've got to get to my daughters."

"Would you like us to call them? Do you have anyone else that can stay with you right now?" Officer Barrett asked.

"No. It's just them. I need to get to them."

The officers looked at each other. Barrett said, "I'm not sure you should be driving. We can collect your daughters and bring them to you if they aren't old enough to drive themselves."

He almost argued until he realized how stupid that would be. First, getting into a car in front of three cops with a blood alcohol level of, well, vodka, wouldn't work out well. But even if they did let him go, how foolish would he be to let his children into a car with him behind the wheel?

"Yeah, okay. I'll give you the address. That would be great." He squinted, eyes focused on the island. In the dark, he couldn't make out what covered it, but something appeared to be moving, clouding the entire land mass. Then it became clearer. It was a mist, and it was growing, expanding, and headed straight toward them.

"Does that look normal to you?"

The officers all turned to where he pointed.

"What?" Burns asked.

"That fog or smoke or whatever that is. It looks all wrong."

Officer Long leaned forward. "What the hell is that?"

Officer Barrett stepped in, putting his hand on Jackson's shoulder. "Come on. Let's get you inside and get that address."

He followed them into the house, but before he entered, he gave the growing sheath one last look. It was just fog. It had to be. But he swore it moved like it was alive, and worse, he felt it was staring at him.

20
YOU CAN FEEL BLOCK ISLAND

As soon as the police car parked in front of Chrissy and Angela's house, another police car pulled onto the road and parked behind them. The officer who drove them home hopped out and opened the back door.

"Teddy Barrett? What are you doing here?" he yelled to the other car.

The second officer got out of his cruiser. "I'm here to pick up Chrissy and Angela Keating."

The sisters looked at each other. Angela felt a tightening knot in her gut.

"Did you find something out about Charlie?" Chrissy asked, scuttling out of the vehicle.

Officer Barrett looked confused, seeing his pick up exit a different police car, but he shook it off, clearly with bigger matters at hand. "Are you Chrissy and Angela?"

Angela stepped out of the car behind Chrissy. "Yes. Did you find Charlie?"

"I'm sorry, but I don't know anything about that. I was sent here to pick you up and bring you to your father's house."

Angela nearly laughed. "My father's house? You couldn't pay me."

"What's going on?" Chrissy asked.

Officer Barrett rubbed his eyes. "We have some things to discuss with you both, and your father shouldn't be alone right now, so he asked us to pick you up. There's a lot going on that we need to talk to you about, but I can't discuss it here."

Chrissy looked at Angela, and for the first time since Angela could remember, it appeared her big sister wanted her younger sibling's opinion, or at least for her to say something.

"We're not on good terms with our father. Can you just explain what this is about?"

The officer took his hat off and rubbed his forehead. "Not out here. But I was unaware you had a strained relationship with your father. If you're not safe or comfortable going over there, can we go inside so I can talk to you? And maybe you have a recommendation for someone else who might be willing to stay with your father for the night?"

"Come on," Chrissy said, heading toward the house. "But good luck finding someone who'll stay with my dad. He's not exactly pleasant company."

Angela waved goodbye to their escort and followed Chrissy and the officer inside. She worried about waking her auntie up. As soon as they entered the kitchen, Angela noticed the blinking light on the voicemail machine. Chrissy and the officer sat at the kitchen table, but Angela checked the message. As eager as she was to find out what this policeman had to say, she worried the missed call involved news on Charlie.

An automated voice told her the time and date of the voicemail. Late last night. So, it wasn't about Charlie. How'd they all go through this morning without noticing a message?

When Brian's voice kicked in, Angela grew angry until she picked up his somber tone. Her hostility toward yet another family member who abandoned her dissipated, and she realized all at once that

Brian was just an older version of her, scared and alone. Hateful of everything.

"Hey, Charlie . . . Hey, Charlie. Listen, I'm not gonna make the trip with you guys tomorrow. I just wanted to tell you something important. Not everyone is made to be a hero. Some of us don't have redemption arcs, you know what I mean? This isn't the movies, and sometimes some of us don't repair, don't come in at the last second and save the day. But you, Charlie. You are a fucking hero. I know you have anxiety and all this other bullshit fucking up your brain, so it's hard to see, but kid, you're a fucking badass. Take care of Chrissy and Angela. Y'all deserved better than me and Dad."

Tears formed in Angela's eyes, not just from the sadness in Brian's voice, but that he called Charlie a hero, and now the hero was missing, disappeared, and while everyone else went full force into finding him, Angela knew deep down that something horrible had happened, that Charlie wasn't coming back. Up until this point, she'd held it together, but the message from a night prior felt like one from the future, a delivery of bad news. The family hero had vanished for good.

Who would be the hero then? It wouldn't be her. Angela knew her place. She kicked and screamed and bit. To those around her, Angela was the monster in the corner, the entity they all feared would one day chomp them down.

And Angela lived with that because she had Charlie. Sure, she hated him most of the time, despised how much he ignored her, but she knew from the depths of her soul that when push came to shove, Charlie would die to protect her. Brian was right. Charlie was a hero. But the hero had left the story.

Chrissy ran to her, wrapping her arms around her little sister as Angela leaned against the wall and cried. Officer Barrett remained seated and said nothing, letting the girls have their emotions. Knowing there was more news to come, Angela fought against the tears long enough to ask, "What do you have to tell us?"

The officer's eyes filled with water. He wiped at them. "Was that your brother Brian?" He pointed to the voicemail machine.

Chrissy nodded.

"Is there an adult at home who can be here for this conversation?"

Angela went to point to the bedroom, but Chrissy put her hand around her sister's arm to stop her. "We live with our aunt, but she's out for the weekend."

"She just leaves you alone for the whole weekend?"

The officer's reaction was exactly why Angela hadn't wanted to lie. Chrissy's fib, probably meant to avoid waking the wrath of their aunt, would only instigate curiosity in the officer. Surely, their living situation would get a future investigation. More problems to pile on another day.

Chrissy shook her head. "No. She never has before. She just—"

Angela held in a smirk. Everything sucked right now, but seeing her sister fumble gave her an ounce of pleasure. "Our aunt is very overprotective of us, but she had a business opportunity, and she originally turned it down, but we all talked her into it and promised her we'd be fine to take care of ourselves for a few days. She left us some money for pizza and the cupboards are full. We're good kids. Not really troublemakers. And Charlie was old enough to watch us." Angela caught her use of past tense a second too late.

The officer ran his fingers along the edge of his hat. "I'm not supposed to have this conversation with children when an adult isn't present, but under the circumstances, I'm going to break the rules a little." He sighed, and the pause was enough to tell a whole story. "Your brother Brian died earlier tonight from an apparent drug overdose."

Chrissy immediately sat down, almost as if her legs couldn't carry the weight of the news. Angela stood frozen, wholly unexpecting what she'd just heard, even after the voicemail, which now became much clearer. It was basically a suicide note. Anger flowed through her. And sadness too. But she didn't break down, didn't fall to the floor in hysterics the way she would if it were Charlie, or Chrissy, or even Auntie. Brian was her brother, and she loved him to some degree, but she hadn't seen him in so long, making him more of a stranger than a relative. He was someone she knew of but didn't know.

Of course, the lack of sadness for him made her sadder *for* him because grief was a mysterious lump on your flesh, a foreign body growing on you. You see it, and know it, and recognize it, and you worry about it. One minute, you can convince yourself it's benign, just an ugly little thing you can learn to deal with, and the next, you're certain it's the start of something bigger, the kind of thing that will eat away at your flesh, devour your bones, crumble you.

It didn't matter how little she knew Brian, how far away he had appeared, because she knew *of* Brian. And while she couldn't agree with his choices, she understood them. The guy hydroplaned, and if anyone understood surviving on the inertia of PTSD, it was Angela. None of them were in control. Never had been. They all spiraled in different directions, but in the end, they all had to meet the fucking wall. One explosion after the next. It was their destiny, a tale set in stone the moment their father opened the door and revealed to them a creature who fed on their sister.

They were doomed.

Chrissy sniffled with her hands over her face. Angela stayed statuesque, not only unsure how to react but worried that if she did react, if she chose her path, whether it be an angry response, an uncaring one, or a sad one, that it would alter the fabric of reality, change not only the future but the past. Whatever movement she made would violate time and space. So she did nothing. Said nothing.

Chrissy lifted her head. "I think I actually would like to go to my dad's if that's okay."

Angela didn't want to go, and of course, no one asked for her opinion, but she'd be damned if she were staying in their house essentially alone thanks to Auntie C's sound sleeping. Chrissy followed the policeman out the door, and Angela trekked behind. As soon as they exited the house, something felt off. When they hopped in the back seat of the cruiser, Angela looked out the back window and saw a dense fog rolling in from the shore.

The car crept forward down their dark side street, and within seconds, the fog had overtaken them, slithering along both sides of the car. It wasn't ordinary fog, grayer, like smoke. And it hadn't come in like an act of nature, but with a purpose. When it had reached the front of the car, it turned on both sides, wrapping around the headlights like two sets of fingers gripping a toy.

"What's happening?" Chrissy asked.

"Bad visibility tonight," Officer Barrett said.

"No. Look. It's changing things."

At first, Angela didn't understand what her sister had meant, but then she noticed it. The houses had changed. She'd sat in the passenger seat of her brother's car and her aunt's car numerous times, staring at the neighborhood houses, and these were not the same ones she remembered seeing. They were older, more decrepit. The paint flecked off the siding, weatherworn, and damaged by time. Even the lawns had lost their green, which was normally natural for the fall, except they had been green. Just this morning. The fall had been unseasonably warm, keeping a lot of the color on most lawns and trees. But beyond the scrim fog, they'd turned yellow, brown, dead, and it had happened in a matter of seconds.

"Something isn't right," Angela said.

"Geez, this fog is something else." Officer Barrett chuckled a nervous little noise. "I can see okay, but it looks like it's swirling around us. Never seen anything like this."

He slammed on the brakes. "What the fuck?"

Chrissy and Angela turned to the front, wondering what caused Officer Barrett to stop the car short.

Angela gripped her sister's arm so tightly her fingernails may have drawn blood. The Langblass stood in front of the car, staring at them.

21
WHEN THE STORM STOPS

As soon as she and Doug arrived back at their house, Tiffany ran upstairs to her room, pulled out her cell, and dialed Charlie's number. Instead of ringing, it screeched at her, a deafening wail in her ears.

She hung up and tried again, and it did the same thing.

"What the hell?"

She hung up and dialed Beth. It rang like normal, which proved whatever glitch had happened wasn't an error from Tiffany's phone, but Charlie's.

Beth didn't answer, though, and that sent Tiffany's stomach spinning with worry and guilt.

She cried, not really at any one thing. Charlie. Chrissy. The shrieking response from Charlie's phone. The monster in her dreams and the one from her past. Could anything go back to normal? Ever. She couldn't see how.

She felt a need to do something but couldn't think of what that something could be. It made her feel small, weak, helpless. Poor Charlie. Was he lost? Scared? Dead?

Something banged down the hall, and she flinched. This was her life now, flinching at every sound, sensing a crawling dread from every shadow. She'd lived through these symptoms before, struggled with them for years before her uncle died. She didn't know if she had the strength for a second go-around, though. A person can only fray for so long before they become nothing but loose strands.

Doug knocked on her door.

"Come in," she said.

He opened the door slowly. "Just checking in."

"We literally got home a minute ago."

He took a big breath and slowly crept toward the rolling office chair in the corner of the room. "Okay. Maybe I just didn't want to be alone."

"Maybe we should just fall asleep watching movies in the living room."

He nodded absently, staring off into the corner of the room. "I don't know how to deal with this, Tiff. Everything that happened today was beyond fucked, and I have a feeling—" He stopped himself, unwilling to finish the sentence.

"—It's about to get a lot worse?"

He put his head down. "I'm terrified. For you. For me. For Charlie."

Tiffany stood up. "When we were little, before all the shit with Uncle Billy, I overheard Dad talking to Mom, and he said Tanner's Switch was a doomed town. I was too little to know that he was talking about economics and shit, but later I asked him what 'doomed' meant. He told me, not realizing I'd overheard the word from him. And for years, I felt like this black cloud hung over all of us. No, not a black cloud, a giant stone, something too heavy for all of us to carry, and one day, our arms would tire out, and we'd be crushed under it. As I got older, I realized how silly that was, but I feel it again now."

He stood up to meet her face-to-face. "What happened to us was screwed up. It wasn't normal."

She nodded her head toward the door and walked out. Doug

followed. They made their way to the living room and sat on the couch.

"What should we watch?" Tiffany asked.

Doug rubbed his eyes. The exercise in distraction would most likely be a failure, but after running away from the island, Tiffany felt the need to try. To try at not trying.

"Something light, I guess."

"*Requiem for a Dream,* then?"

Doug chuckled. "Fuck you. Find a comedy. I'm going to get some chips."

He left for the kitchen, and Tiffany pulled out her cell phone. She dialed Charlie's phone, and again, a shrieking noise broke through. Even when prepared for it, she startled at the sheer volume and pitch of the sound.

She hung up and tried Chrissy, hoping for an update. The horrid sound came again. Maybe it *was* Tiffany's phone after all.

She called Doug's cell to test it. It rang on her receiver, and she heard his cell buzzing on the kitchen table in the next room over.

"Why are you calling me, idiot?" Doug yelled from the kitchen.

"I'm just making sure my phone is working," she yelled back.

"Tiffany? What the fuck?" Doug said with a shivering voice.

Something crashed, like he dropped a dish.

Tiffany stood up to check on him, still holding the phone to her ear. The ringing stopped, and the shrieking took its place. It scared her so much she dropped the phone. "Doug?"

She ran to the kitchen, where potato chips and a shattered bowl decorated the tiling. Doug stood with his back to the fridge, staring out the side door. Tiffany turned to what held his attention. Smoke plumed in from the gap between the bottom of the door and the sill. But it wasn't acting like fire smoke, or even mist. It slithered up and down, snaking in. Tiffany stepped back, worried it was toxic. She looked out the kitchen window and saw the scrim mist breezing past the window.

The foggy fingers crawling into the kitchen were pulsing. Pulsing as if they needed to breathe in and out.

She'd already inhaled fog today, fallen into a spell and lost hours of her life, and now it was back.

"Doug, we need to get out of here."

Doug stood wide-eyed, frozen in place.

"DOUG!"

He snapped out of it just as the living room window shattered. Tiffany screamed. A giant arm swung in through the newly created opening. Giant, pale gray, and bony. Sharp-tipped fingers slashed, ripping into the couch.

"Go!" Tiffany grabbed Doug's arm and led him toward the side door, where the fog crawled in. Before they reached it, the knob of the door collapsed to the floor as a sharp claw smashed the wood around it to bits.

Doug pulled his sister back. "Upstairs."

She followed him, making a big arch around the monster smashing its way through the window. As they ran up the stairs, she said, "This is the dumb thing everyone does in horror movies. Why are we going up?"

"Where else are we going to go? They're everywhere down there."

"Why aren't Mom and Dad waking up?"

"MOM! DAD!" Doug yelled, and then to Chrissy, he said, "I thought there was only one of those things."

"I'm not an expert, Doug."

They ran into Tiffany's room and Doug slammed the door behind them.

He put his hands on her shoulder. Below them, the sounds of crunching and banging persisted. "Listen. I'm going to hide behind your bed. You hide in the closet. When they come in, I'll stand up and yell at them to get their attention away from you. Then, I'll climb onto the roof and jump down to get away. Once they follow me, you need to get the hell out of here."

144

She shook her head, then nodded, then shook her head again. "No. That's a dumb plan. It's so dumb. We just fight. Why do we keep treating these things like they're invincible? I'm sure we can hurt them. And what are we going to do, leave Mom and Dad to fend these fucking things off?"

One of the creatures screeched. By the sound, Tiffany guessed it had fully entered the living room.

"Just get in the closet!"

She listened, not sure if she had another choice. But why weren't her parents waking up? Hopefully the monsters just wanted the kids from the island and wouldn't bother going into their parent's room.

Once she closed the bifold doors, she sat in the corner. Like a child playing hide-and-seek, she took the loose clothes lying on the closet floor and covered herself with them. The door had slats, which provided a way to see out into the bedroom, but only if she were close to the door. Squeezed into the corner, Tiffany was *not* close enough.

She couldn't hear the creatures anymore and wondered if they had left. She nearly yelped out loud when her phone vibrated in her pocket. Luckily, she kept it together. She slowly slid the phone out, worried even the vibrating sound could catch the ear of the creatures. But her heart sank at the sight on her phone screen. Charlie's face slouched in the back seat of Beth's car. A picture Tiffany had taken while Charlie drunkenly slept on his way home. She'd used it as his contact photo. *Charlie calling*, the phone screen read.

Charlie.

Calling.

She didn't know what to do. Monsters were in her house. She couldn't talk without risking the creatures finding her, and she couldn't let the phone keep buzzing either. But it was Charlie calling. Right now, police were probably scouring the island searching for him. Everyone would want to know he was okay. *She* needed to know he was okay.

She slid the bar across the bottom of the screen and slowly

brought it to her ear. With the thinnest whisper she could muster, she said, "Charlie?"

Nothing.

Silence.

She didn't dare whisper his name again.

The wood floors in the upstairs hallway creaked. A gentle sound.

She pressed the phone tighter to her ear, as if doing so would make his voice squeeze out of the phone.

Then, the voice came, that same double voice she'd heard in her seizure dream. Male and female wrapping around each other into one singular voice. "Wash up, Scumbag." She dropped the phone and bit back a scream.

The door to her bedroom crashed open, slamming into the wall.

Tiffany pushed her legs tighter into her torso, trying to make herself smaller. Maybe she could press so tightly she'd flatten into a 2D image, a thin strip of paper that could blow with the wind, get carried away with a storm.

The monster wailed, a deafening war cry blasting through the world. There were no words in its scream, but it said plenty. *I am here to kill. I will find you, and I will rip you to shreds.*

"Come get me, motherfucker," her brother yelled from the far side of the room. The monster hissed and stomped toward the voice. Doug said, "Oh shit," and from there, Tiffany couldn't make out what happened.

Grunting, wailing, Doug swearing, a bang, a crash.

Tiffany slowly crawled to the door and cracked it open. The monster leaned out the window, slashing toward the roof. She didn't know what to do. Save her brother was the obvious choice, but there had been *two* creatures downstairs. One at the front door and one at the window. But now, only one stood in her room. If she left the closet, would the sharp talons of the second monster gore her the second she stepped out? She couldn't see into the hallway, had no idea if the other creature lingered in waiting.

Fog crept in from the hall, quickly filling her room. As it crawled across the walls, it changed the environment, yellowing her white ornate wallpaper. It peeled and flaked as if timeworn. Tiffany flinched as it slipped between the slats in the closet door, wrapping itself around her. It crawled into her nose. She did everything she could to hold her breath, but she was already shaky and near hyperventilating from fear.

Fuck it. If she was going out, she might as well fight for her brother in the process. She stood up and pushed the closet door open. Time for war.

22

THE HARDEST NIGHT

Jackson stood in the living room in a general haze. His wife, burned to death in a factory fire. His oldest daughter, dead at the hands of a monster. His oldest son, dead at the hands of Jackson's neglect. His other son, missing after going back to the island that housed the start of their horror, presumably to find answers or closure, to find some hidden meaning, and that, too, stemmed from Jackson's neglect.

Maybe it all did. Could going through life purposeless spark a fire in a factory twenty miles away? Could it burn up the ones you love?

A headlight flashed through the window as a car turned the corner, snapping Jackson out of his self-loathing funk. But it wasn't the police bringing his two daughters to him. Just a random car passing by. Someone living their life. Maybe going to work or to a girlfriend's house. Maybe to see their children. Who knew? But he guessed whoever drove that vehicle did better than Jackson. It wouldn't take much. The odds were in his favor on that bet.

A high-pitched screech came from Officer Burns' walkie-talkie. It made the same squeal Jackson heard on the phone when he lost touch with the Block Island cop. The abrupt sound gave everyone a jolt. The cop grabbed the walkie from her belt and turned a nob, but it refused to stop screeching. This wasn't the normal obnoxious chirps and burps the police radios usually let out.

"What the hell is wrong with this thing?" she asked.

"Just turn it off," Officer Long said.

"I can't turn my radio off. I'm on the clock."

"It's obviously not working anyway. Just turn it off for a minute and see what happens when you turn it back on."

She relented, turning the switch **<OFF>** and powering the walkie down. It went silent. Everyone took a breath as she placed it on the coffee table.

"That was the loudest I've heard a radio go," Officer Long said.

She nodded. Without her touching it, the walkie came back to life. It played a low static, just a soft crinkling sound. Then, something whispered into it. They all looked at each other.

"How the hell is it picking anything up when it's not even on?" Long asked.

"Do they still like, kind of work when they're off? Do you need to take the batteries out or something?" Jackson asked.

"No," Burns said. "It's off. Like off off. Same as when you click your television off. It doesn't still *kind of* play something. It's off."

They all leaned in, trying to hear the whisper, but it turned out they didn't need to. The voice grew louder and clearer.

"Please. I finally have friends," the voice said, and then it screamed a pained and agonized yell.

Jackson stumbled to his seat, heart beating in his ears. "Give me that."

He grabbed the radio, holding it to his mouth. "Charlie? Charlie?" But he knew deep down it wasn't Charlie at all, just something mimicking his voice. Yet, he couldn't accept it. Wouldn't. Because the implications were too horrid to handle. If it were Charlie speaking and screaming, there was time to save him. If not, well . . .

The two officers gave each other a strange look.

"You have to hit the button to talk, but it's not on," Burns reminded him.

He pressed the button. "Charlie? What's wrong?"

"No! It's not fair. Please!"

"What's not fair, Charlie?"

The walkie went dead again. No sound.

"Come on. Talk to me."

Heavy breathing came through the speaker.

"What? What is it? Charlie, is that you?"

"Welcome home."

The two officers jolted back at the horrific voice, but Jackson turned to stone, frozen in place. That voice hadn't left his ears in four years, but hearing it again in real life made it clear how much memory can wash over our senses, dulling the sounds and feelings behind things. He'd heard those two words every single day, playing out in his brain, but he hadn't remembered just how well that voice cut through his blood, chilling his heart. The way it sharply drove into his spine. How his skin frosted over at the sound.

He gripped the walkie-talkie tightly. "You motherfucker. What did you do? I never should have let this go. I never should have walked away. I should have hunted you down and fucked you up. And that's what I'm going to do. You hear me? If you touched a hair on my kid's head, I will fuck you up. I'm coming for you. You hear me? I am coming for you."

He threw the walkie on the floor and stood up. A tsunami of blood rushed to his skull and speckles of black decorated his vision.

Officer Long stood up and gripped Jackson's arm. "Sir, are you okay? What were those voices? Can you tell us what's going on?"

Jackson pulled away from him, fighting the dizzy spell. He went to the kitchen and opened the fridge. He needed to get out there and save his children, but once the detoxing took hold, he'd be useless, which meant he needed to drink. He knew how ridiculous it sounded, and it probably was, but with a throbbing pain growing in his chest and his heart slamming against his rib cage, he also knew there was some truth in it this time.

He placed a bottle of vodka on the kitchen counter and a two-liter of soda. For a moment, he stared at them, debating if he really needed them or if he was just being an alcoholic asshole. Maybe both answers were correct.

As he took two giant travel tumblers out of the cabinet, Officers Long and Burns whispered in the living room, probably trying to figure out how to approach the madman who spoke to voices on a turned-off radio.

Jackson poured. First, the vodka, filling each tumbler about a third of the way full. Then he used the soda to fill them the rest of the way. The fog rolled past the kitchen window as Jackson shook the tumblers, mixing the poor man's medicinal concoction. He wasn't even just an alcoholic, he was a frat boy dude bro alcoholic.

He took a sip as a shadow passed the window. The detoxing was no longer responsible for his crazed heart rhythms.

"It's here," he whispered.

Burns said, "What the hell is happening outside?"

Officer Long stepped into the kitchen with his cell phone to his ear. He yelped and dropped the phone. Jackson could hear the loud wailing screech coming from the other end of the line from all the way across the kitchen. He kept his eyes looking out the window, waiting for the shadow to return, to make its move.

"I'm going to turn my radio back on and try to get in touch with the station," Burns said from the living room.

Officer Long turned back to her. "Don't do that. Use your cell. Mine isn't working. It's doing the same thing your radio is."

A few seconds later, Jackson heard the high-pitched screech coming from her phone in the living room.

"What the hell is happening?" Officer Long asked. "Is this some kind of weather thing?"

Burns came into the kitchen. "I don't know. Where's Barrett? He should be back by now."

Of course, Jackson knew what they didn't. The monster was here, off the island and hunting for his family. Charlie and his sisters conjured something there tonight and let it loose. And now it was here, and it was going to kill them all.

But Jackson wouldn't let that happen. He'd save his daughters, and together, they'd find Charlie. The monster won once, but never again. He couldn't convince the cops of that, though. They'd never agree to leave until Officer Barrett returned with the kids, and they'd talk in circles about not wanting to miss him on the road, or how they needed to wait until communications were back up before going anywhere.

He'd need to steal their keys, which he didn't believe he could accomplish. He wasn't a professional thief on his best of days, and this was not his best of days. He took a swig from the tumbler, a big one. The vodka hadn't mixed well with the soda yet, despite his half-hearted shaking of the tumbler, so the sip hit hard. Just as he hoped it would. The throbbing in his chest quelled.

He tried to be patient, think up a plan, but time was not on his side. Every second wasted was a chance for the monster to kill his children. No matter what he did, he risked failing them. Robbing cops of their vehicle was a surefire way to spend the night in hand-cuffs while the creature hunted down his flesh and blood.

But the monster was here. At his house. So it wanted him first. He could fight it. He could kill it. Or at the least, he could escape it and get to his daughters.

He turned to the cops, who stood in the kitchen, talking about the communication problem. With no concern for their unimportant conversation, he interrupted them. "Either of you ever have to fire your weapon in the line of duty."

The woman smiled. "In Westerly? No. Almost a few times, but no."

Officer Long frowned. "Hell, I'm in Providence, and I haven't had to fire it yet either. Surprising, I know."

Jackson sipped his drink. He knew how crazed he must look to the two police officers. His eyes were probably glossy and red, his hair a frazzled mess. Was he slurring yet? He didn't know. A nearly empty bottle of vodka sat behind him. He discovered his child had died, and he mixed himself not one but two late-night drinks. But maybe it was good for them to worry about Jackson. He needed them on edge. On edge meant prepared for something to happen. And something *was* going to fucking happen. Any minute. He knew it because he'd seen it. And no one believed him. But they were about to.

"Well, I'd be prepared to break your cherries tonight, friends."

"What does that mean?" Officer Long asked.

Jackson gulped his drink down. "You'll see."

Burns stepped in front of Long. "Why don't you sit down and take a breather? I know this has been the hardest night for you. We understand."

The officers were probably worried Jackson planned to off himself, maybe try to take them out first. "The hardest night?" He took both cups off the counter and sat down as instructed. "No. Not the hardest. It's up there, that's for sure. But do you want to hear about the toughest night?"

They both stared at him. Long crossed his arms around his chest. Burns placed her hands on her hips, one hand close to her firearm. Jackson liked her. She was smart.

"Four years ago, I got a call from Freedell Industries. You know them?"

Long shook his head, while Burns shrugged.

"Yeah, probably not something you'd know offhand. Yet, they're one of the biggest companies in the world. In. The. World. My wife worked for them. She sat in a factory running semiconductors through a machine. Pass or fail. All day long, dropping these computerized bug-looking things through a robot that spat them back out as either a pass or a fail. And she tubed the good ones up and sent them along. The bad ones went in for a closer look to see if they could get fixed and make it through to the other side on the next go-around. Those semiconductors power the world. Cars. Video games. Televisions. Any electronic you can think of. Semiconductors. If my wife made a mistake and packaged up the bad ones in the 'pass' tubes, well that could be a hundred-thousand-dollar mistake. Maybe a whole line of cars might need to be torn into because all of the automatic windows don't roll up or down. Or maybe the latest PlayStation doesn't start up. Who knows?" He took a long sip.

The officers said nothing. Did nothing. They probably had no interest in talks about semiconductors, but they also knew better than to interrupt a man dying of grief.

"Anyway, one day, my wife goes in, sits in her little sphere, surrounded by three or four machines. See, one person ran multiple machines, dropping chips into them one after the next. As she's bundling up packs of chips, a fire spreads behind her. It managed to devour the entire room in seconds. She didn't have a chance." Another swig.

"I'm so sorry," Burns said.

"They assumed one of the machines overheated and caught fire, despite the things having mechanisms to avoid that happening. Wasn't that, though. Corporate had just installed security cameras because they'd rather spend the big bucks monitoring the employees instead of paying them. Maybe if they paid their fucking staff enough to feed their families, they wouldn't have needed to worry about people stealing their fucking semiconductors. Who would steal them anyway? Is there a market for that?" He looked at the officers as if waiting for them to answer his rhetorical question.

The officers shrugged. Long said, "I've never even heard of a semiconductor."

"There's apparently a lot of rules and regulations on electricity, which makes sense, but the company didn't comply with them when they installed this new security system. Wiring was all messed up. Something about wattage and shit. I don't know. Electricity isn't my thing. But apparently, it was a gross violation. Twelve people were in that room. Three died. A few more were severely burned. The rest were lucky."

"Jesus. I'm so sorry," said Burns.

"I can see why that was the worst day of your life." Long shook his head.

Jackson chuckled and sipped his drink. Something smashed against the outside wall. "That wasn't the worst day of my life either."

It smashed again. Burns gripped the butt of her gun. *Good,* Jackson thought. *Smart.*

"What was that?" Long asked.

"The worst day of my life was two months later. After the Freedell company gave us millions of dollars to shut up about their mishap, we moved to Block Island. Quiet as can be. That's when a monster chewed up my daughter right in front of my family."

They both looked at him with confused glances but were too distracted by the loud bangs on the side of the house to make more of it. The window in the living room shattered, and both officers ran to see what it was.

"What the fuck?" Long yelled.

Burns drew her gun. "What the hell is that?"

The creature wailed. Loud whooshing sounds came from the room where it had just broken through. Banging. Crashing. It was probably using those giant fucking claws to destroy everything in its path.

Burns fired, once, twice, before retreating.

Long ran around her, getting to the side door first. "Come on, let's go," he shouted.

Burns stopped and grabbed Jackson. "Let's move," she said. Her eyes were wild, darting everywhere. He saw in her the pure panic that drove through his children the night Wreath died, and it made him happy. Not that he wanted her to suffer as they did, but because finally, someone else knew. Someone else got it.

He grabbed his tumblers and ran with her.

As they exited the house, the fog felt like plastic wrap on his skin, not just a moist mist, but a tangible, material object floating through the atmosphere and clinging to him. They ran down the driveway toward the police cars in the street. Long got to the front of the house first, but just as he reached the end of the lawn, the creature jumped through the window back outside. It charged, driving its claws into Long. The off-duty cop's body hung high above his car, gored by the talons of the monster.

Burns screamed. Jackson grabbed her and pulled her toward her vehicle. "Come on. I need you to help me save my children."

She ran with him. The car beeped as she unlocked the door. He hopped in the shotgun seat as she jumped in the driver's seat. With the press of a button, the car started. Thank God for updates like that. The officer's hands were shaking too much to turn a key properly.

"I guess you believe me now," Jackson said as they peeled out down the road. In the rearview, Jackson kept his eyes on the beast as it chomped into Long just as it had Jackson's daughter four years ago.

23
METAPHORS

C hrissy grabbed Angela and yanked her toward the door as the monster smashed through the windshield with its long arms. Its claws slashed across Officer Barrett's face. Blood splashed onto the back seat as the officer screamed away his last breaths.

Chrissy and Angela screamed too. There were no handles on the back doors, so they couldn't get out. Meanwhile, the monster ducked his head into the front seat and slammed his claws into the plastic partition between the front seat and back. The claws poked through the plastic, separating the entire wall from its base, but the monster's fingers got stuck in it.

As the monster pulled the plastic toward the gaping hole in the front of the car where the windshield had been, Chrissy planned her exit. The Langblass struggled to remove its talons from the partition and, subsequently, remove the partition from the car. The large piece of hard plastic slammed against the dashboard as the monster used its feet on the front of the car to pull itself out.

"Come on." Chrissy jumped into the front seat, thinking she could handle the sight of the dead officer, but she was wrong. His face leaked blood and ooze, no longer recognizable. "Oh Jesus," she said and held in a gag.

The plastic piece smashed against the dashboard, and as the monster pulled back to try again, the piece hit Chrissy in the head. It didn't hurt, but it made her plans difficult. She touched the officer and grimaced. His body bobbed to the side but otherwise stayed in place. "Ew. This is fucking gross."

Slowly, she reached over him and unbuckled his dead body. "Oh shit. Oh shit. Oh shit."

The plastic piece kept rebounding off the dashboard and hitting her.

"Oh, move," Angela said with a huff. She climbed into the front seat, accidentally putting her foot in her sister's face. "Get out of the way."

Chrissy scootched until her back hit the passenger side door. Angela basically sat on her lap. She reached over and opened the driver's side door. With the door open, she pushed the officer out of his seat into the foggy night. The mist had already crept into the police car, but now it barreled in, and Chrissy could taste it. Rotten fish.

"Switch with me," Chrissy said. As Angela slid over Chrissy's body, while Chrissy slipped under her sister's, someone's knee hit a button because the siren wailed into the otherwise hollow night. It echoed into the new, dark world.

Not only did the abrupt wailing set off Chrissy's already frayed nerves, but the reaction the monster had to the sound made it even worse. The Langblass screamed in pain and anger, kicking the front of the car so hard the headlights smashed to bits. It pulled and yanked, trying to free its claws. In the process, it snapped the plastic in half, which allowed the beast to pull the two pieces outside of the car.

"Oh fuck," Chrissy said.

"Start the car, idiot. Go!" Angela yelled. Meanwhile, Angela messed with the buttons until the siren turned off.

Chrissy looked all over, trying to get the lay of the land inside the car, hoping she could learn to drive it. She'd watched Charlie do it, so she had a basic understanding, but the police car had so many more buttons and doohickeys that made any previous knowledge null and void. Doing a ten-piece puzzle was easy, but harder when you drop a million other pieces on top of it.

"Do I have to do everything?" Angela snarked as she reached over and hit a button by the steering wheel. Nothing happened. "What the fuck? Why didn't that work? That's how Auntie starts her car."

The creature stepped on the plastic partition and pulled his arm upward. Its claws slowly slid out of their prison.

Chrissy stepped on the brake and hit the button. She had remembered Charlie always starting the car and forgetting to do that. He'd always giggle and say, "Oops. I forgot to hit the brake."

The engine kicked on. "Okay. Fuck. No time to figure this out."

Chrissy pushed the center stick thing to the R and slammed on the gas just as the creature finished the job of releasing its sharp nails. The car blasted backward much faster than Chrissy expected, and as a reaction, she jerked the wheel, which sent the car nearly toppling over. The back of the car crashed hard into a house. Meanwhile, the monster charged from the front.

In the crash, Angela's head hit the dashboard because she wasn't wearing a seat belt. Luckily, Chrissy didn't crash the car too hard, or the airbags would have deployed, which probably would have broken her sister's neck.

"Ow. You're terrible at this," Angela said.

"Put your damn seat belt on!" Chrissy switched the stick to D. Thank God she'd paid some attention when Charlie drove.

Again, she went too heavy on the gas, but this time it panned out because she drove straight into the monster, who flopped from hood to trunk before flying off the car onto the lawn. Chrissy and Angela screamed and bounced as the state police cruiser flew off the curb onto the road. Angela finally put her belt on.

"Will you slow down?" Angela shouted.

"What don't you understand about I don't know how to drive?" Chrissy yelled over the whipping wind coming in through the gaping hole where the windshield once existed.

Angela put her hands on the dashboard, trying to keep herself stable through all the wild driving. "Which is exactly why you should be going slower."

"If you haven't noticed, there's a giant monster chasing us." She checked the rearview and saw the creature getting up from its fall.

"Yes, I did notice that." And then she added a scream that appeared aimed at no one. "What even is this life?"

Chrissy jerked the wheel then jerked it back in the other direction, zigzagging the car until she corrected herself and the cruiser went straight down the road. "I know, right? Can anything just be normal?"

"It's so goddamned stupid."

"So fucking stupid."

"Like, who else has to deal with this shit? Monsters. Poverty. Moving all the time. A drunk dad. A dead mom. A dead sister. A dead brother." Angela's knuckles turned white as she clutched the dashboard.

Chrissy looked in the rearview where the monster took to a full-on run, chasing after them at an impossible speed. She whipped the wheel, and the tires screeched as they turned onto Route 91. The good thing about 91 was that it went largely straight for a while. Good for speeding. "It's way too much. We shouldn't have to deal with all of this crap. Normal kids just worry about running out of vape juice."

Chrissy hit the gas a little harder, and while she felt more confident driving fast on 91, the fog worried her. What if another car drove from the other direction? What if she slightly veered, steering them straight into a giant tree?

"Charlie was the only normal thing in our lives."

As soon as Angela uttered his name, their venting ended. Nothing else mattered. Charlie. What had happened to him? The monsters found their way off Block Island, hunted them all down. And Charlie remained across that small stretch of ocean, on the plot of land where the Langblass had lived for more than 200 years, according to the woman they spoke to at the station. If the Langblasses were free, what had they done to break from their prison, and what did Charlie's disappearance have to do with it?

She checked the rearview again. Through the mist, she saw the outline of the giant pale creature. It gained on them. How fast was this thing? She stepped on the gas a little harder.

Angela tightened. "Please slow down."

The wind whipped through the opening, smacking them in the face.

"I can't. It's catching up to us."

"Just dodge it, but slow down. You can't drive this fast."

"I have no choice, Angela. Now shut up, you're distracting me."

"You're going to fucking kill us."

"The thing chasing us is going to kill us."

"It'll catch us a lot easier if you crash."

"Shut up and let me concentrate."

She pushed down a little harder on the gas, and as the trees on each side of the road zoomed by, she panicked. She was in over her head, had no idea how to slow down naturally and without skidding out. The car moved too quickly for her to take a turn. And no matter how much speed she put into it, the creature gained. All she could do was keep pushing down until she lost control.

"I don't know what to do," she said, and then repeated, "I don't know what to do." And maybe she wasn't just talking about the driving. If she were reading this in one of her books, she would recognize the metaphor. Not knowing what to do. Spinning out of control. Running from demons. Everything catching up all at once until it crashed. She would crash. It was how this had to play out. And she'd probably die in the process.

"When I say to, hit the brake," Angela yelled.

The monster was so close now it almost touched the trunk with its outstretched hand.

"What? No. We're going too fast."

"Just do it."

Chrissy shook her head. "We'll spin out and probably flip over."

"Just listen to me for once. One."

"No."

"Two."

Chrissy scrunched her face. "No. No. No."

"Three."

She hit the brake, and at the same time, Angela switched the stick to *P*. The car tires screeched, and the car turned hard left until it was sideways on the road. It may have gone up on two tires, but it didn't flip. Both Chrissy and Angela's bodies jerked hard against the seat belts, whipping their heads forward.

The Langblass, still running full force, slammed into the side of the car, rolled over the top, and landed hard on the asphalt, where it continued to roll.

Angela flipped the stick to *D* again. "Take your foot off the brake and go."

Chrissy turned the wheel in the opposite direction they'd been going and hit the gas.

"Now turn down this road."

Chrissy listened, turning down Switch Road, which was another path that went practically straight for a distance while it passed Chariho High School, but a few miles down, it turned into a winding disaster.

"When we get past the school, turn right onto Dawn Lane."

"What's Dawn Lane?"

"Mom used to drive down it all the time when we were kids. The houses always had cool decorations at Christmas and Halloween."

Chrissy shook her head. "I don't remember. Just tell me when."

"Okay."

"Is this a good idea? Shouldn't I be going fast? I don't want to keep having to turn."

"Ugh. Watch a movie once in a while, you fucking book nerd."

As they drove past Chariho High, Chrissy obsessively checked the rearview until Route 91 was out of sight. She thought they may have lost the creature, until she caught a glimpse of it way back beyond the gray mist. For a moment, she had high hopes she'd get away from it, but the bubble burst. It would never stop hunting them. They were going to die. Fighting was only delaying the inevitable.

"Turn right coming up," Angela said.

Chrissy listened. Dawn Lane curved to the left and popped out onto Wood River Junction.

"Turn left here."

"That's going to bring us back to Switch Road. You're just having us do a big *U*."

"Stop arguing."

Chrissy sighed and turned left. Wood River Junction ended at Switch Road, which was the last place Chrissy saw the monster. "Now what? Drive right toward the fucking thing?"

"Do you see it?"

"No."

"Because it saw us go down Dawn Lane, and that's where it is, now go right. Fast. Before it catches up and sees us."

Chrissy turned onto Switch Road again. She drove slower now because they were heading toward the twisty part. The more she drove, the more confident she felt in her ability to do so. But she still panicked at the idea of seeing the creature return in the rearview. So far, so good.

"Jesus, one minute you're Speed Racer, and the next you're a sloth. Hit the gas a little. There's a fucking monster chasing us."

"I'm nervous. This road is too windy."

Once Switch Road ended, they took some more side streets, until they were eventually heading back to Tanner's Switch. As each minute passed, and one road became the next, Chrissy felt confident they'd lost the monster. At least for now. Her fingers still trembled against the steering wheel because a monster had found its way from Block Island to the mainland with the sole mission of killing them, but at least they were safe temporarily.

"I don't want to do this anymore," Angela said.

"I know. Me neither." Tears brewed in her eyes. "Do you think Charlie is dead?"

As soon as Chrissy asked the question, Angela broke down in sobs. "Honestly? Probably. And Brian is. Dad might as well be."

Chrissy put her hand on Angela's back as the girl curled forward and wept into her hands.

"Please keep both hands on the wheel. You aren't a pro yet," Angela muttered through her fingers.

Chrissy chuckled, and that made Angela laugh, until they were both laughing way too hard at what wasn't that funny of a joke.

After wiping her nose on her sleeve, Angela settled down. "Sometimes I really hate you, but I also really love you, and you're all I have left, so please don't die, okay?"

"I'm not planning on it."

An animal ran into the road. Thinking it was the monster, Chrissy screamed, which caused Angela to scream. In an attempt to dodge the creature, Chrissy veered right but cut the wheel too hard, and the car went off the road into a grassy embankment before smashing head-on into a tree. The airbags deployed and hit both girls in the face.

Angela growled an angry hiss. "You're an idiot."

"Some kind of animal ran right out into the road. I thought it was the monster." Chrissy could barely speak, too shaken and frazzled.

"What are we going to do now?"

Chrissy opened her door and pushed herself out. "I don't know. Find another car."

Angela got out of her side and moaned as she stepped onto her feet. "My whole back hurts. I changed my mind, I hope you do die."

Chrissy looked around at the street. "I just realized something."

"What?" Angela reached her arms behind her back to rub it.

"Do you remember seeing another car the entire time we've been on the road?"

"No. But it's after midnight."

"One? You'd think we would have seen at least one. Especially on 91. I can't even remember seeing any other cars parked anywhere."

"What are you saying?"

Chrissy waved her hand around the mist floating all around them. "I don't know. I'm not sure we're home."

"I don't know what you mean."

"I mean, I'm not sure this is the real world."

24

SPIDERWEBS

Tiffany ran from the closet while the monster was leaning out of the bedroom window, focused on her brother. She prayed the second creature wasn't in the hall, ready to impale her from behind. The monster at the window craned its neck, catching Tiffany barreling toward it.

She jumped on her bed and dove, smashing her left shoulder into the thing's back before it had a chance to turn and defend itself.

It hissed and slashed as it toppled forward, falling right off the small sliver of roof outside the dormer window and onto the ground below. It landed with a satisfying thud. The fall barely hurt the thing, though, because it rose to its feet rather quickly.

Tiffany found Doug clinging to the thin strip of roof by his bedroom window. "Okay. All right. We need to get the hell out of here."

He nodded to her. "Yeah. I think I pissed my pants."

The creature growled and jumped, trying to reach them, but Tiffany and Doug stood too high. Thank God for tall houses.

Behind Tiffany, something hissed. She turned quickly to see the second monster in the doorway.

"Oh fuck." She stepped onto the roof, wanting to move slowly out of fear of falling, but lacked the time with the creature in the doorway. Terror shot up her spine. One foot. Two. She made it onto the roof. The monster slashed at the bed, lifting it off the floor and slamming it into the wall. It barreled toward her. She dropped to her knees and used her hands and feet to crawl toward her brother. "It's coming. The other one is coming!" she yelled.

Doug's mouth dropped. "Okay, shit. What do we do?"

She reached him. "We crawl all the way around."

"Why?"

"I don't fucking know, Doug, because what else do we do? Sit here and wait?"

The upstairs monster bent through the window, slashing at the air, just showing aggression for the sake of it.

"Okay, go. Now."

The monster on the ground continued to jump up and down trying to reach them. Its talons hit the roof, but the creature couldn't get the height to bring its arms in and hit them. It didn't matter, though. It followed, and that was threatening enough. It meant they couldn't hide, couldn't sneak away, couldn't jump down, and run into the woods.

Doug got on all fours and crawled in front of Tiffany. He yelled back to her, "Do we just crawl around until we get to Mom and Dad's room?"

"Yeah. We need to get them out of the house too. Do you think they really slept through all this shit?" She hoped so, because the alternative was they barged downstairs to find out the source of all the ruckus, at which point, they surely would have met their end.

Tiffany and Doug crawled around until they reached their parents' room. Tiffany noticed the second floor monster wasn't on the roof chasing them. The ground-level monster stayed below them, though.

The master bedroom light was off, so Tiffany couldn't see

anything inside. As Doug reached the window, he put his hand on the sill to open it.

The window shattered and a giant claw came out. Doug put his hand up defensively, and the claw went right through his palm. He screamed and fell backward off the roof.

"NO!" Tiffany dove, trying to reach him, to grab him, but she wasn't close enough. Doug's limbs flailed as he plummeted. His back hit a giant white oak trunk, and his body flopped forward from the impact. After that, it was all ground. *Thud.*

He lay lifeless on the cold lawn below. Tiffany's eyes filled with water, but she had no time to mourn. Besides her brother, she'd probably lost her parents too. If the monster just smashed through their window, she doubted they stayed sleeping in their bed.

With Doug's blood on its hand, the monster crawled out onto the roof, chasing Tiffany. She only had one place to go. Up. She climbed, headed for the attic window. The second-floor monster realized what she went for and headed back inside. Once she reached the window, the ground-level monster smashed back into the house. They were going to meet her up there.

Which is exactly why she only went in enough to make them think that's where she ran to. These creatures weren't the smartest. She hopped in, waited three or four seconds, and went right back to the roof. Sliding down on her butt, she reached the edge, feet touching the gutter.

Doug lay in the same place. She thought about jumping now that the first monster wasn't right below her, but she didn't think she could make the jump without injury, so she scooted sideways until she reached the wraparound porch on the side of the house. From there, she slid down the porch roof until it lowered close enough to the ground where she felt comfortable jumping. If she were smart, she would have headed right into the woods or the family car, but she didn't. She ran to Doug.

He couldn't have survived the fall, but she had to check. If for no other reason, she couldn't carry on without him.

When she reached him, she dropped to her knees and shook him relentlessly. "Doug. Wake up. Come on, dude. We don't have time for you to nap."

Doug let out a low groan. Tiffany laughed, exhilaration pouring from her lungs. "You're alive. Thank God. Come on, then. Wake up."

She glanced at the house, back at Doug, at the house, back at Doug. She slapped him. "We don't have time, dude. I'm sorry."

He lifted his head a little. "Ohhhh. Oh God. Everything hurts."

"Yeah, perfect. That's fine. Hurting is good. It means you're alive. Let's go. Now."

She put her arm around his back and helped him sit up. He breathed hard, clutching his ribs. "Oh no. I think something's broken."

The attic window smashed open. Glass shards rained down from the roof.

"Yeah, sorry, but we don't have time for you to heal. Please tell me you have the car keys in your pocket."

He grimaced. "I do."

"Good, let's fucking go."

The monster leaned out the window and screamed. She had no idea where the second creature had gone.

She helped Doug to his feet, and he moaned a whole lot more. "Give me the keys."

The monster stepped out on the roof.

Doug fumbled around in his pocket. "Here."

She grabbed the keys from him. "I'll go get the car. Stay here."

She didn't want to leave him alone, but he was going to hobble and slow them both down. It would be smarter to grab the car and drive it through the yard. Besides, they couldn't fight back against these giant fucking things, but a car might be able to.

She ran to the front of the house and jumped in Doug's Camry. As soon as she started it, the second monster lunged through the living room window.

"Oh shit." She reversed a little then put it in drive. With her foot on the gas, the car blasted forward, and the Camry slammed into the creature, pinning it to the house. It bellowed a horrid sound. Its giant mouth opened wide. Now that Tiffany sat so close to it, she realized its massive jaws could swallow her face in a single bite. It had teeth as big as her lower arm, and they were dagger-sharp.

She reversed, and the thing crumbled to the ground. Its legs were nearly flattened, and thin strips of bone protruded from the creature's legs. She didn't have time to make sure it stayed down. The car bumped hard against the lawn as it drove around the house. As she pulled into the backyard, the top of the car dented in as something slammed hard on top of it. The monster must have jumped from the roof. Doug leaned against a tree, holding his chest.

She hit the gas again, flying forward, zooming past Doug, and just before the Camry hit the fence between her house and the neighbors, she slammed on the brakes. The monster flew off the roof, but it dug its sharp claws through the metal, so its body bounced onto the hood, face pressed against the windshield.

Tiffany screamed. The thing opened its mouth and bit the glass. Bit it! Its teeth slid down, putting a hairline slice in the windshield. The slick sound it made sent a nails-on-a-chalkboard shiver up Tiffany's spine.

The creature drew its head back and slammed its forehead into the glass. A spiderweb crack spread across the middle. What could Tiffany do? She was too close to the fence to drive forward. If she reversed, she'd risk running over Doug. Staying in the car meant waiting for the monster to break through and eat her. No matter what she did, she was fucked.

She was back in those shitty motels with her uncle, frozen, incapable of deciding, just letting life pass through her like a soft breeze. She could only stay in place and hope for a *deus ex machina* to swoop in and change her fate.

The monster's forehead smacked against the glass again, and the spiderweb spread.

Tiffany put her hand to the glass, feeling the fissures. She wasn't trying to stop the incoming explosion that would surely come with one more strike. She just wanted to feel it happen. If this was her end, she should at least get as close as possible to every second leading up to it.

The creature drew its head back once more. Tiffany squinted, wanting to protect her eyes from the shards of glass that would come, but also not wanting to completely shut herself off from seeing the destruction.

Time moved slowly. She had the chance, through those nearly closed eyelids, to see the monster's features. Its slick and slimy skin had more cracks and bumps than she had ever noticed before. Somehow, those imperfections made it feel more human, more real. Its ribs poked out from its frame. The creature's neck was thin and long, which made it hard to understand how it was capable of holding the weight of its head.

The monster's forehead flew down, slamming into the windshield. A storm of glass showered onto Tiffany. It cut into her, little lacerations all over her arms, hands, and face. Blood trickled down her cheeks, warm and peaceful. That was how she felt in the moment. If it were time to die, she refused to give the monster her fear. Not in the final seconds. She accepted her fate. Her only hope was that Doug found a way to escape while the creature chewed Tiffany to the bone.

"Before you kill me, can you tell me your story?" Tiffany whispered. "I just need to know why."

The monster hissed and opened its giant mouth. A blast of sea stench hit Tiffany as the creature breathed out. Splashes of warm, slimy saliva slapped against her, mixing with her blood.

"Can't you just feed my curiosity before you end this?"

It turned its head. For a second, Tiffany thought she might have gotten through to the thing, tempered it with her concern. But she realized it only turned its head so it could fit its giant shitty face through the hole it had created in the windshield.

It drove her insane that she wouldn't know anything about the creatures before she died, wouldn't understand why all this happened. Like her first day meeting Charlie, getting half-stories, or no stories at all, made her crazy. That absolute need for answers broke through the calm façade she'd built, and a panic set in. She was about to die. Holy shit. She was going to die.

As the creature dug its head into the car and snapped its jaw, Doug yelled, "Hey, fucker. Over here!"

"No!" Tiffany yelled, but it was too late. The creature ripped its head out from the hole in the windshield and snarled at Doug. Tiffany turned to see her brother standing up behind the car, still clutching his ribs.

"Kill me, you asshole."

"NO!"

The monster leaped over the hood and dove toward Doug. They fell to the ground, out of view. Something crunched, blood splashed, and Doug screamed.

25
GOOD PARENTS

Officer Burns sped down the road, and the monster chased close behind. Officer Long's blood stained the creature's gray skin. As she neared the end of the road, she turned on the sirens and took a sharp left toward the Watch Hill area of Westerly. Jackson could have lived there, could have chosen it as a home for his children instead of Block Island. Stubbornness made a different choice for him.

Taylor Swift lived in Watch Hill, as did Conan O'Brien and a few other celebrities. It would have been a good life for his kids. They'd all be alive.

"Why are you going this way? My daughters are in Tanner's Switch."

Jackson turned and caught the monster falling behind. It was twitching and had its hands over the sides of its head.

"Sorry, I've got my own family."

Jackson shot her an angry look. "What? You're a police officer. On duty. Take me to my children or pull over."

She scoffed. "And you'll what? Walk there?"

"Yes! If I have to!"

The tires screeched as she swerved hard right to turn down a side road. "Look, I don't know what the hell is happening, but this is end-of-the-world shit, so I'm going to get my family and protect them. I'll take you to your daughters after I gather my daughter and husband, and we can all run away and hide together."

"Let me out." He reached for his door handle.

She leaned over and grabbed his arm, stopping him. "Settle down. Think it through. We'll get to your daughters much faster, even after getting my family first, than you would on foot. Don't be an idiot. And are you just going to run through that monster?"

"You're an asshole."

"For caring about my family?"

He put his head down, not having any rebuttal for that, but he wanted to scream, grab her shoulders, and push her out the door. If he thought he stood a chance against her, he might.

"Fuck!" He took a long pull from one of the travel mugs.

She did a double take at him. "Look, I can tell you're a good father—"

Before she could finish whatever sentiment she had planned, Jackson broke out into hysterics. His face turned red as he laughed so hard he thought he might throw up.

"What's so funny?" Burns asked as she turned again, no longer bringing them to Watch Hill but toward the downtown area of Westerly.

"You called me a good father." He held up his two tumblers. "Do I really look like a good parent? Son dies of a drug overdose, another one is missing, and I'm having a drink. If I don't drink, I'll shake, get dizzy, see black spots out of the corners of my eyes, and from what I've read, I could have a seizure, all sorts of dangerous health risks that should require me to go to a detox center. I'd love to be one of those alcoholics in the movies or books that just puts the drink down and ten seconds later becomes an action star, but sadly, if I want to be of any use, I actually have a good excuse to drink for once."

She sighed and clicked the siren off. "You look like you're struggling, but you also seem to care. Now tell me what I'm dealing with. You obviously have experience. What the hell is that thing? I want to protect my family and you, too, but I need to know what that thing is."

He found it remarkable how cool she kept her temperament. He could see the fear in her eyes and the trembling in her fingers, but she talked evenly and thought logically. And she managed to pull that off just a few minutes after seeing her first taste of the creature. Jackson saw it four years ago, and he still hadn't cooled.

Jackson didn't have much he could tell her about the creature, other than he'd seen it in his mind day in and day out for four years, waiting until his marbles spilled off the table again and the thing showed up back in his life. "You know I was a terrible dad long before my wife died. Not terrible. That's the wrong word. I loved my kids, and I spent time with them here and there. But I kept myself busy so I could avoid the frustrating games kids play. And I ignored them a lot while I pursued stupid dream projects.

"I was always trying to make money. Not 'get by' money, 'get rich' money. I always figured if I made enough, I could provide them with all they needed so they wouldn't need it from me. And of course, if I had a lot of money, I'd have more freedom to do things with them on my own terms."

She spun the wheel and turned onto Broad Street, driving past the library and post office, two large, looming buildings. "You sound like most parents, to be honest. I'm guilty of some of those same things with my daughter. You're avoiding my question, though."

He shook his head. "I'm not. This is all answering your question. I promise."

The strips of shops zoomed by on each side. ReReads bookstore, The Brazen Hen, the United Theater.

"My wife, she had a big thing about never going to Block Island. Her family was from there, and I guess they had a lot of tragedy in their past. She didn't even know what those tragedies were, just that they existed. Her father took her off the island against her mother's wishes. He had their names changed, moved them around a lot. When she told me this, she insisted he hadn't kidnapped her, but it sure sounded like it. He made her promise never to go to Block Island, and she kept her word on that.

"I tried to talk her into a vacation there because my parents used to bring me to Block Island all the time as a kid. I loved it. Always had a dream of living on that fucking tiny little island. When she passed away, Freedell gave us a lot of money to shut up about her death, and all those dreams I had of being rich and living on Block Island seemed possible. And I thought maybe I could even find my wife's mother and introduce her to her grandkids."

Burns pulled over by a series of saltbox houses. Most of them looked as if they'd been transformed into apartments.

"Something's wrong here," she said.

"What do you mean?"

She opened the car door and drew her gun. Jackson wasn't sure if he should get out or not. He decided he should. When he stepped out, he followed her eyes as they scanned the neighborhood.

"At first, I thought it was the fog messing with my vision, but that's my apartment." She pointed to a brown saltbox with flecking paint. The steps leading to the porch were crooked, in serious danger of collapsing.

"Okay?" Jackson said. Unsure where she was going with this.

"The landlord just painted it a month ago. And he rebuilt the porch a year and a half ago."

She walked past him, slowly going up the steps. Jackson noticed how shaky her breath had gotten.

Again, he wasn't sure if he should follow, but since she had the gun and he had tumblers, he opted to follow closely.

She used her key on the front door and guided them through a thin hallway toward a door numbered #1. With the gun at her side, she unlocked the door to her apartment and stepped in. "Charlotte? Kingston?" She didn't yell, but she wasn't whispering either.

The fog ran through the house too. A gray, thin cloud wisping through the kitchen and living room.

She glanced at Jackson and pointed to the kitchen walls. "We don't have yellow wallpaper. It was white."

"What exactly are you saying?" Jackson asked, following her into the living room.

She moved faster now, nearly running to the two doors on the other side of the living room. She pushed the first door open. "Charlotte?" Now she yelled.

Boom, right to the second door. "Kingston?"

She turned to Jackson, breathing hard, eyes wild and shining like marbles. "They aren't here."

"Are you sure this is your apartment? I mean, if the wallpaper is a different color?"

She pushed him. Not hard, but definitely filled with emotion. "I know my fucking apartment. My daughter's toys are in there."

She pushed past him and opened another door. A small bathroom. She looked all around. "They aren't here."

Again, she rushed past him and out into the hallway. She darted up a flight of stairs and pounded on door #2, and then she kept climbing until she pounded on #3. "Hey. Anyone here?"

Jackson stayed on the bottom step, sipping on his tumbler. Burns climbed back down to the second level, terror in her eyes. She leaned against the door of apartment #2, breathing hard.

"They probably just got freaked by the weird fog and went to stay somewhere else," he said.

She shook her head, tears dribbling down her cheeks. "You don't get it, do you?"

He shrugged. "What?"

Boom. Before he could process what happened, Officer Burns turned and kicked the second apartment's door open.

"What are you, crazy?"

She stormed in. "Hello? Anyone home?" She ran from room to room, slamming doors open.

"No one here either."

"Okay. What does that mean?"

"Jackson. There wasn't a single fucking car on the road. All communications are gone. My family is gone. My neighbors are gone. I've been yelling in an apartment building where the neighbors freak out if my kid farts."

"Are you saying everyone disappeared?"

She ran past him again, going out the front door. "No. I'm saying we did. This isn't my apartment. Did you see the post office? The stone columns looked cracked. They weren't like that. This isn't real. We're in a dream or something."

He remembered the Block Island cop's words on the phone. "Holy shit."

"What?" She turned to him. "What do you know?"

He shook his head. "I don't know. The cop on Block Island that I called. He told me my kids told him they had slipped into a seven-hour seizure. And they all saw the monster."

She rubbed her face. "Are you telling me that we're having a seizure right now? And this is like some kind of dream world we're experiencing while our bodies—"

"I don't know." He waved his hands in the air, alcohol sloshing in his tumblers. "Do you think I'm an expert at this or something? I don't know a fucking thing."

She grabbed his arm. "Come on. Let's see if your kids are in this weird seizure world." She jumped back in the car, and Jackson followed suit.

As they drove off, she said, "Finish telling me what you *do* know."

"You're going to want to get on Franklin Street until you get to 91."

She nodded.

"We weren't on Block Island long. That's when we saw the monster. It killed my oldest. She was sixteen. Wreath."

"I'm sorry for your loss."

"You've said that a lot tonight."

"You've had a lot of loss."

He glanced out the window, not wanting to make eye contact, ashamed of the amount of death surrounding him. "How could I know Elaina's father warned her away from the island because of monsters? Elaina, she was my wife. Elaina Hempfield. Well, I guess her real name was Mary Vanderline, but her father changed it to Elaina Hempfield. She was a beauty." He lost his train of thought, thinking about his wife smiling in her cheerleader outfit when they were in high school. Always happy, no matter what. Meanwhile, Jackson had swam in a sea of anxiety, always worried they didn't have enough for their family. Elaina never worried about it. She always wanted to put on her best face, even on the worst of days.

He took another swig.

"I'm sorry. And I don't want to be insensitive, but I really need you to focus on telling me what you know about this monster because I need to get back to my family. I'm bringing you to your daughters, and then I'm finding this thing and killing it so I can get back to the normal world. "

"After Wreath died, the police investigated me. I don't know if I was ever a prime suspect. They leaned on me, but not as hard as I expected, honestly. I think they were just exploring all angles. But the media had a field day. And they weren't just cruel to me, but to my kids. We were laughingstocks. The family who said, 'A monster did it!'

"True crime podcasts, websites, they either mocked us or used our story to tell scary real-life tales of terror. It's all over TikTok. But my daughter was dead. It wasn't funny. I blamed myself, but I didn't know where I had fucked up, couldn't place which part of my thinking was responsible for it. I just knew I had somehow poisoned everyone around me. The first finger pointed at the island itself. My dream of moving there. So I took us off the island. I blamed my desire for money, so I gave most of it away. Bought myself a shit little house, sent the kids to live with my sister, saved enough for each of them to go to college, and enough to keep me drinking and fed. I figured, I grew up poor, and you know what? I was happy. As a kid, I was happy. Maybe that 'money is the root of all evil' bullshit was true."

As Officer Burns turned onto Franklin Street, she gave Jackson a suspicious glance. "You don't believe that, do you?"

He shook his head and squeezed off the last drops from the first tumbler. One more to go. "Of course not. But I had just lost my wife and my daughter. I needed something to hate, and money was the answer because the other option was a monster, and that didn't go down easy. Even after seeing it."

"What does this have to do with what you know about it? How does all this help me?"

"I started drinking so I could sleep at night. But I soon realized I was terrified during the day too. So, I just drank all the time. Why not?"

"Because you had children who needed you."

"I had children who needed to stay away from me. I took the island away because it was deadly. I took money away because it brought them the biggest horror of their lives. And I took me away because I was just as much a monster as the thing that ate their sister. Me, Officer Burns. Me. I was poison. The police weren't wrong about that. It doesn't fucking matter if I actually killed my daughter because my decisions did. My thinking. It killed Brian too. 'I didn't mean for it to happen,' is what children say to escape blame. But adults? We should know better.

"So, you want to know about that monster? Here's what I think. It's here because it wants to kill my children. It wants to kill me. I somehow tied it to my family. We're bound now, all of us. My family and the monster. It won't stop until it kills us all. And you had the shit fucking luck of landing on my doorstep the same night the thing figured out how to cross a small slice of ocean, which means you're dead now too. Add it to the fucking tally. Sorry, but I killed you."

He took a long pull from the second tumbler. His head swam. "I killed everyone."

Officer Burns slammed on her brakes. Down the road something moved across the street. It turned toward them, a towering silhouette in the headlights.

A roaring bellow echoed into the tenebrous night, and the beast charged for its prey.

26

VINX

Chrissy and Angela walked away from the car. They were able to start it, but the tires spun out in the mud, and the bent hood wouldn't unwrap from the tree. Angela thought about her sister's comment about them not being in the real world, but she had trouble fully getting it.

The world had changed, certainly wasn't the place they knew, and it sure did seem desolate. But there was that animal that ran into the road.

"Do you think we are in a seizure again?"

"No," Chrissy said, marching ahead of her sister.

"Cool. Nice chat. Where are we going?"

"I don't know. I don't have a playbook. I'm just moving farther away from where we last saw the Langblass."

"Langblass. What a stupid name." Angela jogged to catch up to her sister. "Why aren't you talking to me?"

Chrissy rolled her eyes. "I'm trying to concentrate and think up a plan."

Angela clenched her teeth. She nearly punched a tree as they passed it but thought better of it at the last second. Why punish her knuckles for her sister's bitchy attitude? "Stop talking to me like I'm a nuisance. Last I checked, I'm the one who saved us. You'd be dead if I didn't stop you from speeding down 91."

"You can be helpful and annoying."

"Yeah, and *you* can be smart and an asshole." It wasn't the time for arguing, and after everything they'd endured that night, Angela should remind her sister how much she appreciated her, but she couldn't. Brian was dead. Probably Charlie too. And even with all that loss, Chrissy couldn't change her attitude toward her younger sister? Couldn't be nice for ten minutes? Why did Angela have to be the one to rise above? "You know, you of all people shouldn't act better than anyone. Remember, I know who you are. You're just a dumbass book nerd."

Chrissy didn't miss a beat. "Says the girl who pissed her pants in school."

"Fuck you, how's your dumb jock boyfriend?"

"Fuck you, how's your nonexistent boyfriend?"

"Fuck you, how's your folded up Kevin Bacon poster in your top drawer?"

Chrissy stopped, probably wanting to yell at her sister for snooping but too invested in the one-upping battle. "Fuck you, how's your secret TikTok account where you post minutes-long videos of random cats you see throughout your day?"

"Fuck you, how's your butt? Seriously, I'm concerned because you take a book into the bathroom and sit on the toilet for forty-five minutes. Do you really have that much poop?"

Something barked.

Chrissy screamed and Angela jumped.

"What was that?" Angela wanted to know.

A jingling noise broke through the fog. At first, it was a distant noise, but it grew louder by the second. Both girls looked everywhere, trying to pinpoint where the noise came from.

"What the hell is that?" Chrissy asked.

They both tensed up and reached out for one another. Somehow, they ended up holding hands, bracing for impact from whatever ran their way. The jingling grew louder and louder, and out from the mist, a beast broke through. Tendrils of gray steam pulled away from it as it came into view.

It jumped on Angela, tail wagging, tongue hanging out. She laughed.

"Jesus, that scared me," Chrissy said.

Angela bent down to pet the dog's brown fur. She couldn't make out the breed. He kind of looked like a basset, but she saw a lot of boxer mixed in there. He spun in a circle with excitement and licked her face, jumping on her with his white paws. Yup, he had a lot of boxer in there. "Oh my God. I don't know where you came from, but I love you already."

Chrissy came over to the dog and grabbed its collar, spinning it until she held the tags. "His name is Vinx."

Angela hugged Vinx, and he licked her neck in response. "Vinx. I wonder what it means. Do you want to be my best friend, buddy?"

"You can't keep the dog, Angela."

Angela stood up. "The fuck I can't."

Chrissy muttered something under her breath.

"What?"

"You can't keep the dog, idiot. There's a fucking creature in that mist hunting for us. How well can we hide with a dog that jingles when he walks?"

Angela bent and removed the collar from Vinx's neck.

"Dummy. He's a dog. He'll bark and flip out if the monster comes back."

"Good. He'll protect me."

"He'll get you killed."

Angela tossed the collar into the woods. "Come on, Vinx." She walked around her sister, heading into Tanner's Switch. Vinx followed by her side, and she scratched his head as they walked together.

Chrissy huffed behind them. "Angela, stop being an idiot. This isn't some fun little sibling argument. Your decision here could get us killed, and probably the dog too. Think it through."

Angela put her head down, ignoring her sister. Vinx looked up at her. The dog loved her. Instantly. And she loved him too.

"Angela, stop. Think about it, even if we survive the night—which we probably won't—do you truly believe Auntie will let you keep the dog? Be responsible. You can't feed it. We can all barely feed ourselves. Keeping that dog would be cruel."

Angela snapped around and stormed into her sister's face. "No. You listen. You're an asshole. I'm not trying to be mean, but you are. Charlie, God—" She scrunched her face, unwilling to cry in front of her sister right now. "I'm so worried about him, but you know, he was an asshole too. Brian's dead, and he was an asshole. Dad's an asshole. Wreath, she was the nicest person in the world to everyone in our house except me. I was like five years old, and she was so goddamn mean to me. All the time. Auntie took us in, and she works hard to make sure we have some food in the cupboards, but you think I don't see how much she hates me. This dog has been with me for two seconds and he's already been nicer to me than any of you have. Ever. I'm keeping the fucking dog. I don't give a shit."

Vinx stared up at the conversation, eyes droopy, tongue sticking out. "Come on, Vinx. Let's go through the woods."

She dipped off the road toward the stretch of white oaks and pines, but Vinx stopped short. "What's up, buddy?"

Chrissy stayed rooted in her spot as well. "You're right."

Angela sighed and came back to the dog. "Don't do that, Chrissy. Come on, Vinx." She snapped her fingers and bobbed her head toward the woods. "This way."

Vinx let out a high whine.

"Do what? I'm admitting you're right. I'm an asshole to you, and I'm sorry. And if you want to keep the dog, you should keep the dog."

Angela shook her head and laughed. "I already decided I was keeping the dog. I didn't need your permission for that." She petted

Vinx's head. "You okay, bud. Why don't you want to follow me anymore?"

"Why do you do that? I'm trying to be nice. I'm admitting I suck."

Angela grew frustrated and wondered if the dog had turned on her too. Maybe she couldn't even keep a dog happy. "You don't get to treat me like shit for years and then shrug it off with an apology. I'm sorry. I'm not just going to play nice with you. I did that on Block Island. That's all you get from me."

Chrissy crossed her arms around her chest. "Fine. But there's a monster hunting us down somewhere, so can we at least play nice until this is all over? It's not going to help us to fight the whole time."

"Fine." She gave Vinx a gentle nudge toward the woods. "Buddy? What's wrong?"

Chrissy came up to Angela. She put her hand out. Angela stared at it for a second, not understanding. Then it clicked. She gave her sister a handshake. Before she could pull away, Chrissy pulled her forward and hugged her. Before she knew it, her sister was crying into her neck, and that made her cry too.

It felt so good to be hugged. To be touched at all. To be noticed.

Chrissy said through sobs, "I'm not going to make some stupid proclamation or whatever. Just, I know I was always a jerk to you, but I do love you. That's it. That's all I'll say."

Angela peeled herself away. "Okay. We should keep moving. I don't know why Vinx won't come, though."

Chrissy wiped her face. "Because he doesn't like grass."

Angela chuckled. "What?"

Chrissy laughed too. "He doesn't. I was watching him walk next to you, and every once in a while, his paw would touch the grass on the side of the road, and he'd shake it off and you could see he was upset about it."

"You're kidding."

"I swear. Walk down the road, he'll follow you. But he won't go into the woods."

Angela tested it, walking forward on the asphalt, and sure

enough, Vinx followed, but when she veered toward the woods, the dog stopped.

"Do you not like grass?" She fell over laughing, couldn't hold it in.

Chrissy caught the contagious nature of it and bent over, tears streaming down her face, laughing.

The two of them sat on the side of the road in a fit of laughter. Angela might have cracked up about the dog's aversion to grass on any day of the week, but tonight it was especially potent. Grief did that sometimes, muddled the emotions. It could make you so depressed you can't stop smiling, so anxious you can't stop laughing, and so desperate you bury yourself in a new obsession. Grief was the ultimate detonation. It was a bomb buried deep in the intestines. Mixed with fear, it changed you, removed you from your skin and sucked the meat from your bones until you became nothing but a gaseous ball of dangerous chemicals spewing out in hysterics.

Grief was the kind of laugh that strained your muscles. It hurt to be happy. It hurt to live.

27

PUNK ROCK ANTHEM

As Doug screamed, Tiffany jumped out of the car. Her elbow hit the horn and a loud honk echoed into the foggy night. The monster stood up at the sound and screamed, covering its ears.

"Oh. You hate that?" She slammed on the horn. A continuous, obnoxious honking played, and the monster stumbled backward, screeching in pain. Tiffany laid on the horn until the monster had fallen back a bit.

When she felt she had enough space, she stopped and ran to Doug, but the creature instantly corrected itself and ran to her. "Shit," she said as she ran back to the car and hit the horn again. Once more, the creature fell back and screamed.

She was stuck. The horn separated the beast from her brother, who may or may not be dead already, but if she didn't keep her hand on the horn, it came right back. She needed to get to Doug, to help him into the car.

Looking around, she couldn't find anything she could wedge between the seat and the horn to keep it blaring while she got ou-

and helped Doug. At one point, Doug had an ice scraper lying around on the floor of the car, but she didn't see it now.

"Figure it out, Tiff."

The monster fell back against a tree on the far side of the backyard.

"One, two, three." She ran from the car to Doug. "Come on. No time to talk."

Doug mumbled, which meant he was alive, but his leg had a giant open wound where the monster must have bitten him. It bled hard. Mixed with the broken bones he surely received on the fall off the roof, her brother was in danger of dying very soon. She grabbed his hands and dragged him. He screamed in pain but used his legs (including the chewed-up one) to shimmy himself forward, helping her drag him. Thank God because she'd never have the strength to carry her older brother as dead weight.

"Sorry, I don't have time to do this proper."

The monster charged.

Tiffany dropped Doug, ran back to the car, and hit the horn again. The monster screamed and stumbled back.

"Oh God," she said, letting out a deep breath. "This is too much."

She held her hand on the horn until the monster fell back a ways and then she ran to Doug. He moaned as she pulled him by the arms, getting him all the way to the side of the car. The monster charged again. She took her chances, not wanting to keep doing this over and over again, and knowing she didn't have much time to get Doug somewhere safe, she waited until the last possible second before running back to the horn. The creature's claws whooshed by her face.

She jumped back in the car and hit the horn again. "Idiot," she yelled at herself. She'd let the monster get too close. If it hadn't aimed at her, it would have taken another bite of her brother and most definitely would have killed him in the process. She had to be more careful, and even though Doug didn't have much time, she had to show patience.

Doug was almost to the back door, where she'd have a whole new struggle of getting him into the car.

Two deep breaths and Tiffany steeled herself. She let go of the horn, spun out of the car, and grabbed her brother's arms. This time, she didn't even get a second to pull him. The monster was quick and on to her strategy. She jumped back in the car and hit the horn. The creature bent over and hollered.

Tiffany leaned out of the car with her hand still on the horn. "Doug, I know you don't have the strength, but I really fucking need you to crawl into the back seat.

She pushed her foot up and stepped on the horn, freeing her hand. Twisting around, she extended her body into the back seat, and with her foot planted on the horn, she fumbled with the door handle, hoping to open it enough to help Doug have clearance into the car.

The door opened, but her foot slipped off the horn, and the monster wasn't far behind the car. It let go of its ears and charged, mouth opened wide, and eyes storming with rage.

"No." She turned to hit the horn. Just as her hand landed on the steering wheel, the creature's claws dug into her arm and threw her from the car. "NO!"

The creature turned its head toward Doug. It knew. It knew it could destroy her by killing him, that all of her actions were in service of her brother's safety, that it could kill two birds with one stone.

"NO!" She charged the monster, clutching her injured arm. It raised its huge limb into the air and swiped down, ready to shred Doug to pieces.

Tiffany dove, connecting shoulder and head into the beast's midsection, slamming the thing into the side of the car, which unfortunately closed the back door. Before it had a chance to attack, she slid into the driver's seat and hit the horn again. Blood coated her arm from the open wound the claw left, but otherwise, she was surprised how much it didn't hurt.

The creature screamed and flailed, falling over Doug. Its body slammed into the hard earth. Its foot had landed squarely on Doug's stomach before it fell, and Tiffany worried one last injury from the full weight of the creature might have been enough to kill her brother. Doug hollered in pain. At least he was alive.

With one hand, she pressed on the horn, and with the other, she punched the dashboard. How could she get out of this? Doug could hardly move. The monster, while clearly incapacitated by the loud noise, knew how to recuperate too quickly.

She yelled, "I'll hit this horn forever, asshole. I'm not letting you kill my brother."

The monster rolled on the ground, agonizing over the horn.

"One step at a time," Tiffany said. She jumped out of the car, opened the back door, and jumped back in to hit the horn again. She was quick, and the monster didn't even get the chance to stand up.

"Okay. Good job, Tiff. One more time." She ran from her seat and hoisted Doug up so his upper body leaned against the back of the car, right by the ajar back door. And once again, she jumped right into the driver's side and hit the horn.

The monster had gotten itself on all fours, and even while it screeched in pain and plunged its palms around its ears, it stared at her with contempt. Its snarling lips told her what it planned to do to her if she ever gave it the chance.

"Okay, okay, okay, okay, okay." Boom, she jumped out of the seat and hoisted Doug up. He helped, using his legs to lift himself. She dropped him half on the back seat, his legs still dangling from the car, and she ran back to the front to hit the horn again.

She'd officially given the monster enough time to land on its feet, but it still had a small distance to clear before reaching the car again. Doug was almost in. She could do this. Maybe Doug could help.

"Doug. Can you hear me?" she yelled over the car horn. "Can you just bring your feet in? All you need to do is bring your feet in and stay lying down. Can you do that?"

Doug didn't respond, just mumbled to himself. She wondered if he'd gone delusional from loss of blood.

"Doug, please, I need you to pay attention. You think I'm wailing on this horn for fun?"

"I thought you were writing a punk rock anthem." His sentence came out clear and crisp, enough for her to hear him over the horn, but there was a wetness in his voice, which made her worried he had blood in his lungs. It didn't matter, though. She'd never been so happy to hear him talk.

She couldn't help but laugh at his stupid joke. "Shut the fuck up and get in the car."

Slowly, he shifted until his dangling feet were on the back seat. His body stretched from one side of the car to the other with his knees bent.

"One, two, three, go." She ran out of the car and slammed the back door shut. Then went to jump back in the front, but before she could, the creature dug its claw into her arm again.

28
REDEMPTION

Officer Burns put the car in park right in the middle of Franklin Street. The creature ran, and with its long, lanky legs, it approached them fast.

"What are you doing? Drive," Jackson yelled.

Officer Burns took her gun out. "No. I'm killing this thing. Let's end this."

"Get me to my children first."

She glared at him. "I need to get back to my daughter. If I kill the thing, your kids will be safe too."

She stepped out of the car, but before she could train her gun, the creature had already reached the vehicle. It slashed at the door she used as a shield, and the force of it knocked her flat on her back.

Jackson jumped out of the car and ran around to her side. Halfway across, as he passed the trunk, he nearly stopped and retreated. He wasn't a hero and didn't want to be one. He just wanted to keep his daughters safe. But he also knew he could hardly walk straight, let alone drive, and his best chance at keeping his children safe was with the officer's help.

When he reached her side of the car, the monster stood above her with its claw lodged into her palm. The gun she had held was a few feet behind her. The creature raised its arm, ready for a blow across the woman's face. Jackson didn't have time to grab the gun.

"Hey, fucker! You killed my daughter. You owe me a life."

The creature slowly raised its head and eyed Jackson. As it stared, it tilted its head, sending shivers down Jackson's spine. Seeing the creature this close and having the time to get a good look at it brought a new level of terror. It wasn't just a fleeting thing anymore, a nightmare closing in. It was a real, material object, moving through the world with an intent to kill. Its eyes were hollow gulfs, giant black globes with a celestial sea of red galaxies swimming in the abyss.

Jesus. It was demonic. A hell creature. An alien. A demon from the dark woods.

"Welcome home," it sang in its taunting double voice.

The monster released its talon from Officer Burns' hand and stepped toward Jackson. "Welcome home?" This time it sounded like a question. Jackson understood. It was remembering him.

And those words helped Jackson remember, too, how it taunted him with his own sentence from what he'd meant to be a game played with his children. They had meant to have fun together, God damn it, and this creature turned their lives into a nightmare. Jackson tightened his fists. "Welcome to *my* home. This is where you die."

The creature jumped, slashing its claws at Jackson. Before it could make impact, Jackson fell backward, landing hard on the back of his head. His ears rang. The monster put a palm on Jackson's face, and its claws wrapped around Jackson's head. It squeezed. Jackson couldn't breathe through the thing's tight grip.

The pressure built around his skull. He wondered if he'd suffocate or die from his head exploding like a Gallagher watermelon.

A gunshot went off and the creature screamed. Blood splashed all over Jackson. With his face free again, he saw the creature hold its chest and stumble forward, away from the car, until it fell over hard on the cement.

Jackson stood up, out of breath. Officer Burns stared with her gun still raised, aimed where the creature had been standing before falling over.

"You saved my life," Jackson said.

"And you saved mine. Thank you."

"We should get the fuck out of here."

"GET OUT OF THE WAY!"

Jackson turned to see the monster rising. He ran around the car, back toward his side, and the creature pursued. A few more gunshots went off, but they must not have hit because the creature hadn't slowed.

Officer Burns ran around from the front of the car, trying to get a clear shot of the monster without her police cruiser getting in the way. "DUCK!" she yelled.

Jackson bent low as he ran. The blood rushed to his head, and he felt dizzy. He stumbled into the cruiser. Something sharp hit his side, just below the ribs. It burned. Like a bee sting.

He fell, landing on his knees. His hand touched the wound, and as he pulled away, he saw the blood. So much of it. He looked up at the creature hovering over him.

Boom.

The monster's face exploded. Its blood splattered the car, the cement, and Jackson's face. A loud thump echoed in the night as its body hit the ground.

Officer Burns ran to Jackson's side. "Are you okay? Jesus. We need to get that bandaged."

Jackson went to speak, but he choked instead. Blood cascaded from his mouth, down his chin.

"Oh shit. Oh shit. We need to get you to the hospital."

Jackson bent over, hacking up liquid. He spat and wiped his face. A final cough left his throat. "There is no hospital. We aren't in the real world, remember."

The exertion from talking was bigger than he realized. He couldn't breathe again.

"But I killed it. Shouldn't we go back now? Shouldn't this clear up?"

He didn't answer her, couldn't if he wanted to, but if he had to guess, they were stuck in this in-between world forever, or there were more monsters out there. In which case, his daughters weren't safe.

Since he couldn't speak, he used his blood-soaked hands to write on the side of the car.

GO. He wrote.

If he had the energy he would have written more. "Go save my daughters and quit wasting time with me." But he didn't have that kind of energy or that kind of time.

He fell on his side, right on the injury. A wave of pain throbbed up his spine and into his brain.

Six years ago, Elaina convinced Jackson to pack up the kids for a trip to Vermont. Jackson had protested because they didn't have a lot of disposable income to afford a trip. Elaina's work friend had a cabin up there that she'd inherited from her parents, and she offered to let them stay there for a week in the fall, but trips still cost money in gas, food, and whatever else they might need for a week.

In the end, she won, as she always did because Jackson couldn't resist her excitement. It was infectious. They stuffed the kids into the SUV and drove up for what turned out to be a long week. The kids fought with each other the entire time. Brian bitched about the hikes they took because he just wanted to stay home and play video games. Wreath complained about the lack of cell service. Chrissy never wanted to leave her bed. Angela was only five and needed constant attention and care, which was tough to give because so did the other kids. Charlie was the only well-behaved one, but only because his high anxiety kept him in the corners, and for that, Jackson just felt terrible.

They hardly left the cabin all week. Too much work to get the kids ready to go anywhere. After arguing, getting them prepared and packed, there wasn't much excitement left to go around.

On the last night, Jackson had lain in bed with Elaina, exhausted and frustrated. On top of that, he dreaded having to wake up early to ensure the cabin was properly cleaned and everything was packed up, only to spend the next four hours driving back. Long drives brought him Charlie-level anxiety.

As he tossed and huffed under his blanket, Elaina put her arm around him and whispered, "What's wrong?"

"I knew this trip would be a disaster."

Elaina laughed. "Disaster? It was perfect."

"How can you say that? The kids were miserable the entire time."

"Jackson, kids are always miserable. All we can do is set a good example, show them how happy we can be, and enjoy our time with them."

"It's hard to enjoy our time with them when they're yelling at each other all day."

"Yes, it is. But we're still with them. And one day, you'll be sitting there dying for that opportunity again. Take the worst of what you love because one day, they won't want to see us at all."

"I don't think half of them want to see us now."

Elaina kissed his shoulder. "True. Do you remember the time we went hiking in Acadia in Connecticut? And we somehow got lost. The longer we went trying to find our way out, the more frustrated you got. And you never were mean to me, but I could see the grumpiness setting in, and you were really short. And it just got worse and worse until we finally found the car."

He rolled over to her. "Did I really? I remember getting lost, but I don't remember being grumpy. I do remember us laughing when we found the car, though, because we were never very far from it. I felt like such a doofus."

She chuckled. "Oh, you were fuming mad. Steam out the ears. But you don't remember that, huh? Only the laughing?"

Jackson put his hands behind his head. "All right. I get it. The kids won't remember being miserable, only that they had a family trip. Memory is selective and all that jazz."

She kissed his cheek. "Yes, but more than that, the kids were just like you that day. They're small, Jackson, even Wreath and Brian. When they walk the halls at school, they're small. And they're lost. All the time. And they'll lash out at us. They'll be little jerks sometimes. But when they get older, they'll remember that no matter how much they pushed us, we were always there. We wanted to spend time with them, even at their worst."

Jackson lost the memory as his vision doubled on the asphalt. Officer Burns talked to him, but he couldn't make out the words.

When the monster came back, Jackson almost felt excited, as if it were his opportunity to save his children, to redeem himself. He thought of his wife's words as his breathing grew more ragged and the pain in his chest sharpened.

He would die here. Alone. And he deserved it because he let his children wander the world alone, without a guide, without someone to fall back on. Even now, as his last seconds ticked by, he wasted it feeling sorry for himself. And he spent every day prior to this convincing himself he wasn't capable of being a good father, and he let that be a self-fulling prophecy. He could have just stopped. Just worked at improving. Worked for anything. God, if he'd only just worked.

"I didn't mean for it to happen" was a child's excuse. And it was his excuse as well. The last one, he thought, as the world faded away from him.

I didn't mean for it to happen. Any of it.

29
BATTLEGROUNDS

After their bout of laughter, Angela and Chrissy walked the road again. Angela refused to go without Vinx, and since the dog wouldn't touch grass, they couldn't go into the woods. Chrissy hated being so exposed, but then again, the Langblass probably knew exactly where they were and how to find them. They were prisoners in its world, and it most likely had the keys to every inch.

But the monster also ran as fast as the police cruiser, so if it could find them so easily, why hadn't it?

After half an hour of walking, they reached an intersection that Chrissy recognized. The road crossing led to Tanner's Switch Middle and High School. Exhausted both mentally and physically, Chrissy stopped. Angela sensed it and turned back to her.

"What's up?"

"I can't walk anymore. Everything hurts."

Vinx walked up to her and put his mouth in her palm, sniffing.

"Do we have a choice? We can't just stay here."

Chrissy nodded to the right. "My school is right over there."

Angela shook her head. "No. This place is already my nightmare."

Chrissy closed her eyes. "It's not real school, Angela. No teachers. It'll actually be cool because you can vandalize the place."

Angela shrugged and turned down the road. "All right. Sold. Let's go."

When they arrived at the school, Chrissy prepared to break a window to get in, but it turned out they didn't need to. They were in some kind of rot world, and that meant the school wasn't locked. In fact, the doors were so damaged, Chrissy couldn't keep them closed no matter how hard she tried. But that also meant the Langblass could get in just as easily.

Vinx ran down the hall, excited over something. Angela chased after him, and Chrissy after her.

"Wait, don't just go running. We don't know if the Langblass is in here," Chrissy said. But like always, her sister didn't listen.

The dog made his way to the gym, where he grabbed a softball. Angela laughed. "He just wants to play, I think."

"I don't know if we have time for that."

"Of course we do." Angela chased the dog, who refused to let the ball go. He ran away from her, back out into the corridor. The dog led them both through a set of double doors, where he flew up a staircase until he reached a landing. He turned and dropped the ball, letting it bounce down the steps.

Angela chuckled and tossed the ball back. With his tail going berserk, Vinx caught it and dropped it down the steps again.

"Angela, I'm so tired. I'm super happy you made a friend, and I'm sorry I gave you a hard time about it, but we should fortify this place or something. The monster's going to come for us. We should be prepared."

Angela tossed her head back. "Ugh." She turned to her sister, eyelids drooping. "You just don't get it. I told you, I haven't had a friend in a long time. This is the single best interaction I've had in, I don't know . . . Forever? I don't care if the monster comes. This is me planning my battleground. He can show up and he can kill me. It doesn't matter. Because I'm going to die happy. I spent every fucking day afraid of that thing, hiding in the light. It took my whole life away."

She threw the ball up the steps. "This is me kicking its ass."

Chrissy nodded her head. She'd never felt so alone. She understood Angela's reasoning, but she wanted to live. She wanted to fight. And her sister had planted her feet and taken her stance. Chrissy had to fight alone.

She charged out of the room, back through the double doors, and down the hall. First, she'd need to find something to blockade the front door. She went into the classroom nearest the entrance, looking for a big piece of furniture. She didn't know the room because this was the high school side of the building. She still had classes in the middle school.

There wasn't much. She'd hoped to find a big bookshelf, like in her English class, but all the room housed was student desks and the teacher's desk. While the teacher's desk wasn't much, it would have to do. But she knew the monster could push it with ease.

She put her back against the desk and pushed. It scraped hard on the white, gray, and blue vinyl tile floor. Her muscles ached too much for this. Her strength had been depleted by the most insane day of her life.

After getting it halfway across the room, she gave up. Not just on moving the desk, but on everything. Maybe her sister had it right. This thing had taken Wreath and most likely Charlie. Its reverberating effects took out Brian too. Chrissy slowly lost everything. It took and it took, depriving her of any will to carry on.

She slid to the floor and put her head between her knees. She almost cried, but she lacked the emotional energy.

Behind her, something creaked.

She sat up straight, back against the desk, and peeked around the corner. Footsteps moved down the hall. Slow, but loud. And big. Monster sized.

She got on all fours and crawled across the room, too scared to make a noise. When she reached the classroom door, she slowly pushed it closed, terrified. Her muscles tightened. She was afraid to breathe, too worried her nose might whistle or her mouth might click.

She peeked out. Sure enough, the monster walked down the hall. Chrissy could hear Angela giggling by the stairwell, which meant the monster could, too, and that's where it headed.

She scratched at her neck, trying to summon the gall needed for what she wanted to do. As the monster moved closer to the stairwell's door, Angela didn't quiet down. Her sister had no idea how close death loomed. And maybe Angela had told the truth and didn't care, but Chrissy didn't believe that. It's easy to say those kinds of things.

Chrissy stepped into the hallway. As the monster closed in, she yelled, "HEY!"

It turned and snarled. Then walked toward her. A woozy spell came over her.

Her heartbeat went insane.

Angela must have heard her because she came out of the double doors behind the monster. Chrissy shook her head at her sister.

As the creature stomped toward Chrissy, Angela yelled, "No. Hey. This way."

The monster turned again. "No. Here. Come kill me. Leave her alone," Chrissy yelled.

"After all these years of being an asshole, you don't get to be my hero now. Hey, Banglass or whatever the fuck you're called. Come get me." Angela stomped her feet.

The monster growled and turned toward her, making up its mind. It changed stances, ready to run. Chrissy hurried and slipped her shoe off. Without thought, she picked it up and threw it at the monster, hitting it in the back of the head.

The monster turned and bolted for her like a freight train. Nothing would change its mind now. No matter how much yelling

Angela did, it was going to kill Chrissy first. And Angela did yell, but not at the monster. At Chrissy.

When the creature got close, Chrissy dipped back into the room where she'd moved the teacher's desk and slammed the door shut.

"Oh my God. What did I do?" She ran to the other side of the room and twisted the handle on the window until it was fully open. A fully opened school window meant it angled out about forty-five degrees. Chrissy climbed and got halfway out before getting properly stuck. The door crashed open, and Chrissy's nerves fired like a Fourth of July grand finale. Her body operated on its own, muscles tensing, limbs flailing.

"Get me out of here," she yelled into the night.

The teacher's desk screeched across the floor as the Langblass tossed it like a rag doll.

Chrissy slid down a little further, getting past her hips. Just as her legs snaked out the window, the Langblass swatted at her feet. It hit her one sneakered foot and tore through it, but thankfully the cushion stopped the claw from doing much damage. As she landed hard on her butt, the monster smashed the window. Chunks of plexiglass rained down on her. Thank goodness for safety windows, otherwise she'd be covered in dangerous shards.

She ran toward the back of the school, which she instantly regretted. First, she knew the front door was open, but not the back. Plus, the back of the school was shrouded in darkness. She skirted the wall and swung her arms forward, in hopes they'd touch anything in the way before she ran face-first into it. Her shoeless foot felt the rough gravel on the path, little sharp stones jutting into her soles.

The monster growled behind her, and from the proximity, she could tell it was fully outside and on the move. If it kept pace with a speeding car, she had no shot of outrunning it.

Something ahead squeaked, metal on metal, and light poured out from a newly opened door. Angela leaned on it, back against the panic bar. "Hurry up," she said.

Chrissy ran into the building and Angela slammed the door shut behind her. The Langblass smashed and kicked outside, creating a parade of bangs.

Vinx stood at the landing, ball in his mouth. He dropped it down to them. Angela grabbed it and ran up the stairs. "Come on."

Chrissy followed her. "What are we doing?"

"Killing this fucking thing once and for all," Angela said as she petted Vinx's head. "I changed my mind. If it kills me, so be it, but I'm going out punching."

"Now you're talking. Do you have a plan?"

Angela led them into the school library on the second floor. It was dark and cold. Big swaths of metal shelves housed hundreds of books that emitted a distinct dusty book smell.

"Your favorite place in the world," Angela said.

"You know I haven't even been in this one yet? Why do you think this is a good place to be?" Chrissy kicked her other shoe off. She might as well be even until she got the other one back.

"I don't. I didn't even know I was walking into the library. I'm just checking everything out and looking for weapons." She walked to the front desk and reached over. "See!" She held up a pair of scissors.

Chrissy cringed. "Scissors are probably the best we're going to find, huh?"

"I don't know. Do you guys have a wood shop or anything? My school doesn't have anything that's not wrapped in rubber, so we don't hurt ourselves or the staff."

"Really?"

Angela chuckled. "No, you idiot. I was exaggerating." She went behind the desk and lifted up a keyboard. "You want this? I'll bet you could smash it on the Banglass's face or something."

"It's Langblass, and I hope we can do a little better than a keyboard."

Something crashed down the hall and Vinx barked.

"I think we're out of time," Angela said.

"Yeah."

"Don't die, okay?"

Chrissy nodded. "Yeah, you too."

30
BLOOD LOSS

While the monster dug its claw into her right arm, Tiffany turned the car on with her left hand, hit the gas, and turned into the side yard. The creature stayed attached to her, running along the side of the car. She tried to pull her arm from its talon, but it wouldn't dislodge.

With one hand on the wheel, she had limited ways to fight it off. She moved her arm, the one attached to the creature, and grabbed the door handle. As the car pulled onto the road in front of their house, she attempted to shut the car door, hoping to slam it on the monster's arm, but she couldn't get a good grasp, and the angle was all wrong.

Instead, she pressed on the gas. The creature kept up for as long as it could, but after a short distance, its sharp nail slid out of Tiffany's arm and the monster fell behind. It managed to stay alongside the car, keeping the same speed as the vehicle, but it couldn't manage to stay attached to her. Her arm radiated heat and pain as she reached over and pulled the door shut.

"Wwwwoooooooooooooooo," she yelled. "Holy shit. Holy shit. I can't believe we made it out of there. Hang on, Doug. We're going to the hospital."

She zipped down road after road, turning as much as possible in an attempt to lose the monster. Whenever she saw a road to slip down, she hit the horn, which slowed the creature down. She also hoped it would draw attention, but no one came to her rescue. Eventually, she did lose the monster, but she knew it wouldn't last long. The beast ran faster than Doug's Camry could drive, but as long as she had the horn to slow it down, she could give herself some breathing room. Once she drove Doug to the hospital, she'd have their armed security to keep them safe.

"Doug, you doing okay back there?"

He didn't respond, but she could see his chest moving up and down.

She sped down 91 until it hit Post Road. At one point, she saw some strange things lying in the road around where Post turned into Franklin Street, but she ignored them. They were maybe big garbage bags or piles of clothing. It didn't matter. Not then. She made it to the hospital in record time. It had a small drop-off lane going to the front door where they typically had a valet, but she didn't see anyone. It probably wasn't something they offered this late at night.

"Stay here for one second, Doug," she said, as she ran out of the car.

The front lobby was desolate. She ran to the admissions area and rang the bell on each desk. Where were they? Shouldn't someone be on duty?

"Hello?" she yelled. Panicked, she ran to the double doors, which she knew from past experience would be locked. A security officer had to buzz people in, or a nurse could use her key card. She slammed on the door, pounding her fist into it, just needing to get someone's attention, but to her surprise, the door opened upon impact. Since when were they unlocked?

She ran in. "Hello?"

There was no one. The nurses' station was empty.

"What the fuck?"

She ran around the stations, peeking into every room. They were all empty. No nurses. No patients. No doctors. No security. No janitors. No one.

"What the fuck?" she repeated.

She stood frozen for a moment, lost and out of ideas. Her arm dripped blood onto the floor.

"Okay. I have to do this myself." She ran to the nurses' station and looked around. There wasn't much. In a back room, she found basic supplies and grabbed as much gauze as she could. Without time or patience, she did a slipshod job of wrapping her wound just to get it covered. She didn't worry about the tiny cuts on her other arm or face. Those weren't bleeding much.

She found some bottles of rubbing alcohol and antibacterial ointment and ran back to the car. Doug made a grumbling sound as she opened the back door. She couldn't do anything for his rib, which she prayed hadn't caused any internal bleeding, but she could at least clean his leg and hand and wrap them up. Just like her arm, Doug's injuries would need stitches, but the gauze was better than nothing.

"Okay, Doug. Listen to me. There's no one here to protect us, so I'm just going to do my best to slow your bleeding and then we gotta get the fuck out of here before the monster comes back. You need to be your strong badass self, okay?"

She poured the alcohol on his leg. It sizzled and foamed. Doug didn't react at all. Using some Dunkin' Donuts napkins Doug had left in the center console, she dried it off, and gooped as much antibacterial ointment as she could on the bite marks, then wrapped the gauze around his leg. Every tiny noise, a whistle from the wind, a leaf rolling by, made Tiffany jolt, ruining her concentration. The wrapping wouldn't do much, and she could already see the blood leaking through, but she didn't know what else to do. Medicine wasn't her field of expertise. She didn't even know the difference between Tylenol and Advil.

After finishing his leg, she repeated the process on his hand.

Back in the driver's seat, she contemplated where to go. "Where the hell is everyone? This is crazy."

Doug made a crackling noise like he was trying to talk, but nothing came out.

"*Shhhh.* You just rest."

She started the car and headed out of the Westerly Hospital parking lot, unsure where she planned to go. Once she got back on Post Road, she formulated a plan. She again passed the two strange lumps in the road, getting a better look this time, and nearly fell out of her own skin. She stopped the car. It was foolish to get out, but she couldn't stop herself. She needed a better look.

A monster lay dead in the middle of the road, and next to it, a man lay equally as dead. Blood pooled around their bodies. How many monsters were there? But the scene told her something else. The monsters could be killed.

She jumped back in the car and drove off, unhappy to head in this direction, toward where her monster would be coming from, but she had no choice. As soon as she could, she dipped off the main road and took side streets until she reached the place she wanted to go, making sure to bypass roads she'd taken on her way to the hospital.

All the lights were off in Charlie's house, but Tiffany didn't care. She would wake Chrissy and Angela up if she had to. As she exited the car, she got an uncontrollable shiver. It was so dark. So quiet. No one anywhere. She noticed a police cruiser parked across the way, but she assumed the officer who drove it probably went wherever the nurses and doctors went.

She locked the car, which made a loud honk. She winced at her mistake. Hopefully she didn't just alert a nearby monster. She couldn't just leave Doug in there with the doors unlocked, though.

She gently tapped on the front door first. Not wanting to make more noise if she didn't have to. To her surprise, just like at the hospital, the door opened. When someone's front door opened without needing the handle turned, it felt pretty ominous. Especially this late at night.

Tiffany's options were in short supply, so she went into the kitchen. She knew they lived with an aunt, and from what Charlie had explained, she sounded grumpy. But again, as her brother potentially died in the back seat, she didn't much care.

"Hello?"

"HEY!"

Tiffany jumped and her heart shot into her lungs. Someone had shouted to her from outside. She shot around to see a female police officer running toward her.

"I wasn't breaking in."

"Are you Chrissy or the other one?"

Tiffany put her hand on the door handle, getting a little nervous. "Ah, I'm Tiffany."

"Tiffany? Who the hell is Tiffany?" The cop spread her fingers out and pinched the sides of her eyes. She had a bandage around her hand, and blood dripped out of it, much like Doug's careless wound covering.

"I'm Tiffany. What's going on?"

"You're here. How are you here?"

"I drove here. My brother's in the back seat. He's really injured. Can you help?"

"I mean, how are you here? In this world?"

Tiffany stepped back. "What?"

"Have you not noticed there's no one out here? The whole world is just gone."

She relaxed, getting it now. "Yes. I tried taking my brother to the hospital, and no one's there. Can you help him?"

The woman shook her head like she was rattling out marbles. "Jesus. Yeah. Where is he?"

Tiffany pointed and walked to the car. "He fell off our roof and he kept holding his chest. I think he might have broken a rib or something." She stopped, which made the police officer do the same. "And I don't know how to say this, but something bit him in the leg."

The cop put her hand on Tiffany's shoulder. "A monster. I got it."

"You've seen them too?" She held up her wounded hand as she walked to the car and opened the back door.

"Yes. I thought there was only one. I killed it. I assumed once I did, this fog would clear up and I'd be back in the real world, but that doesn't seem to be happening. If you had a monster, too, there must be more of them. I've heard some fucking stories tonight, man." She bent into the car for a few seconds, assessing, and popped back out.

"So, where's your monster?" the officer asked.

"What?"

"Was it chasing you? Is it close? Did you kill it?"

Tiffany looked down the road. "There were two. I don't know if I killed the first one. I hit it with my car and pinned its legs to my house. I definitely broke those legs, but I don't know if it died from it. The second one chased us, but I lost him on some back roads on the border between Tanner's Switch and Richmond, but then I drove all the way to Westerly Hospital and back here. So I have no idea where it is."

The cop moved around her, heading toward her car. "Okay, so we have no idea how much time we have. We'll have to make do." She opened the trunk and pulled out a large first aid kit. "Your brother's wound needs better wrapping, but you did a good job getting something on there. The bad news is if he does have a broken rib, there's not much I can do for it, but I doubt he does. In my experience, broken ribs are usually very painful when you lie down. People with broken ribs want to sit up. It feels better."

As the officer moved away from her cruiser, Tiffany noticed the word GO written on the side in what looked like blood. "What's that?"

"I told you, it's been a night."

Tiffany followed her back to the Camry. "That's good, then, right? That my brother's able to lie down? So he should be okay?"

"Well, from what I can see, sure. I don't know what other injuries he might have. He could be bleeding internally, or who knows? But if I had to guess, I think he's probably got a bruised rib cage and lots of bleeding from that wound. Also, from the black and blue on his temple and the goose egg on his hairline, probably a concussion."

"Okay," Tiffany said as she hopped into the front seat, going in backward, so she could watch the police officer tend to her brother.

"No. No. You stay out there and keep an eye out for the monster. Yell as loud as you can if you see it. There's no neighborhood to wake up."

Tiffany nodded her head. The advice made sense. It was good. She had something to do, something important, something to keep her mind occupied, focused. And the news on her brother sounded promising too.

She stood outside the car and worked to wrap her head around the evening. The thin veil of fog slithered and rolled around her. A gentle breeze felt nice on her skin. Yesterday, she was a normal teen. She had friends, a girlfriend, a nice family. Then she went to Block Island. She wished she could call Beth, apologize, cry to her, beg her for help on all the upcoming sleepless nights.

She hoped Beth slept sweetly in the real world, the one outside all the fog, and she hoped when Beth woke up, she would wear her forgiveness shoes. Tiffany owed her a hell of an apology.

The ocean was somewhere behind her, way too far away to see from here, but she smelled its briny breath and felt its breeze between her fingers. She prayed to it, asking it to return Charlie to her.

The officer, still in the car bandaging her brother, interrupted Tiffany's thinking. "Do you have any idea where Chrissy and the other one would go if they weren't home?"

"Angela."

"Yes, Angela. Chrissy and Angela. Do you know where they could be?"

Tiffany shook her head. "No. If not here, I have no idea. Unless they went back to Block Island to find Charlie."

The officer huffed. "Well, you came down the opposite side of the road, so you didn't see the gruesome scene on the other end. A state police officer came to their house tonight to deliver them to their father. His name was Officer Barrett. He never made it back. I know why, now. His body is at the end of the road. Monster got him good. No sign of the girls, though, or his car. Lots of glass. And the partition was removed. My guess is the girls have that car. Unless you think the monster drove it away."

Tiffany shrugged. "I don't think so."

"Which gives me high hopes they're okay. So I say we drive around a little bit and see if we can't find that car."

"I guess that sounds like a plan. What about my brother?"

"Well, I got his leg wrapped. Looks like he sprained his ankle too. I want to check on his ribs and head really quickly, but after that, we can get him into the back of the cruiser."

"Okay," Tiffany said.

"On the drive, I'd love it if you could give me some backstory here."

"What do you mean?"

"I mean, we're in some weird fog world created by monsters set on killing this family." She pointed to the house. "I'm stuck in it because I happened to be at their father's house when it all went down. So why are you and your brother here?"

Tiffany nodded. "Yeah. That's gonna be a long story."

"Uh-huh." The officer went into the back seat.

Tiffany thought about Charlie again, how their visit to the art studio was the catalyst for all of this. She wondered if Milicent made it home okay. If there was a cop dead at the end of the road, it meant a lot of collateral damage related to their trip.

She tensed. "Officer?"

"It's Burns. Or you can call me Meghan." The officer sat half in the car, doing something in the back seat.

"Fine. Meghan."

"Yeah?"

"The monster is here."

31
KINGDOM COME

Chrissy ran behind the librarian's desk. "Quick. Find me something better than a keyboard."

They both opened drawers. Angela eyed Vinx staring at the door with his hackles raised and teeth snarling. The monster moved closer, and she'd be damned if she let the Banglass thingy hurt her dog.

Chrissy tossed stuff from the desk drawers. "Aha. Another pair of scissors."

"How many pairs of scissors does the librarian need in your school? What the hell are they cutting?"

Angela tapped Chrissy's arm and bobbed her head toward the shelves. Chrissy nodded and they snuck over, hiding behind the stacks. Of course, this was a high school library, so the stacks were only four shelves deep, but that should be enough for bobbing and weaving around.

"Vinx. Come here," Angela whispered. The dog didn't listen. He continued to snarl by the door.

"Vinx!" she whispered again, but a little louder.

"Fuck." She put the scissors down and ran to the dog. Her sister objected behind her, but she ignored it.

When she reached Vinx, she wrapped her arms around his body and waddled back to the shelves with him. "You need to be quiet. I know you want to fight, but you can't. Not with this thing."

Chrissy pointed to a door behind the librarian's desk. "Maybe you should put him in there until this is over, so he doesn't get hurt."

"Good idea." She lifted the dog again and waddled with him toward the door. Halfway there and she was out of breath. When she finally got to the door, she brought the dog all the way to the handle so she could twist it while keeping him in her arms. The door popped open, revealing a small, square room filled with supplies and books. She walked the dog in about halfway and ran to the door, but the dog followed.

"No. Vinx. Stay in here." She slid through the narrow opening and shut the door. Meanwhile, the doors at the main entrance crashed open, and without a second wasted, the monster came at her.

She didn't have time to think, and she didn't even have her scissors to use on it. The creature moved like a bullet, but before it reached her, Chrissy lunged at it, scissors in hand, and drove them into the creature's arm.

It slashed its injured arm, backhanding Chrissy so hard in the face, she flew backward into a shelf. The scissors fell out of the creature's skin. Books tumbled to the floor. Blood dripped down Chrissy's nose. Angela took the keyboard off the librarian's desk and smashed it across the monster's face. It snapped in half, and the monster barely blinked.

"Well, you were right, Chrissy."

The monster swatted at her. She dodged it by jumping backward, barely escaping the thing's sharp claws, and she pulled a muscle in her calf.

Chrissy ran at it again, jumping on its back. While it struggled to remove her, Angela hobbled toward the shelves and grabbed the scissors she had left on the floor. Chrissy wrapped her hands around the monster's neck, and it extended its arms back to try to claw at her. Angela ran as best she could, ignoring the pain in her leg, and plunged the scissors wherever they landed. They hit the creature in its upper torso.

It roared again and slashed at Angela. Luckily, she was too close and only felt the brute force of its forearm instead of its dagger-shaped fingers. The blow knocked her into the wall, which hurt. She flopped to the floor upon impact.

From all the creature's flailing, Chrissy's grip loosened. As the Langblass shook itself, Chrissy rocked from side to side, her legs flying in each direction.

Angela stood up, a little dizzy. Vinx barked up a storm behind the door. Chrissy hung on by a thread.

Angela stumbled, looking for the scissors that had fallen from the creature's arm. She only had a few seconds. Chrissy wouldn't last much longer. She turned around the desk and accidentally kicked them. The scissors slid across the floor, landing back by the book-shelves. She hobbled for them, and on the way, her sister screamed behind her. Something thudded.

She picked up the scissors and turned to see her sister on top of a computer desk, curled up in a fetal position. The monster made its way toward Chrissy. Angela ran with the scissors raised above her head, ready to plunge them into the monster's heart, but it predicted her movements and turned in time to grab Angela by the top of the head. It lifted her in the air, squeezing her skull. She swatted at it, trying to stab, but the thing's arms were too long. The creature opened its giant mouth and moved in for a bite. Angela kicked her leg up, landing it right on the thing's forehead. With all the force she had in her, she used her leg to keep it back. The creature lifted its face, trying to bite the foot on its forehead. Angela drove the scissors up and into the monster's lower arm.

It screamed and dropped her, then with a forceful rage, swatted her in the head, knocking her down. This hit hurt a lot more than the first, and it took a second to snap back to reality. She felt out of sorts, not quite there. Her vision blurred.

Chrissy ran from the table she'd been laid out on, a vague shape running across the library. The monster, a fuzzy, tall white entity in front of Angela, screeched. Her sister smashed into the monster's leg, and the beast fell to the floor with a loud smash.

"C'MON!" Chrissy's voice was low and distorted, a demonic sound.

Angela looked at her, confused. The ringing in her ears faded and her vision coalesced.

"C'MON!"

Angela tried to stand but almost fell over, as though her legs had turned to seaweed in a current.

"C'MON!"

The white shape returned, rising above her sister.

"C'MON!"

What was it? What was that thing?

"COOOMMMEEE OOONNN!"

"Welcome home." The two voices came together and infiltrated Angela's muddled brain, bringing reality back to her. The library. Her sister. The monster.

The monster! It stood behind Chrissy.

"COME ON!"

"CHRISSY!" Angela yelled.

The monster's claw drove into Chrissy's back and the tip protruded through the other side. Blood shot out of Chrissy's stomach, spraying Angela's pants. Chrissy's face turned to shock, pale white. Her eyes grew two sizes bigger. Her mouth dropped.

"Run," she whispered, then the monster ripped its claw free. Chrissy flopped to the floor.

Angela listened. She ran faster than she ever had.

32
LOST AND FOUND

Tiffany shivered at the sight of the monster. She'd faced it already—two of them, in fact—but she'd run out of steam, and Doug was immobile and unconscious in the back seat of his car. She had nothing left to give.

The officer stepped in front of her. "Get in the car and protect your brother. I'll take care of this thing."

Tiffany had no interest in arguing the cop's points. She was happy to let the lady do all the heavy lifting. To Tiffany's surprise, Doug was awake in the back seat.

"DOUG!" She almost jumped on him for a hug but stopped herself before she injured him further. "You're alive."

Outside the car, the monster let out its intimidating screech. Two gunshots fired.

"Ugh," Doug said.

Tiffany teared up. "You don't need to talk. I just can't tell you how good it is to see you with your eyes opened."

"It fucking hurts." He chuckled, which turned into a cough, and as he hacked up a lung, his face turned red and he grimaced, clutching his chest.

"Dude, stop. Rest. Don't talk. Just let me rant about how much I love my brother while you chill the fuck out."

The monster growled.

"Oh fuck. What's going on now?" Doug's eyes were glossy and red.

"Don't worry. There's a cop now. She's got a gun."

Doug rested his head on the back door. "That's good. I didn't want to have to kick its ass myself."

Now it was Tiffany's turn to laugh.

Another gunshot went off. Tiffany got nervous. If the gun could take the thing down, why was it taking so long?

Something banged against the car with so much force, the whole vehicle shifted. Doug's head slammed hard on the car door. "Ow, fuck."

The creature ran by the back of the car. Tiffany's heart sped up, and she prayed the cop could finish this. Doug closed his eyes.

The monster stood by the door where Doug rested. A single slash from the creature's powerful claws could kill her brother right now, but the creature didn't notice them in the vehicle, or at least didn't care. The policewoman stood on the other side of the car with her gun raised, but Tiffany guessed she refrained from firing out of fear she might accidentally hit one of the siblings.

Maybe the monster had known they were in the car and used them as a human shield. She hated the idea of it, but she had to do something. Or maybe not. Could she help the officer, or would she just make the scene more difficult?

The creature jumped on top of the car and in one swift motion smashed into the cop. The woman crumbled to the asphalt and her gun skidded across the road. Within a second, the creature spun around and bent low, its face at the driver's side window where Tiffany sat backward, facing her brother.

The monster's hot breath hit the window and a blast of steam came between them.

Tiffany froze, terrified.

"Wash up, Scumbag," it sang.

Anger flared inside Tiffany's guts. The taunting nature of the creature's tone made her furious.

"Oh, fuck you." She shoved the car door open, smashing the creature in the face. It hadn't expected that, and a look of shock landed in its wide, black eyes.

If she weren't so horrified and scared, she would have gained great satisfaction from that face. But the monster was huge and supernaturally strong, so while the door shot might have hurt, it didn't slow it down. The creature thrashed and the door slammed in Tiffany's face. With a second thrash, it had broken through the window and reached in for her.

Why hadn't she considered using the horn? She was too tired, too out of it, and wasn't thinking straight. When she'd hopped in the car, her brother had awoken, stealing her thinking, and she'd accepted that an adult—one with a weapon—had things under control. Now, it was too late. The monster's arm swatted around the driver's seat.

Tiffany shimmied into the passenger seat, opened the door, and spilled out onto the sidewalk in front of Charlie's house. Her only objective was to move the fight away from her brother. The creature jumped on top of the hood and over to Tiffany's side. Before the thing could land, Tiffany made her way to the back of the car. Cat and mouse.

The policewoman sat up, groggy and out of it. Tiffany ran past her, hoping to reach the gun before the monster killed her. Her arm throbbed from her wound, and as she ran and her heartbeat increased, it became more noticeable. It shot pain into her shoulder, and she worried she might be having a heart attack.

The monster growled behind her, letting Tiffany know it wasn't far behind. The thing could keep pace with cars for a short distance, so she had no shot of outrunning it.

A loud crash went off behind her. She knew peeking would potentially slow her down, but she had to look. The monster had fallen but was on the way back up. The officer had her arms wrapped around its lower leg.

Tiffany had to hurry and get the gun before the creature retaliated on the cop. She'd seen the weapon sliding but missed exactly where it landed, and in the dead of night on a dimly lit street with fog rolling around, it proved difficult to see.

"Come on. Where are you?"

She quickly glanced back at the cop, who held the monster's wrists while it tried to slash at her. Burns had impressive strength if she could hold the monster back as well as she did.

Tiffany examined the street, searching for the weapon, when she noticed a glint under the police cruiser. "Oh no." She tilted her head to get a better view and saw the gun resting midway between both front tires.

"Fuck." She had no choice, so she dropped down and crawled under the car. As she reached for it, she gave another look toward the ensuing fight. The cop still clung to the monster's wrists, but it held both arms up high, dangling her in the air. She tried to kick at him, but with its long arms, she didn't have the range. The monster slammed her into Doug's car, and she lost her grip, falling to the ground.

Without hesitation, the monster turned and ran toward Tiffany.

"Fuck. Fuck. Fuck." She scooted out from under the car with the gun. She needed room to maneuver her hands. Wiggling out, she watched as the monster came closer and closer.

It grabbed her ankle and opened its jaws wide. Tiffany pulled her arm out from under the car and fired directly into the creature's mouth.

Its lifeless body collapsed on top of her. She lay there, shaken to her core, trembling. Blood and gore slipped out of its mouth onto her clothes. She didn't move. Couldn't.

She'd once been lost, stolen by a family member, forced to travel the East Coast. She'd once been found, brought home to a caring family, introduced to new friends who loved her and kept her safe.

And now she was lost again, and no amount of love could save her, could shine a light on the scared girl tucked into the dark corner. This would break her. Today ended her in some way. If she survived, she'd go on, but she'd never be the same Tiffany again. The whole night stretched her thin, pulling and pulling, barely giving her a second to comprehend the mess she'd fallen into, but this final shot, the blast of the gun, and the body falling on top of her snapped her. Stretched too far. She had once been lost. Then found. And now she was gone for good.

The policewoman groaned across the street. She sat upright on the side of Doug's car, holding her arm.

Tiffany rolled out from under the monster. "Are you all right?"

The cop nodded. "I'll be fine. You?"

Tiffany stood up. "No. I'll never be fine again."

The cop looked around. "Either that wasn't the last of them, or we're fucked for life."

Tiffany handed the gun back to the cop. The officer had a much sturdier hand than she did. "Well, let's go find the rest and kill them because I'd like to get my brother to a hospital, and my arm is starting to really hurt."

The cop stood up, wincing and groaning as she did. "Okay. Let's get your brother to my car and see if we can't find Chrissy and Angela."

33
ANGELA'S WORLD

Angela ran out of the library and down the second-floor hallway, hating herself for leaving Chrissy and Vinx behind. She had faith the monster wouldn't hurt the dog, and she doubted her sister survived the attack, but she needed to find a way back into the library to check. Her leg still ached, but it improved as the minutes ticked by.

She turned into the first door she came across, hoping to hide before the monster left the library and spotted her. As soon as the automatic lights turned on, she lost her breath.

"Of course," she whispered.

The girls' bathroom.

She ran into a stall, hoisted herself on top of the toilet, and removed the tank lid, brandishing it at nothing, just waiting for the thing to appear.

She knew the monster would find her, that it could somehow sense her location, otherwise it never would have found her and Chrissy at the school after they'd lost it in Richmond.

It didn't take long.

The door to the bathroom opened, banging hard on the wall.

Angela flinched. The monster was taller than the stall walls, so she could see its head, and once it moved closer, it would see her without needing to open the door.

She stepped off the toilet as the monster crept closer. She realized that inside the stall, she wouldn't have enough room to pull the tank lid back and get a good strike. As she considered how to correct this, the monster stepped in front of her stall.

Boom.

His claw drove through the metal door and ripped it open. She'd never get a good hit from inside, so she held the tank lid with both hands and charged, using all her force to slam it into the thing's body. It stumbled backward until she had it pinned to the wall.

She stayed as close to its body as she could, so it wouldn't have the opportunity to slash her with its incredibly long claws. The monster screeched and fell sideways, causing Angela to slip too. It hit the ground and she landed on top of it with the tank lid between them. Their faces touched, and the monster's slick skin left an oily residue on her cheek.

And then she fell into a dream, seeing the monster's life in quick flashes.

A thick forest. Screaming women. A boat. Block Island. Murder. Murder. Murder. Always young men or women, dying by the Langblasses. Chomp chomp chomp.

A group of people in a circle in the middle of the woods.

The monsters were with them. With them. Not attacking. Not eating. With them.

As soon as Angela pulled her head back, she lost the visions.

"I don't give a fuck about your world," she said, as she stood up and jumped on the tank lid in one swift motion.

The monster heaved as her full weight landed on its chest. The tank lid slipped off the monster, and Angela crashed onto the hard linoleum floor. She crawled forward, slowly rising to her feet, and dashed out of the bathroom, knowing it wouldn't take the Langblass much time to recover.

But as she entered the hallway, she changed her mind, turning back into the girls' bathroom. The monster rolled on the ground. Angela walked around it, grabbed the tank lid, lifted it high above her head, and yelled, "This is my world." She drove the tank lid down onto the monster's head. It screamed and held up its lanky arms.

She lifted the lid and did it again. And again. Blood oozed from the creature's head.

The tank lid hit the linoleum with a loud bang, and Angela dashed out of the bathroom and back to her sister in the library. Chrissy lay on the floor, shivering. Blood pooled around her.

Vinx continued to bark behind the door. "Come on, Chrissy. I killed the monster. You need to stay alive."

Chrissy's skin had turned porcelain white, lips purple. She shook uncontrollably.

"I told you not to die. Why don't you ever listen to me?"

Chrissy eked out a small laugh and blood shot from her mouth.

Angela stroked Chrissy's hair. "Fuck. I don't know what to do."

She ran to the phone, wondering if the world would have righted itself now that the monster had died. But there was no dial tone, just a wailing screech.

"Fuck!' she yelled at nothing.

The library door crashed open, and the monster, now covered in its own blood, stood at the threshold.

34
SEARCH PARTY

After Tiffany and Officer Burns brought Doug to the back seat of the cruiser, they drove around a series of Tanner's Switch neighborhoods, looking for Barrett's police cruiser. Tiffany remained shaken from the last monster attack, a feeling that would probably never subside. On top of that, her worry for Doug kept her stomach in knots.

"Nice area over here," Burns said absently.

Tiffany snorted. "Don't lie. Tanner's Switch is a shithole. It's one of the poorest towns in the state."

Burns frowned. "Yeah, but it's still scenic. Lots of beautiful woods. Plus, it's an anomaly. Typically, crime rates and low income correlate, but Tanner's Switch has very low crime rates despite its economic challenges."

Tiffany smirked. "You've been very helpful, and I'm so glad I ran into you, but if you don't mind, what a shitty thing to say. First, you sound like a textbook. Second, crime rates correlate to poverty but also to population density, and Tanner's Switch has a low population rate. But yes, thank you for saying it in the kindest way possible: Y'all broke asses aren't a bunch of heathens. Remarkable!"

Burns' face turned red. "That's not what I meant. I'm sorry."

"I know you didn't, and I'm sorry. I'm just on edge. But let me tell you something about Tanner's Switch. Did you ever hear the story of the girl who found a dead body behind the old Wellman's house?"

"No."

"Within the next week, her coworkers and family all wound up dead. Not all of them in The Switch, but still. No one ever found out what happened to those people, but everyone around here knows. How about the two girls at the abandoned amusement park?"

Burns shook her head.

"They were teens when I was just a kid. Both of them were mean assholes. One of them was like a major criminal. Violent. The other pushed her friend off an abandoned Ferris wheel. She was arrested for it. And her defense claimed—and I am not making this up—that she was possessed by the evil spirit of a dead bird."

"Wow."

"Yep. Then there was the woman who was obsessed with Carli Long, the internet star. I don't think I need to get into that one. I know you've heard the story. Everyone in the world has. You have the alien sightings in the seventies, the nuclear reactor accident in Richmond, which led to a bunch of folks in Tanner's Switch claiming they saw glowing objects in their yards despite being miles and miles from where the reactor killed that dude. I could go on and on all day."

"With the exception of the Carli Long one, I hadn't heard about any of those."

"No? How about the one where a family moved to Tanner's Switch from Block Island after claiming their sibling was eaten by a monster, only to have the entire town turn into a creepy fog land filled with monsters picking them off one by one and taking out every person associated with them on the way?"

Burns glared at her. "Yeah. Yeah, I know that one."

"Makes all the urban legends and fairy tales about this shithole feel a little more real." Tiffany put her feet on the glovebox door.

"So what are you saying? Tanner's Switch is really unsafe, despite the numbers?"

Tiffany looked in the rearview to get a peek at Doug. He slept soundly. "Did you know we have over twenty sightings a year of lamppost monsters? LAMPPOSTS! The goofiest, fakest monsters in the history of television. Folks around here see them all the time."

"Do you believe people really see lamppost monsters?"

"After today? I believe anything. I believe everything. You want to know the truth about Tanner's Switch? It's been rotting since the tracks stopped rolling through. Economically, the town died and then, poof, so did the people. We've all been dead since we were born. Tanner's Switch is doomed. It always has been. It's decay. It's death. It just fucking festers and bubbles and slowly it eats away at all of us. If we don't get killed by monsters, we find another way to die young. Do you know what the life expectancy in Tanner's Switch is? First, do you know what the life expectancy in America is?"

Burns shrugged.

"In America, it's seventy-seven years. In the best states, like Hawaii, it can go as high as eighty. In the worst state, it's like, seventy-one. I think that award goes to Mississippi. In Rhode Island, it's seventy-eight. So we're ahead of the national average. But Tanner's Switch? Luckily, we have a low population because our life expectancy is sixty-eight. Sixty-eight! Do you know how many tragically young deaths have to occur to bring the entire town's population that low?"

"Shit, that's bleak."

"Try living here."

Tiffany stared out the window. Trees zipped by. She'd lived in Tanner's Switch her entire life. Watched as the income levels flat-lined, but the cost of living skyrocketed. She saw the small shops close down as more and more folks opted for a trip to Walmart in Westerly. She watched the few wealthy people who lived in the area use their influence to avoid paying their fair share of taxes. She witnessed the old lady at the gas station get older until she passed away and her daughter took over ringing people up for their cigarettes and sodas. She watched new houses go up, only to have them dropped into the hands of rich assholes who rented the houses out as vacation properties—*Just five short miles from the ocean!*—instead of letting people move to the area. She watched the rot seep in, take hold of them, and the townspeople argued about cleaning it up because it meant they'd have to adapt.

The monsters came in and out. The apparitions, the death, the chemicals, the smells, the demons. They came in and out. And the whole town died on their hills.

"There!" Tiffany shouted. Burns slammed on the brakes. Hidden by an embankment and wrapped around a tree, Barrett's car rested.

They ran out of the car, checking the abandoned police cruiser.

"They aren't here. They must have taken off on foot," Tiffany said.

"Unless the monster ate them."

Tiffany ignored her, pointing down the road. "If I were them, I'd head that way. Back toward their house. And our high school is just down a side road a little ways up."

"Okay. See if Barrett's car starts."

Tiffany hopped in and hit the button under the steering wheel. Despite the damage done, it started right up.

"Can you back it out?"

Tiffany put it in reverse and gave it gas, but the wheels spun in the mud, and the car stayed put.

"Let me try," Burns said.

Tiffany went back into the road, standing by the other cruiser. She checked in on her brother while Burns tinkered with Barrett's. The engine roared, and the wheels moved a few centimeters back and forth. Finally, with a loud shattering sound, the car released from the tree and mud. Burns brought the car up to the road, and Tiffany again admired the cop's ability to accomplish.

Burns kept the car running but stepped out. "All right. You drive Barrett's car. It's in terrible shape and may not run for long, but it's the best we got. If we find Chrissy and Angela, we're going to need both cars, though, especially with your brother out in the back seat.

Tiffany nodded. She wondered if the cop knew she didn't have a license. It probably didn't matter under the circumstances.

Burns drove slowly down the road, allowing Tiffany to keep up in the beat-up cruiser and probably to keep an eye out for the girls too.

After a few minutes, they drove past the road Tanner's Switch High School resided on. Tiffany glanced at it as they drove by. She could make out small fragments of the front façade from her angle.

They continued to crawl toward Chrissy's house.

"Wait!" Tiffany shouted as if Burns could hear her. Realizing her error, she clicked her high beams on and off and stopped the car.

Burns hit the brakes and yelled out the window, "What's up?"

"The lights are on at the school," Tiffany yelled to her.

35
HOW IT ENDS

Angela's fear turned to anger. She'd had more than enough. The monster snarled in the doorway, and she never wanted to smash a head in as badly as she did now, which was saying something because she often wanted to smash people's heads in.

"Welcome home," it sang.

"No. Shut up. You don't get to say that ever again. Fuck you."

It ran toward her, slower than typical. She'd messed it up good with the tank lid. She ran toward the bookshelves, wanting to keep the action away from her sister. The monster followed her path, and while she had slowed it down, it still kept a good pace thanks to its long legs. She dipped down one aisle and then the next.

"I've been running from you all my life. You think you can wear me down now? I'll never slow down."

As she reached one side of a shelf where the monster moved on the opposite side, she pushed the shelves. It wasn't enough to knock the whole structure down as she'd hoped, but it did manage to drop some books on the creature.

"I never want to hear your shitty song again. I want to go to the bathroom in peace." She ran around an endcap into another aisle, and the monster pursued. It gained on her.

As she ran out of the aisle, the monster walked only a few steps behind. She stopped to push the last shelving unit over, hoping to knock it down on the creature behind her, but again, it didn't topple, only dropped some books on the Langblass's head.

She turned to run into the next aisle when the monster slashed at her. She thought she had the clearance, but she was wrong. The claws whipped across her back, tearing her shirt and skimming her skin. She fell to the ground and slid across the linoleum.

"You'll never win. I saw you every time I closed my eyes. I hid from you. I hid from my life because of you. You already killed me. You can't win."

The Langblass tilted its head, confusion washing over it. "Welcome home?"

"AAAAAAHHHHHHHH!" She jumped up and tackled the monster, punching it in the face. While she managed to knock it over, it quickly recovered. Even with the major head damage, it outpowered her. Within seconds, it had rolled over and got on top of her.

Angela and the Langblass engaged in a power struggle, her pushing its giant hands away from her face while it pushed hard to bring its claws down.

A pair of scissors sailed across the linoleum, landing next to Angela. Her sister stared, still lying on the floor, bleeding out. Angela wanted to reach for them but doing so meant letting go of the creature's hand.

The Langblass opened its huge mouth, drool dripping on Angela's face. The foul scent of dead ocean overtook her. She cringed and turned away from it.

The school intercom crackled to life, and a high-pitched whine played over the speakers. Feedback. The monster flopped off Angela, gripping its ears, roaring with rage. Angela rolled over and grabbed the scissors.

As the monster screamed in agony, she got on her knees by the Langblass's head and plunged the scissors into its eye, and then ripped them right out.

It screamed and flailed even more. Its legs kicked a shelving unit, knocking the whole aisle over. One set of shelves collapsed onto the next, a series of dominoes, until the entire middle section of the library was on the floor.

She drove the scissors into the creature's neck. It gurgled and whined. She did it again, this time to its chest.

Its claws latched onto her wrist, and she fell into one of its dreams again.

Three Langblasses tied up in the cabin of a boat. They rocked with the rumbling waves. A man and woman sat in front of the creatures, old-fashioned guns at their side. They held contempt in their eyes. The creatures, on the other hand, were steel-faced. They had no reaction to the humans. The man looked ready to shoot them. The woman had tears dribbling down her face.

Angela pulled away and stuck the scissors into the Langblass's neck once more. Blood coated her hand.

"Welcome home?" the creature asked.

Angela fell over, exhausted. "No," she said. "Never."

Someone shouted, "Hello?" from the hallway.

Until Angela heard the voice, it hadn't clicked that someone else must have been in the school to turn the intercom on.

"Hello?" they asked again.

The library doors kicked in.

"Oh my god." A female officer immediately ran to Chrissy. "Oh my God, she's lost a lot of blood."

"Angela?' Tiffany ran to her.

Angela sat up and leaned against the wreckage of the shelves the monster had created. "Hey, Tiff. How was your day?"

Tiffany wrapped her arms around Angela and hugged her. Angela noticed the bloody gashes on Tiffany's arms and realized she must have seen the monster too. "We have to get Chrissy to the hospital," Angela said.

Tiffany pulled away and examined the room. "The mist hasn't cleared. There's no one left."

"What?"

"The mist. We aren't in the real world anymore. We hoped when the monsters all died, the mist would clear and we'd return home, but the mist isn't clearing, which means there's either more monsters somewhere, or we're stuck here forever."

Tiffany's words ran through Angela's mind in a confused and jumbled mess.

"Wait. There's more than one of those things?"

Tiffany eyed the dead creature next to them. "I'm up to a four count."

Angela stood up on unstable legs. Her stomach whirlpooled. "I can't do more of these things."

The officer stood up. "She needs help I can't provide here. We need to get her to the hospital. I'm not a doctor, but at least they have supplies and I can do something for her. I used a lot of my supplies on your brother. This girl could die soon."

Angela brushed past Tiffany. "Let's move then." She unlocked Vinx from the back room and he barged out with his tail going insane.

The officer moved fast. They found blankets in the nurse's office and used them to build a makeshift stretcher for Chrissy. With Doug in the back of the officer's car, they had to put Chrissy in the back of the wrecked cruiser. Burns drove that car with Angela riding shotgun, while Tiffany drove behind, escorting her brother with Vinx in shotty.

Burns drove the cruiser as if racing in a high-speed chase, with the lights and sirens raising hell.

"The sirens will keep the monster back. Tiffany figured that out. She said the horn really upset one of those things at her house. It was her idea to make feedback on the intercom. When we reached the school, Tiffany caught that the lights were on, so we stopped to see if you ended up there. As soon as we entered, we heard the monster roar. Tiffany remembered the noise thing and figured it would mess the creature up until we found you. I planned to shoot it, but thanks to you, I didn't need to."

Angela slowly turned to her. "I'm sorry. Who are you?"

"Long story. I've been looking for you all night, though."

Angela turned back to her sister. Chrissy looked worse than before, her skin a weird waxy color. Her breath came out in sharp, harsh bursts. It was the only way Angela could tell she wasn't looking at a dead body. "Is she gonna make it?"

The officer shook her head. "I don't know. I hope so. It would be really helpful if we had doctors."

"So, you think the fog means there's more of those things out there?"

"Yeah, because the other option is we're stuck here forever, and I refuse to accept that."

Angela rested her head back and crossed her arms. "I kind of refuse to accept that I have to deal with another one of those things, too, though."

36
PRIVY

O fficer Carmen walked through some woods on the north side of the island, feet crunching on leaves. The fog made the search for Charlie even more difficult. His flashlight beam scanned the perimeter, back and forth, as he kept up his march.

Some of the local help had already called it a night, giving up on the search, but Carmen refused to stop just yet. The state officers stayed on the island, but they were losing steam. The whole search was unorthodox, and if it weren't for Carmen's fervency, it never would have happened as quickly as it did. Charlie's disappearance was connected to his sister's and Molly Mix's disappearance, and although Carmen didn't believe in the supernatural, even he was a little spooked by the constant similarities of the monster claims. Because he hadn't solved Wreath's disappearance, Carmen felt personally indebted to Charlie and the rest of the Keating family.

"Officer Carmen," someone said. A figure walked toward him from his left flank.

He turned the flashlight, and the man put his arm over his eyes. "Carmen, it's me, George Stephens."

George stepped closer. His gray hair was disheveled, eyes drowning in dark bags. He was barefoot, but that wasn't unusual for the old weirdo.

"George, what are you doing out here? If you're helping with the search, you need to check in at the station. Don't need you going missing too."

George moved closer. "No, sir. I don't need to join the search. I know exactly what happened to that boy. I saw him early today walking down the road over there."

Carmen stood up straight. "Why didn't you tell us earlier?"

As George took another step, Carmen could see his bloodshot eyes, not the victims of alcohol as they usually were, but of sadness. "Officer, you're a good man. You're going to learn a lot about this island tonight, and I'm sorry for that. I'm sorry for it all. I think I may be responsible for everything that's happening, and I figured it was high time to end it."

"George? What are you talking about?" Carmen slid his hand around his waist, nearing his gun.

"I could have stopped that boy from going into the cemetery. I should have. I debated on it when I was talking to him. I knew what those monsters were doing and what the result would be, but I also knew if this shit was ever going to end, this was how."

"I need you to speak a little clearer. I'm not following."

George sniffled. Tears rolled down his face. "The deal was always the firstborn. Those were the terms. Both families agreed to it. The Mixes and the Vanderlines. They gave up their firstborn to the monsters to keep those beasts trapped on the island. Not just on the island but in their own little worlds. But how could that last? How could it, Officer?" He stopped as if waiting for Carmen to actually answer a question that made no sense.

Carmen said nothing.

"We all had a job. Generations of us, God damn it. We all made sure the Mixes and Vanderlines kept their word. Until we didn't. These things get passed down, year after year, and when you haven't witnessed it yourself, you stop believing. No one cared anymore because who thought it was real? Of course, part of that *helped* keep it going. If you ain't afraid of monsters, you don't hide from them. But Mary's dad, he knew, and he ruined everything. Left the island before the monsters could get her. And none of us stopped him." He openly wept now, his words coming out in a whimper, "We should have stopped him, but gosh, we didn't want the blood on our hands either, even if it meant opening the world to so much more of it later on. And then tonight, I let them take that boy so I could wash my hands clean."

Carmen pinned the light right in George's eyes. "You're rambling. This isn't making any sense. Is Charlie in the graveyard?"

George looked up, his weak, sad face changing to one of anger. "Once Mary died off the island, and those things didn't have their firstborn as promised, they just had to spill the blood of any one person from each family in the graveyard. Don't you get it? They're free now. They're in both worlds. Theirs and ours. You know you can only kill them in their world, right? 'Course, other than when they'd come here for the firstborns, they can only kill us in their world too. But that's what they do. They bring you in with the mist."

"Okay, I've had enough of this. Are you saying the boy was in the graveyard?" Carmen walked quickly toward the graves but kept his sight on George.

"You're going toward them, Carmen. You'll get all of your answers soon. I'm sorry. I'm so sorry."

Carmen left the woods and entered the small field where the *Palatine* graves lay. He shined his flashlight all over. "Charlie?" While the fog made it hard to see, Carmen didn't notice any signs of struggle.

As he stepped into the center of the gravesite, the fog changed, moving like a snake around his ankles. It poofed around him, then dissipated, and when he could see again, everything had changed. He wasn't sure how, exactly, but the landscape looked off, tilted on its axis, rotten. The tree roots were darker, the leaves not the beau-

tiful colors of fall but a crisp dead brown. The gravestones themselves came out of the ground at an angle, crooked little cutting teeth
emerging from the gums of the earth.

Something breathed loudly, a deep exhale, and the woods
crunched with the sound of movement in front of him.

"Charlie?"

As a figure emerged from the shrouded forest, Carmen gasped. It
was huge with long, lanky limbs. Its face housed a gaping mouth
with black orbs for eyes.

"You're real," was all Carmen could spill from his lips.

It stepped closer to him.

"You're in its world now," a voice said from behind.

Officer Carmen snapped his head around to see George standing
on the outskirts of the field with his hands in his pockets, cool as
can be.

"That fog, it takes us to the thin space just outside our world. It's
where they live most of the time. But they can bounce back and forth
easily. You're lucky. Before they freed themselves, when they didn't
have much power, it would cause you quite the seizure to get in
between. Now you're vulnerable, though. Now they can hurt you."

Carmen turned back to the monster as it walked closer, tilting its
head left and right, examining him.

"What are you?"

George laughed behind him. "And this one's just a youngin'. Used
to just be three of them. They had a couple of offspring over the
centuries. Not sure why they don't reproduce more than that."

The creature leaped forward, landing right in front of Carmen.
The officer flinched. The monster sniffed him, snarled, and lifted its
massive, clawed hand. Carmen closed his eyes, waiting for impact,
too shocked to react otherwise.

"Don't kill him yet, little guy. Show 'em. Officer Carmen's a good
man. He deserves to know the truth before he departs," George said.

Carmen opened his eyes as the creature opened its hand and
slowly moved its palm toward the officer. Carmen squinted,

squishing up his face, waiting for the slimy creature's hand to hit his skin.

"Welcome home," the creature said in a gentle voice, but the tone of it, the way it came out as two voices instead of one, sent a shock wave down Carmen's spine.

As soon as the creature's palm made contact, Carmen fell into a series of visions, whooshing through not only his mind but flowing through his bloodstream, as if it truly transported him to the world of the past.

The monsters lined up on the outskirts of the forest, all with their hands tied behind them.

"Those ropes really gonna keep them there?" a large man with a fisherman's beard asked.

"Honestly, the ropes are more symbolic. Molly's got them roped up in their minds. That's what matters," a man in a rain jacket said. He stood tall, sucking on a pipe.

The large man with the beard looked over at a woman sitting by a contained fire. She slouched and rubbed her fingers together. "Mary, come over and meet Mr. Mix."

The woman either hadn't heard him or chose to ignore him.

The bearded man turned to Mr. Mix and said, "Don't mind her, she's more than willing to do what must be done to keep these things from getting free, but the price is haunting her."

Mr. Mix put his hand on the man's shoulder. "Well, let her know we aren't happy about it either, but it's the way these things work. Molly is a woman of great power, but nothing comes without a price, and when she has to create something as large as binds between worlds, the price comes heavy."

"I understand. We understand. We wouldn't have made the trip otherwise."

Mr. Mix took a puff from his pipe. "These creatures had their day in the Black Forest and could have kept having it, but they overstepped. They've enough power to turn our world into theirs, rotting it from the soil to the sky. Someone had to be brave enough to pay the toll."

"Yessir," the bearded man said.

"Trust me, if our family could have made the sacrifice alone, we would have accepted to keep you from bearing the cross, but one can't feed three."

A woman walked into the field from the woods, wearing a black cloak. She pulled her hood off, revealing long, slick black hair. When she looked up, the bearded man gasped. Her eyes were glowing red.

Mr. Mix said, "Molly, our guests have arrived."

"I see that."

The woman by the fire noticed the new arrival and ran to her husband's side.

Molly said, "Mr. and Mrs. Vanderline, it's a pleasure to make your acquaintance. I apologize it has to happen under these circumstances."

Mrs. Vanderline stepped forward. "I'm sorry. It's been a long trip. I agreed to this with good intentions, but I've had time to think about it, and I just don't know that I understand. What does firstborn mean? If I have twelve children, will all eleven survivors have to feed their firstborn to these demons?"

Molly smiled. She had an ethereal quality to her face, the way her eyes glowed, and her smile stretched like a galaxy. "Your second born will always be responsible for the next generation's sacrifice. And it's imperative you have a second born, as it is equally imperative they do as well. If the line ends, so does the compromise."

The woman nodded, tears filling her eyes. "I'm sorry. It's hard to accept I'm poisoning my bloodline for generations to keep these awful beasts appeased."

Molly puffed out her chest. "You're not. You're giving to the greater good and not allowing these things to turn our world into theirs. You're saving all life as we know it. If they're ever set free, given free rein to release their veil, they'll first take out their viciousness on our families, and once they've gotten their revenge, they'll devour everyone else.

"What I'm going to cast will keep them on this island, and it will keep them in their realm, stuck forever, only to come out to feed once every generation. The world will never know of their existence from this point forward. Some with great vision will see the Langblasses out of the corner *of their eyes, but it'll be nothing more than a scary story for them to pass on to their children."*

Mr. Vanderline hugged his wife. "She's just tired."

Molly tilted her head. "I know what they did to your child in those woods. And I know it seemed easy to promise your firstborn when you'd already lost her. But now you're realizing the reverberating effects of your choice. It's not just the child you've already lost. But remember, it isn't just you that will be sacrificing. My husband and I will also be poisoning our bloodline, as you so eloquently put it, and this isn't our first sacrifice in the name of protecting our world from others. This is what we do. This is who we are."

Something cracked. A fissure broke through the vision until Carmen was in a different place. A fog world.

The creatures walked the shoreline. They looked defeated, broken. A woman stood on the shore. She turned, revealing her face. Mrs. Vanderline. She was much older than in the last vision, probably by decades. Her cheeks were wet and red. She pulled out a small blade and brought it to her neck. With a swift motion, the blade danced across her flesh, and her neck spilled crimson on the soft beach sand.

The monsters stopped and watched as the woman twitched to her death. Within a few minutes, shorebirds came and picked at her corpse. One of them plucked out the woman's eye.

Another crack. Another fissure in the vision.

The monsters stood within the fog, walking throughout the island. People walked all around them, tourists visiting the island, shopping, laughing. Modern times. And the monsters watched. The people surrounding them were completely unaware of the creatures' existence.

One of the beasts slashed at a person, and his claws went right through them, unable to connect. It hollered a sorrowful cry.

Another fissure came, cracking through the foundation of the vision.

A monster lay on the ground, screaming in pain, as a little monster came out of her.

Another fissure.

The monsters stood on the shoreline, the same three from the first vision and now two others. Smaller ones. As boats drifted by in the distance, the creatures pounded on an invisible wall, screaming and crying, doing everything in their power to break through.

The monster removed his palm from Officer Carmen's forehead. "All this time," Carmen said.

Behind him, George cleared his throat. "All this time. We've been dripping blood into the ocean since before your daddy's daddy was born."

The monster pointed to the side, aiming his finger toward some unknown destination shrouded in the night's charcoal sky, made even more impossible to see thanks to the gray fog. "Welcome home," it cried. "Welcome home."

George stepped over to Officer Carmen's side.

"I'm ready," George said.

The monster snarled and slashed George's neck. Blood sprayed on Carmen's face.

"Jesus," Carmen said and drew his gun, but before he could use it, the creature drove his claw through the officer's chest.

Carmen went to scream, but only a low whistle left his throat. As his body slid off the creature's massive talon, he lifted his arm, putting the muzzle to the monster's mouth.

A gunshot fired.

And two bodies fell to the earth.

37
CLOWN FISH

Burns drove down Franklin Street, and Angela noticed two lumps lying in the road. One of them was a monster, the other harder to distinguish. As they neared the lumps, they disappeared. Completely vanished. The fog thinned.

Headlights shined ahead of them in the distance. Lights flickered on from the streetlamps.

The farther they drove, the more the fog dissipated until fully gone.

"Holy shit," Burns said.

"Is it clearing?" Angela could barely contain her excitement. If they were back in the real world, her sister stood a chance of surviving.

She turned to look out the back window to see if Tiffany stayed behind. The rules of crossing in and out of the real world were a weird-ass mystery, and she had no idea if Tiffany would exit it the same way they just had. Sure enough, the second cruiser sped behind them.

When they reached the hospital, Burns ran out of the car. Angela wept at the sight of a man smoking a butt by the entrance, and through the large front windows, two women worked behind desks. Did that mean the monsters were gone for good? That her sister would survive?

Teams of people rushed around her. A stretcher—a real one—carried Chrissy into the hospital. Another came for Doug. Angela didn't know what to do. Was she allowed past the double doors? No one seemed to notice her. No one asked. She had claw marks down her back. Surely nothing more than scratches. Maybe she should ask to get them checked, but she didn't.

With both cars abandoned, she walked over to the second cruiser and found what she worried she might find. Vinx was gone.

Burns came out shortly after, phone at her ear. She had tears in her eyes as she hung up. She smiled at Angela. "I just woke my husband up and made him check that our daughter was asleep in her bed. He thought I was crazy. I need to get home to her, but I gotta talk to you and Tiffany first."

"How's my sister?"

"I'm not sure. I think it'll be a while until they have answers for you, to be honest."

Angela nodded.

"Where's the dog?" Burns asked.

"Gone. With the mist."

"Shit. I'm sorry."

Angela threw her hands up in the air. "The dog had two tags. Two."

"Huh?"

"My sister checked the tag. That's how we found out his name was Vinx. But there was a second tag. It said, *If lost, please return to Kendall O'Connor.* Then it had an address. He was never my dog."

Burns bit her bottom lip, clearly unsure what to say. "Still sucks. I'm sorry."

"It doesn't. We don't own something just because we need it. It never belonged to me. Sometimes a girl and a dog meet, and it's not destiny or the beginning of a lifelong friendship. It's just a whole lot of luck that they were both there for each other when they needed that for a little bit."

"I think I get it. You're way too smart for your age."

"Officer, my mother died when I was nine. My oldest sister too. Last night, I found out my oldest brother died. My other brother disappeared, and I'm pretty sure he's dead too. Who knows what will happen to Chrissy—"

The officer opened her mouth to say something but thought better of it. Angela decided not to pursue it.

"The point is, I'm used to relationships being short-lived."

Tiffany came out of the hospital with her hands wrapped around her abdomen.

"How are you holding up?" Burns asked her.

Tiffany offered a small smile. "Okay. My arm's fine. They got it all stitched up and gave me antibiotics."

"And your brother?"

"He'll be fine. How's Chrissy?"

Angela stepped in. "Don't know yet."

Burns grabbed them both by the shoulder. "When you were in there? What did you tell them happened?"

Tiffany pulled her arm away. "I didn't. I avoided giving answers, and they weren't happy about it. They called my parents, who are on their way to pick me up. I have no idea what kind of story to tell."

"Yeah, that's what I want to talk to you both about. We need a story. I have no idea how to make one stick. From the eyes of the people who didn't get sucked into a different world, here's what they'll piece together. Doug's injured from a fall. Tiffany has multiple stab wounds, as does Chrissy, but not from any kind of weapon they'd recognize. Charlie disappeared. Two police officers and Mr. Keating are also gone. And we drove to the hospital in one of those officer's cars."

"Wait. What?" Angela asked.

Burns caught her mistake and mouthed the word, "Fuck." She rubbed her temples. "I'm sorry, Angela. I wanted you to find out a better way than this."

She had no response, but Tiffany and Burns waited for her to say something. To divert the conversation and to keep her brain from wrapping around the new revelation, Angela said, "We either tell the truth and look like crazy people, or we say there was a serial killer. We'll create our own *Friday the 13th* story and use what happened to my sister as part of it. It'll make the media feel like shit for what they did to us four years ago. 'Serial killer dresses as a monster and terrorizes family, comes back four years later for murder spree.'"

Burns pulled at her ponytail. "There's probably a million reasons why that story wouldn't work, but I'm too exhausted to think of them. Stick with that, don't give any details. In fact, fucking flat out refuse to answer anything. You're both suffering right now, and the police will be sensitive to that. But they will want a story. Just tell them you were terrorized by a man in a mask, and you can't talk about it. Cry a lot. Say you can't remember. Too traumatized. Details equals screwing up our story. Got it?"

They both nodded.

"Good. Eventually, we'll need to give them a lot more, but we can meet up and clean up the details another time. For now, go be with your families. I'm sorry for everything you've had to go through."

Angela flinched when the cop awkwardly jumped forward and hugged them. Once in the embrace, though, she didn't want Burns to let go. Tiffany's hand wrapped around Angela's back, and the three were locked in a group hug. When it ended, the cool autumn air hit Angela's skin, making her feel naked. Exposed.

Shortly after, Burns drove off to be with her family. Tiffany's parents came and took her inside to visit Doug. Angela sat alone in the waiting room. In the center of the Westerly Hospital waiting area, a fish tank housed a half dozen beautiful, colorful fish. A clown fish swam from one end to the other, and she stared at it until her eyes blurred. One end to the other. One end to the other. One end to the other. Over and over.

After a few hours, she had to pee. And she did. She peed alone in the public restroom and felt nothing. Not anger, not grief, not even fear. For a few minutes, she'd run dry of emotions.

38

CORNERS

A FEW MONTHS LATER

Chrissy stood at the bottom of the steps leading to Tanner's Switch Middle School. Kids brushed past her on both sides. When a student brushed shoulders with her, her heart spun into overdrive. Each step in front of her stretched in her mind, growing impossibly long.

Almost two months had passed since she last attended school. The isolation during recovery only exaggerated her already growing anxiety and terror of her surroundings.

She closed her eyes and breathed in deep. She could run away from this, fly home, and not a single person would blame her. No one would stop her from taking more time. But if she did, if she didn't fight her instinct to run, she'd retreat further and further into her shell, and she'd end up just another victim of the Langblass.

Her breath caught in her throat as she ascended the stairs. A student pulled on one of the double doors, and it banged hard against the outside railing. Chrissy flinched.

The thin strips of hallways inside the school sharped the

250

cacophony of teenage chatter, focusing it and pushing it on Chrissy. Her chest caved in, strangling her heart. Lockers slammed. Hastings opened his locker about fifteen feet away, pulling out some texts and shoving them into his bookbag. Luckily, he hadn't seen her yet.

He'd called numerous times and visited the hospital with flowers. She always refused the company, too terrified of showing anyone her scars.

The bell rang and she flinched, jolting backward and banging the back of her skull on the wall. The pressure in her chest grew, tightening. She couldn't breathe. Her limbs trembled and her teeth chattered.

People looked at her as they passed, unsure what to make of the full-blown panic attack happening in front of them.

She turned and ran, heading straight into the girls' bathroom. A few students walked out, giggling to each other.

She flew into a stall and shut the door, locking herself in. Outside of a gentle drip from the sink, it was quiet.

She sat on the toilet seat and rested her head against the back wall. With her eyes shut, she let air come into her lungs and out through her nose. Her hand went to her chest, so she could feel her heart rate simmering.

She opened her eyes. Maybe she wasn't ready for this, but if she could escape to the bathroom when needed, then maybe she could use it as a crutch to get through the day. At least within the confines of a stall, she could be alone.

Alone.

Her heart sped back up, beating hard against her ribs.

Alone.

Tears formed in the corners of her eyes. Slowly, she turned her head toward the far corner of the bathroom.

Alone.

The Langblass did not hover in the corner as it had for so many years with Angela. But if Chrissy looked away, would it appear, forming from her fear? Would it coalesce, recreate itself and finish

251

the job on her family? What if more of them existed? How could they ever be sure? Would she forever be trapped in a revenge cycle?

She stared at the empty corner.

How could she look away?

How?

How could she ever?

Her eyes blurred. She glanced away, bringing her eyes to another corner, then another, and then the last before bringing herself back to the first again.

She wiped snot from her nose and cried.

Jesus. She could never look away. Not for long. The corners owned her.

39
LEFTOVERS

The microwaved dinged. Angela carried the plate of spaghetti to the kitchen table. It looked like shit. They were out of sauce, so the only flavor on the plate was the dried sauce caked to the noodles from when her aunt cooked it a few days ago.

As soon as she sat, someone knocked at the door. She left her plate and answered it.

"Hi," Tiffany said. Angela found her delivery too friendly for someone she hadn't seen or talked to in months.

Nonetheless, she waved Tiffany in as she went back to her plate. "Sorry, I'm just about to eat. I don't have anything to offer. Do you want something to drink, at least?"

Tiffany rubbed her arm. "Ah, I could go for a glass of water, but I don't want you to have to get up. Just tell me where the cups are."

Angela pointed to the cupboard to the left of the sink. Tiffany opened it and grabbed a plastic cup.

"I didn't expect to see you when I opened the door."

Tiffany turned the sink on and filled her cup. "Yeah. I'm sorry I haven't been by. I wanted to. And Burns kept calling about the story, and the police, and the fucking news. We've already given our story a thousand times, and she keeps nagging me to make sure I still have all the details. I just kind of sunk into myself, and then when I felt like I really wanted to connect with you guys, I didn't know how. Ya know? It felt like this open wound and the more I ignored it, the bigger it grew. And then today, I figured I should do something about it."

Angela took a bite of her hard noodles. "What have you been up to? I mean, besides all that."

Tiffany shook her head as she grabbed a chair from the table and sat across from Angela. "Avoidance, mostly. I try to spend time with my girlfriend so I can feel normal, but she grills me as much as the police. It's really hard to hang out with people who don't have a fucking clue."

Angela swallowed another bite down. "I get it. How's Doug?"

"Physically? Fine. Mentally? Fucked-up. How about you? How are you holding up?"

Angela laughed and shook her head.

"Fair enough. How's Chrissy? I don't see her in school."

"After surgery, she got sepsis. She's just getting back on her feet. Her boyfriend or ex-boyfriend or whatever he is keeps calling. I think she might be practicing the avoidance thing you talked about too. She keeps to herself mostly."

Tiffany sipped her water. "How about you two? Do you get along better?"

Angela frowned. "Not really. I mean, I guess. I think we're less mean to each other, but we're still totally different people. It's not like we're going to magically become best buds because of everything that happened."

Tiffany stared at her. At first, it made Angela uncomfortable, but then she realized Tiffany's eyes were filling with water. "I just thought once it was over, we'd all end up okay, but I'm not okay," she said.

Angela nodded. "Why would you think it would be okay?" She

sighed and put her fork down. "I guess that's not fair to you. I've done this before. It just gets worse. You asked how I'm doing. Well, both of my brothers are dead, and I can only outwardly mourn one. The other I'm supposed to pretend to hold out hope for. We can't even have a funeral for him. My father's dead, and I have to pretend I don't know that either. And for whatever reason, even though I hated that man for so long, his death really hurts."

She choked up, cleared her throat.

"I always hoped he'd show up at the door one day all sobered up and we'd fix everything, like our family would somehow just get back together. And he had some money squirreled away for us, at least some of it, but who knows when we'll see it, if ever. For now, he's just 'missing.'"

She picked her fork up again and stabbed at her spaghetti.

"The one thing I did think would get better is the way I was always scared, but it didn't. It might even be worse. I can pee alone now, so there's that, but every loud noise makes my chest ache until I can't breathe, and I feel like I'm going to pass out. Kids at school were talking about how they're building a pop-up escape room nearby based on original Caleb Jones stories. You know, the old horror director guy, and all I could think was, *I'll never be able to do normal shit.* If I tried to do an escape room, I'd end up curled in a ball in the bathroom hyperventilating and bawling my eyes out."

The fork stabbed harder.

"I wake up screaming in the middle of the night. So does Chrissy, who needs the rest more than anyone. And I worry about her because she's all I have left."

Stab. Stab. Stab.

"And I'm still eating leftover spaghetti, and I'll be poor forever. Like, I can't even function in school, so I have no hopes of using my brain to get some big degree that'll buy me a nice house one day. I'll be this fucked-up adult who can't hold a steady job, moving from one shit place to another, and I'll be eating the same shitty leftovers in kitchens just like this one for the rest of my life."

She slammed the fork down and tossed it across the table.

"Welcome home, right? Welcome home."

Tiffany put her hand on Angela's. "Hey, it's okay. I mean, it's not, but it is."

"I'm sorry I just dumped that on you." Angela's hands trembled, and she couldn't make them stop.

Tiffany chuckled. "Don't be. It feels good to know I'm not the only one who's fucked-up." She sighed. "Angela?"

"Yeah."

"I could use a friend."

Angela put her head down and sobbed. "Me too." She looked up and hugged Tiffany. "I hate these two words, but I kind of want to own them. Welcome home."

Tiffany sobbed in her ear. "Welcome home."

Long live Vinx!

Thank you so much for reading On a Clear Day, You Can See Block Island.

Did you know when you join my Patreon, depending on the tier, you can get access to my books months before they release. On top of that, I offer all sorts of cool perks and rewards, like special edition variant covers you can only get on Patreon, monthly zoom meetings with the crew, a group chat, exclusive stories you can't find anywhere else, and all sorts of other awesome rewards.

Want to hear the awesome playlist for this book, curated by Kylee Jones? Check it out here:

ACKNOWLEDGMENTS

Writing a novel is a lonely affair. It's not just the sitting hunched over a computer typing up words, but also all those moments outside of writing where your head is in the game, and not focused on your life otherwise. That's why Nolan and Becky always get top billing on these acknowledgments. Their patience, understanding, support, and endless love fuel these pages, and keep me going.

Dagan Legg Boyd designed the cover of this book, the chapter headers, and the scene break elements. Its one of the most beautiful covers I've ever seen, and I'm incredibly thankful for the amazing work she did.

Danielle Yeager edited these pages. I promise you, it was a messy, comma-filled book before she touched it.

Luke Spooner designed the variant covers that are only available on my Patreon, and he did an amazing job with it.

My author friends provided me with tons of insight, tips, and more importantly friendship and inspiration. Nick Roberts!!!, John Durgin, Felix Blackwell, and Sammy Scott. (Sammy, keep on fighting dude).

Megan Stockton, Joshua MacMillan, Jae Mazer, Chaz Williams, Ben Young, Caleb Jones, Duncan Ralston, Dan Franklin, Andrew Van Wey, Lisa Vasquez, you're all amazing people, tremendous writers, and even better friends.

Kristina Lee saved me from a terrible mistake by coming up with a solution that didn't leave me so drowning in debt, I never would have been able to publish this book. On top of that, she's become my impromptu assistant, organizing my chaotic life. She also happens to be an amazing friend.

Kylee Jones made the killer playlist that accompanies this book, and she knocked it out of the park. Kylee, by the way, is one of the coolest people on the planet. You'll find her an answer on Jeopardy! someday. I'll take

Molly Mix and Meghan Burns lent their names to these pages. Thanks for letting me create weird characters with your names.

Kendall O'Connor is my biggest fan, and she will throw down if you try to dispute this. With her permission, we gave her pup Vinx eternal life in On a Clear Day. Long live Vinx! Thanks for being a friend to Kendall when she needed you, because now we all need her.

Catie McGuinness always inspires me, and her friendship has made me a better person, and thus, a better writer.

So many booktokers have been a huge part of my career, and without their amazing work, I wouldn't be where I am. @CandyAppleReads, @GhostlyReads, @APageCastingWitch, @Books_booze_horror, @TheSpineofMotherhood, @ChazReadsHorror, @ForTheLoveofBookmarks, @Deven_Reads, @Anna.Reads.Horror, @msmaisied, @letsgofrightseeing, @GrimDreadful, and so many more.

My lovely weirdos in Books of Horror. You wacky sons of guns. I love you.

STAND ALONE NOVELS:

Bunker Dogs

On a Clear Day, You Can See Block Island

We Are All Dead, Anyway (COMING 2024)

THE WINTER SAGA

Winter's Myths

Winter's Legacy

Winter's End (COMING SOON)

SHORT STORIES

Grackles on the Feeder

Through Flickering Lights, a Silhouette

About the Author

Gage Greenwood is the best-selling author of the Winter's Myths Saga, and Bunker Dogs. He's a proud member of the Horror Writers Association and Science Fiction and Fantasy Writers association.

He's been an actor, comedian, podcaster, and even the Vice President of an escape room company. Since childhood, he's been a big fan of comic books, horror movies, and depressing music that fills him with existential dread.

He lives in New England with his girlfriend and son, and he spends his time writing, hiking, and decorating for various holidays.

Find out more, or contact me: www.gagegreenwood.com

facebook.com/gagegreenwoodauthor

instagram.com/gagegreenwood

patreon.com/gagegreenwood

threads.net/@gagegreenwood

tiktok.com/@gagegreenwoodauthor

Printed in Great Britain
by Amazon

37901384R00158